GW00372811

Adventures of a Gentleman Thief

Maurice Leblanc

Cherry Stone Publishing, an imprint of
Sweet Cherry Publishing Limited
Unit 36, Vulcan House,
Vulcan Road,
Leicester, LE5 3EF
United Kingdom

First published by Cherry Stone Publishing in 2021
2021 edition

2 4 6 8 10 9 7 5 3 1

ISBN: 978-1-78226-542-9

© Sweet Cherry Publishing

Adventures of a Gentleman Thief:
The Crystal Stopper

Originally written in French by Maurice Leblanc.

Cover design by Jess Brown

www.cherrystonepublishing.com

Printed and bound in Turkey
T.IO006

The Crystal Stopper

Maurice Leblanc

CHERRY STONE
PUBLISHING

The
Arrests

The two boats fastened to the little pier that jutted out from the garden lay rocking in its shadow. Here and there lighted windows showed through the thick mist on the margins of the lake. The Enghien Casino opposite blazed with light, though it was late in the season, the end of September. A few stars appeared through the clouds. A light breeze ruffled the surface of the water.

Arsène Lupin left the summer house where he was smoking a cigar and, bending forwards at the end of the pier:

"Growler?" he asked. "Masher? Are you there?"

A man rose from each of the boats, and one of them answered:

"Yes, governor."

"Get ready. I hear the car coming with Gilbert and Vaucheray."

He crossed the garden, walked round a house in process of construction, the scaffolding of which loomed overhead, and cautiously opened the door on the avenue de Ceinture. He was not mistaken: a bright light flashed round the bend and a large, open motor car drew up, from whence sprang two men in great coats, with the collars turned up, and caps.

It was Gilbert and Vaucheray: Gilbert, a young fellow of twenty or twenty-two, with an attractive cast of features and a supple and sinewy frame; Vaucheray, older, shorter, with grizzled hair and a pale, sickly face.

"Well," asked Lupin, "did you see him, the deputy?"

"Yes, governor," said Gilbert, "we saw him take the 7.40 tram for Paris, as we knew he would."

"Then we are free to act?"

"Absolutely. The Villa Marie-Therese is ours to do as we please with."

The chauffeur had kept his seat. Lupin gave him his orders:

"Don't wait here. It might attract attention. Be back at half-past nine exactly, in time to load the car unless the whole business falls through."

"Why should it fall through?" observed Gilbert.

The motor drove away; and Lupin, taking the road to the lake with his two companions, replied:

"Why? Because I didn't prepare the plan; and, when I don't do a thing myself, I am only half-confident."

"Nonsense, governor! I've been working with you for three years now ... I'm beginning to know the ropes!"

"Yes, my lad, you're beginning," said Lupin, "and that's just why I'm afraid of blunders ... Here, get in with me. And you, Vaucheray, take the other boat ... That's it ... And now push off, boys ... and make as little noise as you can."

Growler and Masher, the two oarsmen, made straight for the opposite bank, a little to the left of the casino.

They met a boat containing a couple locked in each other's arms, floating aimlessly, and another in which a number of people were singing at the top of their voices. And that was all.

Lupin shifted closer to his companion and said, under his breath:

"Tell me, Gilbert, did you think of this job, or was it Vaucheray's idea?"

"Upon my word, I couldn't tell you: we've both of us been discussing it for weeks."

"The thing is, I don't trust Vaucheray: he's a low ruffian when one gets to know him ... I can't make out why I don't get rid of him ..."

"Oh, governor!"

"Yes, yes, I mean what I say: he's a dangerous fellow, to say nothing of the fact that he has some rather serious peccadilloes on his conscience."

He sat silent for a moment and continued:

"So you're quite sure that you saw Daubrecq the deputy?"

"Saw him with my own eyes, governor."

"And you know that he has an appointment in Paris?"

"He's going to the theatre."

"Very well; but his servants have remained behind at the Enghien villa ..."

"The cook has been sent away. As for the valet, Leonard, who is Daubrecq's confidant, he'll wait for his master in Paris. They can't get back from town before one o'clock in the morning. But ..."

"But what?"

"We must reckon with a possible flight of fancy on Daubrecq's part, a change of mind, an unexpected return, and so arrange to have everything finished and done within an hour."

"And when did you get these details?"

"This morning. Vaucheray and I at once thought that it was a favourable moment. I selected the garden of the unfinished house which we have just left as the best place to start from; for the house is not watched at night. I sent for two mates to row the boats; and I telephoned you. That's the whole story."

"Have you the keys?"

"The keys of the front door."

"Is that the villa which I see from here, standing in its own grounds?"

"Yes, the Villa Marie-Therese; and as the two others, with the gardens touching it on either side, have been unoccupied since this day week, we shall be able to remove what we please at our leisure; and I swear to you, governor, it's well worthwhile."

"The job's much too simple," mumbled Lupin. "No charm about it!"

They landed in a little creek whence rose a few stone steps, under cover of a mouldering roof. Lupin reflected that shipping the furniture would be easy work. But, suddenly, he said:

"There are people at the villa. Look ... a light."

"It's a gas-jet, governor. The light's not moving."

The Growler stayed by the boats, with instructions to keep watch, while the Masher, the other rower, went to the gate on the avenue de Ceinture, and Lupin and his two companions crept in the shadow to the foot of the steps.

Gilbert went up first. Groping in the dark, he inserted first the big door key and then the latch key. Both turned easily in their locks, the door opened and the three men walked in.

A gas jet was flaring in the hall.

"You see, governor ..." said Gilbert.

"Yes, yes," said Lupin, in a low voice, "but it seems to me that the light which I saw shining did not come from here ..."

"Where did it come from then?"

"I can't say ... Is this the drawing-room?"

"No," replied Gilbert, who was not afraid to speak pretty loudly, "No. By way of precaution, he keeps everything on the first floor, in his bedroom and in the two rooms on either side of it."

"And where is the staircase?"

"On the right, behind the curtain."

Lupin moved to the curtain and was drawing the hanging aside when, suddenly, at four steps on the left, a door opened and a head appeared, a pallid man's head, with terrified eyes.

"Help! Murder!" shouted the man.

And he rushed back into the room.

"It's Leonard, the valet!" cried Gilbert.

"If he makes a fuss, I'll out him," growled Vaucheray.

"You'll jolly well do nothing of the sort, do you hear, Vaucheray?" said Lupin, peremptorily. And he darted off in pursuit of the servant. He first went through a dining room, where he saw a lamp still lit, with plates and a bottle around it, and he found Leonard at the further end of a pantry, making vain efforts to open the window:

"Don't move, sport! No, kid! Ah, the brute!"

He had thrown himself flat on the floor, on seeing Leonard raise his arm at him. Three shots were fired in the dusk of the pantry and then the valet came tumbling to the ground, seized by the legs by Lupin, who snatched his weapon from him and gripped him by the throat:

"Get out, you dirty brute!" he growled. "He very nearly did for me ... Here, Vaucheray, secure this gentleman!"

He threw the light of his pocket-lantern on the servant's face and chuckled:

"He's not a pretty gentleman either ... You can't have a very clear conscience, Leonard; besides, to play flunkey to Daubrecq the deputy ...! Have you finished, Vaucheray? I don't want to hang about here for ever!"

"There's no danger, governor," said Gilbert.

"Oh, really? So you think that shots can't be heard?"

"Quite impossible."

"No matter, we must look sharp. Vaucheray, take the lamp and let's go upstairs."

He took Gilbert by the arm and, as he dragged him to the first floor:

"You ass," he said, "is that the way you make inquiries? Wasn't I right to have my doubts?"

"Look here, governor, I couldn't know that he would change his mind and come back to dinner."

"One's got to know everything when one has the honour of breaking into people's houses. You numskull! I'll remember you and Vaucheray ... a nice pair of gossoons!"

The sight of the furniture on the first floor pacified Lupin and he started on his inventory with the satisfied air of a collector who has looked in to treat himself to a few works of art:

"By Jingo! There's not much of it, but what there is, is pucka! There's nothing the matter with this representative of the people in the question of taste. Four Aubusson chairs ... A bureau signed 'Percier-Fontaine,' for a wager ... Two inlays by Gouttieres ... A genuine Fragonard and a sham Nattier which any American millionaire will swallow for the asking: in short, a fortune – And there are curmudgeons who pretend that there's nothing but faked stuff left. Dash it all, why don't they do as I do? They should look about!"

Gilbert and Vaucheray, following Lupin's orders and instructions, at once proceeded methodically to remove the bulkier pieces. The first boat was filled in half an hour; and it was decided that the Growler and the Masher should go on ahead and begin to load the motor car.

Lupin went to see them start. On returning to the house, it struck him, as he passed through the hall, that he heard a voice in the pantry. He went there and found Leonard lying flat on his stomach, quite alone, with his hands tied behind his back:

"So it's you growling, my flunkey? Don't get excited: it's almost finished. Only, if you make too much noise, you'll oblige us to take severer measures ... Do

you like pears? We might give you one, you know:
a choke-pear!"

As he went upstairs, he again heard the same sound
and, stopping to listen, he caught these words, uttered in
a hoarse, groaning voice, which came, beyond a doubt,
from the pantry:

"Help ... Murder! Help ...! I shall be killed ...! Inform
the commissary!"

"The fellow's clean off his chump!" muttered Lupin.
"By Jove! To disturb the police at nine o'clock in the
evening: there's a notion for you!"

He set to work again. It took longer than he expected,
for they discovered in the cupboards all sorts of valuable
knick-knacks which it would have been very wrong to
disdain and, on the other hand, Vaucheray and Gilbert
were going about their investigations with signs of
laboured concentration that nonplussed him.

At long last, he lost his patience:

"That will do!" he said. "We're not going to spoil the
whole job and keep the motor waiting for the sake of the
few odd bits that remain. I'm taking the boat."

They were now by the waterside and Lupin went down
the steps. Gilbert held him back:

"I say, governor, we want one more look round five
minutes, no longer."

"But what for, dash it all?"

"Well, it's like this: we were told of an old reliquary,
something stunning ..."

"Well?"

"We can't lay our hands on it. And I was thinking ...
There's a cupboard with a big lock to it in the pantry ...

You see, we can't very well …" He was already on his way to the villa. Vaucheray ran back too.

"I'll give you ten minutes, not a second longer!" cried Lupin. "In ten minutes, I'm off."

But the ten minutes passed and he was still waiting.

He looked at his watch:

"A quarter-past nine," he said to himself. "This is madness."

And he also remembered that Gilbert and Vaucheray had behaved rather queerly throughout the removal of the things, keeping close together and apparently watching each other. What could be happening?

Lupin mechanically returned to the house, urged by a feeling of anxiety which he was unable to explain; and, at the same time, he listened to a dull sound which rose in the distance, from the direction of Enghien, and which seemed to be coming nearer … People strolling about, no doubt …

He gave a sharp whistle and then went to the main gate, to take a glance down the avenue. But, suddenly, as he was opening the gate, a shot rang out, followed by a yell of pain. He returned at a run, went round the house, leapt up the steps and rushed to the dining room:

"Blast it all, what are you doing there, you two?"

Gilbert and Vaucheray, locked in a furious embrace, were rolling on the floor, uttering cries of rage. Their clothes were dripping with blood. Lupin flew at them to separate them. But already Gilbert had got his adversary down and was wrenching out of his hand something which Lupin had no time to see. And Vaucheray, who was losing blood through a wound in the shoulder, fainted.

"Who hurt him? You, Gilbert?" asked Lupin, furiously.

"No, Leonard."

"Leonard? Why, he was tied up!"

"He undid his fastenings and got hold of his revolver."

"The scoundrel! Where is he?"

Lupin took the lamp and went into the pantry.

The manservant was lying on his back, with his arms outstretched, a dagger stuck in his throat and a livid face. A red stream trickled from his mouth.

"Ah," gasped Lupin, after examining him, "he's dead!"

"Do you think so ...? Do you think so?" stammered Gilbert, in a trembling voice.

"He's dead, I tell you."

"It was Vaucheray ... it was Vaucheray who did it ..."

Pale with anger, Lupin caught hold of him:

"It was Vaucheray, was it ...? And you too, you blackguard, since you were there and didn't stop him! Blood! Blood! You know I won't have it ... Well, it's a bad lookout for you, my fine fellows ... You'll have to pay the damage! And you won't get off cheaply either ... Mind the guillotine!" And, shaking him violently, "What was it? Why did he kill him?"

"He wanted to go through his pockets and take the key of the cupboard from him. When he stooped over him, he saw that the man unloosed his arms. He got frightened ... and he stabbed him ..."

"But the revolver shot?"

"It was Leonard ... he had his revolver in his hand ... he just had strength to take aim before he died ..."

"And the key of the cupboard?"

"Vaucheray took it ..."

"Did he open it?"

"And did he find what he was after?"

"Yes."

"And you wanted to take the thing from him. What sort of thing was it? The reliquary? No, it was too small for that ... Then what was it? Answer me, will you ...?"

Lupin gathered from Gilbert's silence and the determined expression on his face that he would not obtain a reply. With a threatening gesture, "I'll make you talk, my man. Sure as my name's Lupin, you shall come out with it. But, for the moment, we must see about decamping. Here, help me. We must get Vaucheray into the boat ..."

They had returned to the dining room and Gilbert was bending over the wounded man, when Lupin stopped him:

"Listen."

They exchanged one look of alarm... Someone was speaking in the pantry ... a very low, strange, very distant voice ... Nevertheless, as they at once made certain, there was no one in the room, no one except the dead man, whose dark outline lay stretched upon the floor.

And the voice spake anew, by turns shrill, stifled, bleating, stammering, yelling, fearsome. It uttered indistinct words, broken syllables.

Lupin felt the top of his head covering with perspiration. What was this incoherent voice, mysterious as a voice from beyond the grave?

He had knelt down by the manservant's side. The voice was silent and then began again:

"Give us a better light," he said to Gilbert.

He was trembling a little, shaken with a nervous dread which he was unable to master, for there was no doubt possible: when Gilbert had removed the shade from the lamp, Lupin realised that the voice issued from the corpse itself, without a movement of the lifeless mass, without a quiver of the bleeding mouth.

"Governor, I've got the shivers," stammered Gilbert.

Again the same voice, the same snuffling whisper.

Suddenly, Lupin burst out laughing, seized the corpse and pulled it aside:

"Exactly!" he said, catching sight of an object made of polished metal. "Exactly! That's it ...! Well, upon my word, it took me long enough!"

On the spot on the floor which he had uncovered lay the receiver of a telephone, the cord of which ran up to the apparatus fixed on the wall, at the usual height.

Lupin put the receiver to his ear. The noise began again at once, but it was a mixed noise, made up of different calls, exclamations, confused cries, the noise produced by a number of persons questioning one another at the same time.

"Are you there ...? He won't answer. It's awful ... They must have killed him. What is it ...? Keep up your courage. There's help on the way ... police ... soldiers ..."

"Dash it!" said Lupin, dropping the receiver.

The truth appeared to him in a terrifying vision. Quite at the beginning, while the things upstairs were being moved, Leonard, whose bonds were not securely fastened, had contrived to scramble to his feet, to unhook the receiver, probably with his teeth, to drop it and to appeal for assistance to the Enghien telephone-exchange.

And those were the words which Lupin had overheard, after the first boat started:

"Help ...! Murder ...! I shall be killed ...!"

And this was the reply of the exchange. The police were hurrying to the spot. And Lupin remembered the sounds which he had heard from the garden, four or five minutes earlier, at most:

"The police! Take to your heels!" he shouted, darting across the dining room.

"What about Vaucheray?" asked Gilbert.

"Sorry, can't be helped!"

But Vaucheray, waking from his torpor, entreated him as he passed:

"Governor, you wouldn't leave me like this!"

Lupin stopped, in spite of the danger, and was lifting the wounded man, with Gilbert's assistance, when a loud din arose outside:

"Too late!" he said.

At that moment, blows shook the hall door at the back of the house. He ran to the front steps: a number of men had already turned the corner of the house at a rush. He might have managed to keep ahead of them, with Gilbert, and reach the waterside. But what chance was there of embarking and escaping under the enemy's fire?

He locked and bolted the door.

"We are surrounded ... and done for," spluttered Gilbert.

"Hold your tongue," said Lupin.

"But they've seen us, governor. There, they're knocking."

"Hold your tongue," Lupin repeated. "Not a word. Not a movement."

He himself remained unperturbed, with an utterly

calm face and the pensive attitude of one who has all the time that he needs to examine a delicate situation from every point of view. He had reached one of those minutes which he called the 'superior moments of existence', those which alone give a value and a price to life. On such occasions, however threatening the danger, he always began by counting to himself, slowly – "One ... Two ... Three ... Four ... Five ... Six" – until the beating of his heart became normal and regular. Then and not till then, he reflected, but with what intensity, with what perspicacity, with what a profound intuition of possibilities! All the factors of the problem were present in his mind. He foresaw everything. He admitted everything. And he took his resolution in all logic and in all certainty.

After thirty or forty seconds, while the men outside were banging at the doors and picking the locks, he said to his companion:

"Follow me."

Returning to the dining room, he softly opened the sash and drew the Venetian blinds of a window in the side-wall. People were coming and going, rendering flight out of the question.

Thereupon he began to shout with all his might, in a breathless voice:

"This way ...! Help ...! I've got them ...! This way!"

He pointed his revolver and fired two shots into the tree-tops. Then he went back to Vaucheray, bent over him and smeared his face and hands with the wounded man's blood. Lastly, turning upon Gilbert, he took him violently by the shoulders and threw him to the floor.

"What do you want, governor? There's a nice thing to do!"

"Let me do as I please," said Lupin, laying an imperative stress on every syllable. "I'll answer for everything ... I'll answer for the two of you ... Let me do as I like with you ... I'll get you both out of prison ... But I can only do that if I'm free."

Excited cries rose through the open window.

"This way!" he shouted. "I've got them! Help!"

And, quietly, in a whisper:

"Just think for a moment ... Have you anything to say to me ...? Something that can be of use to us?"

Gilbert was too much taken aback to understand Lupin's plan and he struggled furiously. Vaucheray showed more intelligence; moreover, he had given up all hope of escape, because of his wound; and he snarled:

"Let the governor have his way, you ass! As long as he gets off, isn't that the great thing?"

Suddenly, Lupin remembered the article which Gilbert had put in his pocket, after capturing it from Vaucheray. He now tried to take it in his turn.

"No, not that! Not if I know it!" growled Gilbert, managing to release himself.

Lupin floored him once more. But two men suddenly appeared at the window; and Gilbert yielded and, handing the thing to Lupin, who pocketed it without looking at it, whispered:

"Here you are, governor ... I'll explain. You can be sure that ..."

He did not have time to finish. Two policemen and others after them and soldiers who entered through every door and window came to Lupin's assistance.

Gilbert was at once seized and firmly bound.

Lupin withdrew:

"I'm glad you've come," he said. "The beggar's given me a lot of trouble. I wounded the other; but this one ..."

The commissary of police asked him, hurriedly:

"Have you seen the manservant? Have they killed him?"

"I don't know," he answered.

"You don't know ...?"

"Why, I came with you from Enghien, on hearing of the murder! Only, while you were going round the left of the house, I went round the right. There was a window open. I climbed up just as these two ruffians were about to jump down. I fired at this one," pointing to Vaucheray, "and seized hold of his pal."

How could he have been suspected? He was covered with blood. He had handed over the valet's murderers. Half a score of people had witnessed the end of the heroic combat which he had delivered. Besides, the uproar was too great for anyone to take the trouble to argue or to waste time in entertaining doubts. In the height of the first confusion, the people of the neighbourhood invaded the villa. One and all lost their heads. They ran to every side, upstairs, downstairs, to the very cellar. They asked one another questions, yelled and shouted; and no one dreamt of checking Lupin's statements, which sounded so plausible.

However, the discovery of the body in the pantry restored the commissary to a sense of his responsibility. He issued orders, had the house cleared and placed policemen at the gate to prevent anyone from passing in or out. Then, without further delay, he examined the spot and began his inquiry. Vaucheray gave his name; Gilbert refused to give his, on the plea that he would only speak in the presence of a lawyer. But, when he was accused of the murder, he informed against Vaucheray, who defended himself by denouncing the other; and the two of them vociferated at the same time, with the evident wish to monopolise the commissary's attention. When the commissary turned to Lupin, to request his evidence, he perceived that the stranger was no longer there.

Without the least suspicion, he said to one of the policemen:

"Go and tell that gentleman that I should like to ask him a few questions."

They looked about for the gentleman. Someone had seen him standing on the steps, lighting a cigarette. The next news was that he had given cigarettes to a group of soldiers and strolled towards the lake, saying that they were to call him if he was wanted.

They called him. No one replied.

But a soldier came running up. The gentleman had just got into a boat and was rowing away for all he was worth. The commissary looked at Gilbert and realised that he had been tricked:

"Stop him!" he shouted. "Fire on him! He's an accomplice!"

He himself rushed out, followed by two policemen, while the others remained with the prisoners. On reaching the bank, he saw the gentleman, a hundred yards away, taking off his hat to him in the dusk.

One of the policemen discharged his revolver, without thinking.

The wind carried the sound of words across the water. The gentleman was singing as he rowed:

"Go, little bark, Float in the dark ... "

But the commissary saw a skiff fastened to the landing-stage of the adjoining property. He scrambled over the hedge separating the two gardens and, after ordering the soldiers to watch the banks of the lake and to seize the fugitive if he tried to put ashore, the commissary and two of his men pulled off in pursuit of Lupin.

It was not a difficult matter, for they were able to follow his movements by the intermittent light of the moon and to see that he was trying to cross the lakes while bearing towards the right – that is to say, towards the village of Saint-Gratien. Moreover, the commissary soon perceived that, with the aid of his men and thanks perhaps to the comparative lightness of his craft, he was rapidly gaining on the other. In ten minutes he had decreased the interval between them by one half.

"That's it!" he cried. "We shan't even need the soldiers to keep him from landing. I very much want to make the fellow's acquaintance. He's a cool hand and no mistake!"

The funny thing was that the distance was now diminishing at an abnormal rate, as though the fugitive had lost heart at realising the futility of the struggle. The policemen redoubled their efforts. The boat shot across the water with the swiftness of a swallow. Another hundred yards at most and they would reach the man.

"Halt!" cried the commissary.

The enemy, whose huddled shape they could make out

in the boat, no longer moved. The sculls drifted with the stream. And this absence of all motion had something alarming about it. A ruffian of that stamp might easily lie in wait for his aggressors, sell his life dearly and even shoot them dead before they had a chance of attacking him.

"Surrender!" shouted the commissary.

The sky, at that moment, was dark. The three men lay flat at the bottom of their skiff, for they thought they perceived a threatening gesture.

The boat, carried by its own impetus, was approaching the other.

The commissary growled:

"We won't let ourselves be sniped. Let's fire at him. Are you ready?" And he roared, once more, "Surrender ... if not ...!"

No reply.

The enemy did not budge.

"Surrender! Hands up! You refuse? So much the worse for you ... I'm counting ... One ... Two ..."

The policemen did not wait for the word of command. They fired and, at once, bending over their oars, gave the boat so powerful an impulse that it reached the goal in a few strokes.

The commissary watched, revolver in hand, ready for the least movement. He raised his arm:

"If you stir, I'll blow out your brains!"

But the enemy did not stir for a moment; and, when the boat was bumped and the two men, letting go their oars, prepared for the formidable assault, the commissary understood the reason of this passive attitude: there was no one in the boat. The enemy had escaped by swimming, leaving in the hands of the victor a certain number of the stolen articles, which, heaped up and surmounted by a jacket and a bowler hat, might be taken, at a pinch, in the semi-darkness, vaguely to represent the figure of a man.

They struck matches and examined the enemy's cast clothes. There were no initials in the hat. The jacket contained neither papers nor pocketbook. Nevertheless, they made a discovery which was destined to give the case no little celebrity and which had a terrible influence on the fate of Gilbert and Vaucheray: in one of the pockets was a visiting-card which the fugitive had left behind ... the card of Arsène Lupin.

At almost the same moment, while the police, towing the captured skiff behind them, continued their empty search and while the soldiers stood drawn up on the bank, straining their eyes to try and follow the fortunes of the naval combat, the aforesaid Arsène Lupin was quietly landing at the very spot which he had left two hours earlier.

He was there met by his two other accomplices, the Growler and the Masher, flung them a few sentences by way of explanation, jumped into the motor car, among Daubrecq the deputy's armchairs and other valuables, wrapped himself in his furs and drove, by deserted roads, to his repository at Neuilly, where he left the chauffeur. A taxicab brought him back to Paris and put him down by the church of Saint-Philippe-du-Roule, not far from which, in the rue Matignon, he had a flat, on the entresol-floor, of which none of his gang, excepting Gilbert, knew, a flat with a private entrance. He was glad to take off his clothes and rub himself down; for, in spite of his strong constitution, he felt chilled to the bone. On retiring to bed, he emptied the contents of his pockets, as usual, on the mantelpiece. It was not till then that he noticed, near his pocketbook and his keys, the object which Gilbert had put into his hand at the last moment.

And he was very much surprised. It was a decanter-stopper, a little crystal stopper, like those used for the bottles in a liqueur stand. And this crystal stopper had nothing particular about it. The most that Lupin observed was that the knob, with its many facets, was gilded right down to the indent. But, to tell the truth, this detail did not seem to him of a nature to attract special notice.

"And it was this bit of glass to which Gilbert and Vaucheray attached such stubborn importance!" he said to himself. "It was for this that they killed the valet, fought each other, wasted their time, risked prison ... trial ... the scaffold!"

Too tired to linger further upon this matter, exciting though it appeared to him, he replaced the stopper on the mantelpiece and got into bed.

He had bad dreams. Gilbert and Vaucheray were kneeling on the flags of their cells, wildly stretching out their hands to him and yelling with fright:

"Help! Help!" they cried.

But, notwithstanding all his efforts, he was unable to move. He himself was fastened by invisible bonds. And, trembling, obsessed by a monstrous vision, he watched the dismal preparations, the cutting of the condemned men's hair and shirt-collars, the squalid tragedy.

"By Jove!" he said, when he woke after a series of nightmares. "There's a lot of bad omens! Fortunately, we don't err on the side of superstition. Otherwise ...!" And he added, "For that matter, we have a talisman which, to judge by Gilbert and Vaucheray's behaviour, should be enough, with Lupin's help, to frustrate bad luck and secure the triumph of the good cause. Let's have a look at that crystal stopper!"

He sprang out of bed to take the thing and examine it more closely. An exclamation escaped him. The crystal stopper had disappeared ...

Eight from Nine Leaves One

Notwithstanding my friendly relations with Lupin and the many flattering proofs of his confidence which he has given me, there is one thing which I have never been quite able to fathom, and that is the organisation of his gang.

The existence of the gang is an undoubted fact. Certain adventures can be explained only by countless acts of devotion, invincible efforts of energy and powerful cases of complicity, representing so many forces which all obey one mighty will. But how is this will exerted? Through what intermediaries, through what subordinates? That is what I do not know. Lupin keeps his secret; and the secrets which Lupin chooses to keep are, so to speak, impenetrable.

The only supposition which I can allow myself to make is that this gang, which, in my opinion, is very limited in numbers and therefore all the more formidable, is completed and extended indefinitely by the addition of independent units, provisional associates, picked up in every class of society and in every country of the world, who are the executive agents of an authority with which, in many cases, they are not even acquainted. The companions, the initiates, the faithful adherents – men who play the leading parts under the direct command of Lupin – move to and fro between these secondary agents and the master.

Gilbert and Vaucheray evidently belonged to the main gang. And that is why the law showed itself so implacable in their regard. For the first time, it held accomplices of Lupin in its clutches – declared, undisputed accomplices – and those accomplices had committed a murder. If the murder was premeditated, if the accusation of deliberate homicide could be supported by substantial proofs, it meant the scaffold. Now there was, at the very least, one self-evident proof, the cry for assistance which Leonard had sent over the telephone a few minutes before his death:

"Help ...! Murder ...! I shall be killed ...!"

The desperate appeal had been heard by two men, the operator on duty and one of his fellow-clerks, who swore to it positively. And it was in consequence of this appeal that the commissary of police, who was at once informed, had proceeded to the Villa Marie-Therese, escorted by his men and a number of soldiers off duty.

Lupin had a very clear notion of the danger from the first. The fierce struggle in which he had engaged against society was entering upon a new and terrible phase. His luck was turning. It was no longer a matter of attacking others, but of defending himself and saving the heads of his two companions.

A little memorandum, which I have copied from one of the notebooks in which he often jots down a summary of the situations that perplex him, will show us the workings of his brain:

"One definite fact, to begin with, is that Gilbert and Vaucheray humbugged me. The Enghien expedition, undertaken ostensibly with the object of robbing the Villa Marie-Therese, had a secret purpose. This purpose obsessed their minds throughout the operations; and what they were looking for, under the furniture and in the cupboards, was one thing and one thing alone: the crystal stopper. Therefore, if I want to see clear ahead, I must first of all know what this means. It is certain that, for some hidden reason, that mysterious piece of glass possesses an incalculable value in their eyes. And not only in theirs, for, last night, someone was bold enough and clever enough to enter my flat and steal the object in question from me."

This theft of which he was the victim puzzled Lupin curiously.

Two problems, both equally difficult of solution, presented themselves to his mind. First, who was the mysterious visitor? Gilbert, who enjoyed his entire confidence and acted as his private secretary, was the only one who knew of the retreat in the rue Matignon. Now Gilbert was in prison. Was Lupin to suppose that Gilbert had betrayed him and put the police on his tracks? In that case, why were they content with taking the crystal stopper, instead of arresting him, Lupin?

But there was something much stranger still. Admitting that they had been able to force the doors of his flat – and this he was compelled to admit, though there was no mark to show it – how had they succeeded in entering the bedroom? He turned the key and pushed the bolt as he did every evening, in accordance with a habit from which he never departed. And, nevertheless – the fact was undeniable – the crystal stopper had disappeared without the lock or the bolt having been touched. And, although Lupin flattered himself that he had sharp ears, even when asleep, not a sound had waked him!

He took no great pains to probe the mystery. He knew those problems too well to hope that this one could be solved other than in the course of events. But, feeling very much put out and exceedingly uneasy, he then and there locked up his entresol flat in the rue Matignon and swore that he would never set foot in it again.

And he applied himself forthwith to the question of corresponding with Vaucheray or Gilbert.

Here a fresh disappointment awaited him. It was so clearly understood, both at the Santé Prison and at the Law Courts, that all communication between Lupin and the prisoners must be absolutely prevented, that a multitude of minute precautions were ordered by the prefect of police and minutely observed by the lowest subordinates. Trusted policemen, always the same men, watched Gilbert and Vaucheray, day and night, and never let them out of their sight.

Lupin, at this time, had not yet promoted himself to the crowning honour of his career, the post of chief of the detective service, and, consequently, was not able to take steps at the Law Courts to insure the execution of his plans. After a fortnight of fruitless endeavours, he was obliged to bow.

He did so with a raging heart and a growing sense of anxiety.

"The difficult part of a business," he often says, "is not the finish, but the start."

Where was he to start in the present circumstances? What road was he to follow?

His thoughts recurred to Daubrecq the deputy, the original owner of the crystal stopper, who probably knew its importance. On the other hand, how was Gilbert aware of the doings and mode of life of Daubrecq the deputy? What means had he employed to keep him under observation? Who had told him of the place where Daubrecq spent the evening of that day? These were all interesting questions to solve.

Daubrecq had moved to his winter quarters in Paris immediately after the burglary at the Villa Marie-Therese and was now living in his own house, on the left-hand side of the little Square Lamartine that opens out at the end of the avenue Victor-Hugo.

First disguising himself as an old gentleman of private means, strolling about, cane in hand, Lupin spent his time in the neighbourhood, on the benches of the square and the avenue. He made a discovery on the first day. Two men, dressed as workmen, but behaving in a manner that left no doubt as to their aims, were watching the deputy's house. When Daubrecq went out, they set off in pursuit of him; and they were immediately behind him when he came home again. At night, as soon as the lights were out, they went away.

Lupin shadowed them in his turn. They were detective-officers.

"Hullo, hullo!" he said to himself. "This is hardly what I expected. So the Daubrecq bird is under suspicion?"

But, on the fourth day, at nightfall, the two men were joined by six others, who conversed with them in the darkest part of the Square Lamartine. And, among these new arrivals, Lupin was vastly astonished to recognise, by his figure and bearing, the famous Prasville, the erstwhile barrister, sportsman and explorer, now favourite at the Elysée, who, for some mysterious reason, had been pitchforked into the headquarters of police as secretary general, with the reversion of the prefecture.

And, suddenly, Lupin remembered: two years ago, Prasville and Daubrecq the deputy had had a personal encounter on the place du Palais-Bourbon. The incident made a great stir at the time. No one knew the cause of it. Prasville had sent his seconds to Daubrecq on the same day; but Daubrecq refused to fight.

A little while later, Prasville was appointed secretary general.

"Very odd, very odd," said Lupin, who remained plunged in thought, while continuing to observe Prasville's movements.

At seven o'clock Prasville's group of men moved away a few yards, in the direction of the avenue Henri-Martin. The door of a small garden on the right of the house opened and Daubrecq appeared. The two detectives followed close behind him and, when he took the rue-Taitbout train, jumped on after him.

Prasville at once walked across the square and rang

the bell. The garden gate was between the house and the porter's lodge. The portress came and opened it. There was a brief conversation, after which Prasville and his companions were admitted.

"A domiciliary visit," said Lupin. "Secret and illegal. By the strict rules of politeness, I ought to be invited. My presence is indispensable."

Without the least hesitation he went up to the house, the door of which had not been closed, and, passing in front of the portress, who was casting her eyes outside, he asked, in the hurried tones of a person who is late for an appointment:

"Have the gentlemen come?"

"Yes, you will find them in the study."

His plan was quite simple: if any one met him, he would pretend to be a tradesman. But there was no need for this subterfuge. He was able, after crossing an empty hall, to enter a dining room which also had no one in it, but which, through the panes of a glass partition that separated the dining room from the study, afforded him a view of Prasville and his five companions.

Prasville opened all the drawers with the aid of false keys. Next, he examined all the papers, while his companions took down the books from the shelves, shook the pages of each separately and felt inside the bindings.

"Of course, it's a paper they're looking for," said Lupin. "Banknotes, perhaps ..."

Prasville exclaimed:

"What rot! We shan't find a thing!"

Yet he obviously did not abandon all hope of discovering what he wanted, for he suddenly seized the four bottles in a liqueur-stand, took out the four stoppers and inspected them.

"Hullo!" thought Lupin. "Now he's going for decanter stoppers! Then it's not a question of a paper? Well, I give it up."

Prasville next lifted and examined different objects; and he asked:

"How often have you been here?"

"Six times last winter," was the reply.

"And you have searched the house thoroughly?"

"Every one of the rooms, for days at a time, while he was visiting his constituency."

"Still ... still ..." And he added, "Has he no servant at present?"

"No, he is looking for one. He has his meals out and the portress keeps the house as best she can. The woman is devoted to us ..."

Prasville persisted in his investigations for nearly an hour and a half, shifting and fingering all the knick-knacks, but taking care to put everything back exactly where he found it. At nine o'clock, however, the two detectives who had followed Daubrecq burst into the study:

"He's coming back!"

"On foot?"

"Yes."

"Have we time?"

"Oh, dear, yes!"

Prasville and the men from the police office withdrew, without undue haste, after taking a last glance round the room to make sure that there was nothing to betray their visit.

The position was becoming critical for Lupin. He ran the risk of knocking up against Daubrecq if he went away, or of not being able to get out if he remained. But, on ascertaining that the dining room windows afforded a direct means of exit to the square, he resolved to stay. Besides, the opportunity of obtaining a close view of Daubrecq was too good to refuse; and, as Daubrecq had been out to dinner, there was not much chance of his entering the dining room.

Lupin, therefore, waited, holding himself ready to hide behind a velvet curtain that could be drawn across the glazed partition in case of need.

He heard the sound of doors opening and shutting. Someone walked into the study and switched on the light. He recognised Daubrecq.

The deputy was a stout, thickset, bull-necked man, very nearly bald, with a fringe of grey whiskers round his chin and wearing a pair of black eye glasses under his spectacles, for his eyes were weak and strained. Lupin noticed the powerful features, the square chin, the prominent cheekbones. The hands were brawny and covered with hair, the legs bowed; and he walked with a stoop, bearing first on one hip and then on the other, which gave him something of the gait of a gorilla. But the face was topped by an enormous, lined forehead, indented with hollows and dotted with bumps.

There was something bestial, something savage, something repulsive about the man's whole personality. Lupin remembered that, in the Chamber of Deputies, Daubrecq was nicknamed 'The Wild Man of the Woods' and that he was so labelled not only because he stood aloof and hardly ever mixed with his fellow-members, but also because of his appearance, his behaviour, his peculiar gait and his remarkable muscular development.

He sat down to his desk, took a meerschaum pipe from his pocket, selected a packet of caporal among several packets of tobacco which lay drying in a bowl, tore open the wrapper, filled his pipe and lit it. Then he began to write letters.

Presently he ceased his work and sat thinking, with his attention fixed on a spot on his desk.

He lifted a little stamp box and examined it. Next, he verified the position of different articles which Prasville had touched and replaced; and he searched them with his eyes, felt them with his hands, bending over them as though certain signs, known to himself alone, were able to tell him what he wished to know.

Lastly, he grasped the knob on an electric bell-pull and rang. The portress appeared a minute later.

He asked:

"They've been, haven't they?"

And, when the woman hesitated about replying, he insisted:

"Come, come, Clemence, did you open this stamp box?"

"No, sir."

"Well, I fastened the lid down with a little strip of gummed paper. The strip has been broken."

"But I assure you ..." the woman began.

"Why tell lies," he said, "considering that I myself instructed you to lend yourself to those visits?"

"The fact is ..."

"The fact is that you want to keep on good terms with both sides ... Very well!" He handed her a fifty-franc note and repeated, "Have they been?"

"Yes."

"The same men as in the spring?"

"Yes, all five of them ... with another one, who ordered them about."

"A tall, dark man?"

"Yes."

Lupin saw Daubrecq's mouth hardening; and Daubrecq continued:

"Is that all?"

"There was one more, who came after they did and joined them ... and then, just now, two more, the pair who usually keep watch outside the house."

"Did they remain in the study?"

"Yes, sir."

"And they went away when I came back? A few minutes before, perhaps?"

"Yes, sir."

"That will do."

The woman left the room. Daubrecq returned to his letter writing. Then, stretching out his arm, he made some marks on a white writing tablet, at the end of his desk, and rested it against the desk, as though he wished to keep it in sight. The marks were figures; and Lupin was able to read the following subtraction sum:

$9 - 8 = 1$

And Daubrecq, speaking between his teeth, thoughtfully uttered the syllables:

"Eight from nine leaves one … There's not a doubt about that," he added, aloud. He wrote one more letter, a very short one, and addressed the envelope with an inscription which Lupin was able to decipher when the letter was placed beside the writing tablet:

To Monsieur Prasville, Secretary general of the Prefecture of Police.

Then he rang the bell again:

"Clemence," he said, to the portress, "did you go to school as a child?"

"Yes, sir, of course I did."

"And were you taught arithmetic?"

"Why, sir …"

"Well, you're not very good at subtraction."

"What makes you say that?"

"Because you don't know that nine minus eight equals one. And that, you see, is a fact of the highest importance. Life becomes impossible if you are ignorant of that fundamental truth."

He rose, as he spoke, and walked round the room, with his hands behind his back, swaying upon his hips. He did so once more. Then, stopping at the dining room, he opened the door:

"For that matter, there's another way of putting the problem. Take eight from nine; and one remains. And the one who remains is here, eh? Correct! And Monsieur supplies us with a striking proof, does he not?"

He patted the velvet curtain in which Lupin had hurriedly wrapped himself:

"Upon my word, sir, you must be stifling under this! Not to say that I might have amused myself by sticking a dagger through the curtain. Remember Hamlet's madness and Polonius' death: 'How now! A rat? Dead, for a ducat, dead!' Come along, Mr. Polonius, come out of your hole."

It was one of those positions to which Lupin was not accustomed and which he loathed. To catch others in a trap and pull their leg was all very well; but it was a very different thing to have people teasing him and roaring with laughter at his expense. Yet what could he answer back?

"You look a little pale, Mr. Polonius ... Hullo! Why, it's the respectable old gentleman who has been hanging about the square for some days! So you belong to the police too, Mr. Polonius? There, there, pull yourself together, I shan't hurt you! But you see, Clemence, how right my calculation was. You told me that nine spies had been to the house. I counted a troop of eight, as I came along, eight of them in the distance, down the avenue. Take eight from nine and one remains: the one who evidently remained behind to see what he could see. Ecce homo!"

"Well? And then?" said Lupin, who felt a mad craving to fly at the fellow and reduce him to silence.

"And then? Nothing at all, my good man ... What more do you want? The farce is over. I will only ask you to take this little note to Master Prasville, your employer. Clemence, please show Mr. Polonius out. And, if ever he calls again, fling open the doors wide to him.

Pray look upon this as your home, Mr. Polonius. Your servant, sir ...!"

Lupin hesitated. He would have liked to talk big and to come out with a farewell phrase, a parting speech, like an actor making a showy exit from the stage, and at least to disappear with the honours of war. But his defeat was so pitiable that he could think of nothing better than to bang his hat on his head and stamp his feet as he followed the portress down the hall. It was a poor revenge.

"You rascally beggar!" he shouted, once he was outside the door, shaking his fist at Daubrecq's windows. "Wretch, scum of the earth, deputy, you shall pay for this! Oh, he allows himself! Oh, he has the cheek to! Well, I swear to you, my fine fellow, that, one of these days ..."

He was foaming with rage, all the more as, in his innermost heart, he recognised the strength of his new enemy and could not deny the masterly fashion in which he had managed this business. Daubrecq's coolness, the assurance with which he hoaxed the police officials, the contempt with which he lent himself to their visits at his house and, above all, his wonderful self-possession, his easy bearing and the impertinence of his conduct in the presence of the ninth person who was spying on him: all this denoted a man of character, a strong man, with a well-balanced mind, lucid, bold, sure of himself and of the cards in his hand.

But what were those cards? What game was he playing? Who held the stakes? And how did the players stand on either side? Lupin could not tell. Knowing nothing, he flung himself headlong into the thick of the fray, between adversaries desperately involved, though he himself was in total ignorance of their positions, their weapons, their resources and their secret plans. For, when all was said, he could not admit that the object of all those efforts was to obtain possession of a crystal stopper!

One thing alone pleased him: Daubrecq had not penetrated his disguise. Daubrecq believed him to be in the employ of the police. Neither Daubrecq nor the police, therefore, suspected the intrusion of a third thief in the business. This was his one and only trump, a trump that gave him a liberty of action to which he attached the greatest importance.

Without further delay, he opened the letter which Daubrecq had handed him for the secretary general of police. It contained these few lines:

Within reach of your hand, my dear Prasville, within reach of your hand! You touched it! A little more and the trick was done … But you're too big a fool. And to think that they couldn't hit upon any one better than you to make me bite the dust. Poor old France! Goodbye, Prasville. But, if I catch you in the act, it will be a bad lookout for you: my maxim is to shoot at sight. Daubrecq

"Within reach of your hand," repeated Lupin, after reading the note. "And to think that the rogue may be writing the truth! The most elementary hiding places are the safest. We must look into this, all the same. And, also, we must find out why Daubrecq is the object of such

41

strict supervision and obtain a few particulars about the fellow generally."

The information supplied to Lupin by a private enquiry office consisted of the following details:

ALEXIS DAUBRECQ, deputy of the Bouches-du-Rhone for the past two years; sits among the independent members. Political opinions not very clearly defined, but electoral position exceedingly strong, because of the enormous sums which he spends in nursing his constituency. No private income. Nevertheless, has a house in Paris, a villa at Enghien and another at Nice and loses heavily at play, though no one knows where the money comes from. Has great influence and obtains all he wants without making up to ministers or, apparently, having either friends or connections in political circles.

"That's a trade docket," said Lupin to himself. "What I want is a domestic docket, a police docket, which will tell me about the gentleman's private life and enable me to work more easily in this darkness and to know if I'm not getting myself into a tangle by bothering about the Daubrecq bird. And time's getting short, hang it!"

One of the residences which Lupin occupied at that period and which he used oftener than any of the others was in the rue Chateaubriand, near the Triomphe. He was known there by the name of Michel Beaumont. He had a snug flat here and was looked after by a manservant, Achille, who was utterly devoted to his interests and whose chief duty was to receive and repeat the telephone messages addressed to Lupin by his followers.

Lupin, on returning home, learnt, with great astonishment, that a woman had been waiting to see him for over an hour:

"What! Why, no one ever comes to see me here! Is she young?"

"No ... I don't think so."

"You don't think so!"

"She's wearing a lace shawl over her head, instead of a hat, and you can't see her face ... She's more like a clerk ... or a woman employed in a shop. She's not well-dressed ..."

"Whom did she ask for?"

"Monsieur Michel Beaumont," replied the servant.

"Queer. And why has she called?"

"All she said was that it was about the Enghien business ... So I thought that ..."

"What! The Enghien business! Then she knows that I am mixed up in that business ... She knows that, by applying here ..."

"I could not get anything out of her, but I thought, all the same, that I had better let her in."

"Quite right. Where is she?"

"In the drawing-room. I've put on the lights."

Lupin walked briskly across the hall and opened the door of the drawing-room:

"What are you talking about?" he said, to his man. "There's no one here."

"No one here?" said Achille, running up.

And the room, in fact, was empty.

"Well, on my word, this takes the cake!" cried the servant. "It wasn't twenty minutes ago that I came and had a look, to make sure. She was sitting over there. And there's nothing wrong with my eyesight, you know."

"Look here, look here," said Lupin, irritably. "Where were you while the woman was waiting?"

"In the hall, governor! I never left the hall for a second! I should have seen her go out, blow it!"

"Still, she's not here now..."

"So I see," moaned the man, quite flabbergasted.

"She must have got tired of waiting and gone away. But, dash it all, I should like to know how she got out!"

"How she got out?" said Lupin. "Well that's easy enough, it's not rocket science."

"What do you mean?"

"She got out through the window. Look, it's still ajar. We are on the ground-floor ... The street is almost always deserted, in the evenings. There's no doubt about it."

He had looked around him and satisfied himself that nothing had been taken away or moved. The room, for that matter, contained no knick knack of any value, no important paper that might have explained the woman's visit, followed by her sudden disappearance. And yet why that inexplicable flight?

"Has any one telephoned?" he asked.

"No."

"Any letters?"

"Yes, one letter by the last post."

"Where is it?"

"I put it on your mantelpiece, governor, as usual."

Lupin's bedroom was next to the drawing-room, but Lupin had permanently bolted the door between the two. He, therefore, had to go through the hall again.

Lupin switched on the electric light and, the next moment, said:

"I don't see it ..."

"Yes ... I put it next to the flower bowl."

"There's nothing here at all."

"You must be looking in the wrong place, governor."

But Achille moved the bowl, lifted the clock, bent down to the grate, in vain: the letter was not there.

"Oh blast it, blast it!" he muttered. "She's done it ... she's taken it ... And then, when she had the letter, she cleared out ... Oh, the conniving little ...!"

Lupin said:

"You're mad! There's no way through between the two rooms."

"Then who did take it, governor?"

They were both of them silent. Lupin strove to control his anger and collect his ideas. He asked:

"Did you look at the envelope?"

"Yes."

"Anything particular about it?"

"Yes, it looked as if it had been written in a hurry, or scribbled, rather."

"How was the address worded ...? Do you remember?" asked Lupin, in a voice strained with anxiety.

"Yes, I remembered it, because it struck me as funny ..."

"But speak, will you? Speak!"

"It said, 'Monsieur de Beaumont, Michel.'"

Lupin took his servant by the shoulders and shook him:

"It said 'de' Beaumont? Are you sure? And 'Michel' after 'Beaumont'?"

"Quite certain."

"Ah!" muttered Lupin, with a choking throat. "It was a letter from Gilbert!"

He stood motionless, a little pale, with drawn features. There was no doubt about it: the letter was from Gilbert. It was the form of address which, by Lupin's orders, Gilbert had used for years in corresponding with him. Gilbert had at last – after long waiting and by dint of endless artifices – found a means of getting a letter posted from his prison and had hastily written to him. And now the letter was intercepted! What did it say? What instructions had the unhappy prisoner given? What help was he praying for? What stratagem did he suggest?

Lupin looked round the room, which, contrary to the drawing-room, contained important papers. But none of the locks had been forced; and he was compelled to admit that the woman had no other object than to get hold of Gilbert's letter.

Constraining himself to keep his temper, he asked:

"Did the letter come while the woman was here?"

"At the same time. The porter rang at the same moment."

"Could she see the envelope?"

"Yes."

The conclusion was evident. It remained to discover how the visitor had been able to effect her theft. By slipping from one window to the other, outside the flat? Impossible: Lupin found the window of his room shut. By opening the communicating door? Impossible: Lupin found it locked and barred with its two inner bolts.

Nevertheless, a person cannot pass through a wall

by a mere operation of will. To go in or out of a room requires a passage; and, as the act was accomplished in the space of a few minutes, it was necessary, in the circumstances, that the passage should be previously in existence, that it should already have been contrived in the wall and, of course, known to the woman. This hypothesis simplified the search by concentrating it upon the door; for the wall was quite bare, without a cupboard, mantelpiece or hangings of any kind, and unable to conceal the least outlet.

Lupin went back to the drawing-room and prepared to make a study of the door. But he at once gave a start. He perceived, at the first glance, that the left lower panel of the six small panels contained within the cross-bars of the door no longer occupied its normal position and that the light did not fall straight upon it. On leaning forwards, he saw two little tin tacks sticking out on either side and holding the panel in place, similar to a wooden board behind a picture frame. He had only to shift these. The panel at once came out.

Achille gave a cry of amazement. But Lupin objected:

"Well? And what then? We are no better off than before. Here is an empty oblong, eight or nine inches wide by sixteen inches high. You're not going to pretend that a woman can slip through an opening which would not admit the thinnest child of ten years old!"

"No, but she can have put her arm through and drawn the bolts."

"The bottom bolt, yes," said Lupin. "But the top bolt, no: the distance is far too great. Try for yourself and see."

Achille tried and had to give up the attempt.

Lupin did not reply. He stood thinking for a long time. Then, suddenly, he said:

"Give me my hat ... my coat ..."

He hurried off, urged by an imperative idea. And, the moment he reached the street, he sprang into a taxi:

"Rue Matignon, quick ...!"

As soon as they came to the house where he had been robbed of the crystal stopper, he jumped out of the cab, opened his private entrance, went upstairs, ran to the drawing-room, turned on the light and crouched at the foot of the door leading to his bedroom.

He had guessed right. One of the little panels was loosened in the same manner.

And, just as in his other flat in the rue Chateaubriand, the opening was large enough to admit a man's arm and shoulder, but not to allow him to draw the upper bolt.

"Hang!" he shouted, unable any longer to master the rage that had been seething within him for the last two hours. "Blast! Shall I never have finished with this confounded business?"

In fact, an incredible ill luck seemed to dog his footsteps, compelling him to grope about at random, without permitting him to use the elements of success which his own persistency or the very force of things placed within his grasp. Gilbert gave him the crystal stopper. Gilbert sent him a letter. And both had disappeared at that very moment.

And it was not, as he had until then believed, a series of fortuitous and independent circumstances. No, it was manifestly the effect of an adverse will pursuing a definite object with prodigious ability and incredible boldness, attacking him, Lupin, in the recesses of his safest retreats and baffling him with blows so severe and so unexpected that he did not even know against whom he had to defend himself. Never, in the course of his adventures, had he encountered such obstacles as now.

And, little by little, deep down within himself, there grew a haunting dread of the future. A date loomed before his eyes, the terrible date which he unconsciously assigned to the law to perform its work of vengeance, the date upon which, in the light of a wan April morning, two men would mount the scaffold, two men who had stood by him, two comrades whom he had been unable to save from paying the awful penalty ...

The Home Life of Alexis Daubrecq

When Daubrecq the deputy came in from lunch on the day after the police had searched his house he was stopped by Clemence, his portress, who told him that she had found a cook who could be thoroughly relied on.

The cook arrived a few minutes later and produced first-rate characters, signed by people with whom it was easy to take up her references. She was a very active woman, although of a certain age, and agreed to do the work of the house by herself, without the help of a manservant, this being a condition upon which Daubrecq insisted.

Her last place had been with a member of the Chamber of Deputies, Comte Saulevat, to whom Daubrecq had at once telephoned. The count's steward gave her a perfect character, and she was engaged.

As soon as she had fetched her trunk, she set to work and cleaned and scrubbed until it was time to cook the dinner.

Daubrecq dined and went out.

At eleven o'clock, after the portress had gone to bed, the cook cautiously opened the garden gate. A man came up.

"Is that you?" she asked.

"Yes, it's I, Lupin."

She took him to her bedroom on the third floor, overlooking the garden, and at once burst into lamentations:

"More of your tricks and nothing but tricks! Why can't you leave me alone, instead of sending me to do your dirty work?"

"How can I help it, you dear old Victoire? When I want a person of respectable appearance and incorruptible morals, I think of you. You ought to be flattered."

"That's all you care about me!" she cried. "You run me into danger once more; and you think it's funny!"

"What are you risking?"

"How do you mean, what am I risking? All my characters are false."

"Characters are always false."

"And suppose Monsieur Daubrecq finds out? Suppose he makes enquiries?"

"He has made enquiries."

"Eh? What's that?"

"He has telephoned the steward of Comte Saulevat, in whose service you say that you have had the honour of being."

"There, you see, I'm done for!"

"The count's steward could not say enough in your praise."

"He does not know me."

"But I know him. I got him his situation with Comte Saulevat. So you understand ..."

Victoire seemed to calm down a little:

"Well," she said, "God's will be done ... or rather yours. And what do you expect me to do in all this?"

"First, to put me up. You were my wet nurse once. You can very well give me half your room now. I'll sleep in the armchair."

"And next?"

"Next? To supply me with such food as I want."

"And next?"

"Next? To undertake, with me and under my direction, a regular series of searches with a view ..."

"To what?"

"To discovering the precious object of which I spoke to you."

"What's that?"

"A crystal stopper."

"A crystal stopper ... Saints above! A nice business! And, if we don't find your confounded stopper, what then?"

Lupin took her gently by the arm and, in a serious voice:

"If we don't find it, Gilbert, young Gilbert whom you know and love, will stand every chance of losing his head; and so will Vaucheray."

"Vaucheray I don't mind ... a dirty rascal like him! But Gilbert ..."

"Have you seen the papers this evening? Things are looking worse than ever. Vaucheray, as might be expected, accuses Gilbert of stabbing the valet; and it so happens that the knife which Vaucheray used belonged to Gilbert. That came out this morning. Whereupon Gilbert, who is intelligent in his way, but easily frightened, blithered and launched forth into stories and lies which will end in his undoing. That's how the matter stands. Will you help me?"

Thenceforth, for several days, Lupin moulded his existence upon Daubrecq's, beginning his investigations the moment the deputy left the house. He pursued them methodically, dividing each room into sections which he did not abandon until he had been through the tiniest nooks and corners and, so to speak, exhausted every possible device.

Victoire searched also. And nothing was forgotten. Table legs, chair rungs, floorboards, mouldings, mirror and picture frames, clocks, plinths, curtain borders, telephone holders and electric fittings: everything that an ingenious imagination could have selected as a hiding place was overhauled.

And they also watched the deputy's least actions, his most unconscious movements, the expression of his face, the books which he read and the letters which he wrote.

It was easy enough. He seemed to live his life in the light of day. No door was ever shut. He received no visits. And his existence worked with mechanical regularity. He went to the Chamber in the afternoon, to the club in the evening.

"Still," said Lupin, "there must be something that's not orthodox behind all this."

"There's nothing of the sort," moaned Victoire. "You're wasting your time and we shall be bowled out."

The presence of the detectives and their habit of walking up and down outside the windows drove her mad. She refused to admit that they were there for any other purpose than to trap her, Victoire. And, each time that she went shopping, she was quite surprised that one of those men did not lay his hand upon her shoulder.

One day she returned all upset. Her basket of provisions was shaking on her arm.

"What's the matter, my dear Victoire?" said Lupin. "You're looking green."

"Green? I dare say I do. So would you look green ..."

She had to sit down and it was only after making repeated efforts that she succeeded in stuttering:

"A man ... a man spoke to me ... at the fruiterer's."

"By jingo! Did he want you to run away with him?"

"No, he gave me a letter ..."

"Then what are you complaining about? It was a love letter, of course!"

"No. 'It's for your governor,' said he. 'My governor?' I said. 'Yes,' he said, 'for the gentleman who's staying in your room.'"

"What's that?"

This time, Lupin had started:

"Give it here," he said, snatching the letter from her. The envelope bore no address. But there was another, inside it, on which he read:

Monsieur Arsène Lupin, c/o Victoire.

"The devil!" he said. "This is a bit thick!" He tore open the second envelope. It contained a sheet of paper with the following words, written in large capitals:

EVERYTHING YOU ARE DOING IS USELESS AND DANGEROUS ... GIVE IT UP.

Victoire uttered one moan and fainted. As for Lupin, he felt himself blush up to his eyes, as though he had been grossly insulted. He experienced all the humiliation which a duellist would undergo if he heard the most secret advice which he had received from his seconds repeated aloud by a mocking adversary.

However, he held his tongue. Victoire went back to her work. As for him, he remained in his room all day, thinking.

That night he did not sleep.

And he kept saying to himself:

"What is the good of thinking? I am up against one of those problems which are not solved by any amount of thought. It is certain that I am not alone in the matter and that, between Daubrecq and the police, there is, in addition to the third thief that I am, a fourth thief who is working on his own account, who knows me and who reads my game clearly. But who is this fourth thief? And am I mistaken, by any chance? And ... oh, rot ...! Let's get to sleep!"

But he could not sleep; and a good part of the night went in this way.

At four o'clock in the morning he seemed to hear a noise in the house. He jumped up quickly and, from the top of the staircase, saw Daubrecq go down the first flight and turn towards the garden.

A minute later, after opening the gate, the deputy returned with a man whose head was buried in an enormous fur collar and showed him into his study.

Lupin had taken his precautions in view of any such contingency. As the windows of the study and those of his bedroom, both of which were at the back of the house, overlooked the garden, he fastened a rope ladder to his balcony, unrolled it softly and let himself down by it until it was level with the top of the study windows.

These windows were closed by shutters; but, as they were bowed, there remained a semi-circular space at the top; and Lupin, though he could not hear, was able to see all that went on inside.

He then realised that the person whom he had taken for a man was a woman: a woman who was still young, though her dark hair was mingled with grey; a tall woman, elegantly but quite unobtrusively dressed, whose handsome features bore the expression of weariness and melancholy which long suffering gives.

"Where the deuce have I seen her before?" Lupin asked himself. "For I certainly know that face, that look, that expression."

She stood leaning against the table, listening impassively to Daubrecq, who was also standing and who was talking very excitedly. He had his back turned to Lupin; but Lupin, leaning forwards, caught sight of a glass in which the deputy's image was reflected. And he was startled to see the strange look in his eyes, the air of fierce and brutal desire with which Daubrecq was staring at his visitor.

It seemed to embarrass her too, for she sat down with lowered lids. Then Daubrecq leant over her and it appeared as though he were ready to fling his long arms, with their huge hands, around her. And, suddenly, Lupin perceived great tears rolling down the woman's sad face.

Whether or not it was the sight of those tears that made Daubrecq lose his head, with a brusque movement he clutched the woman and drew her to him. She repelled him, with a violence full of hatred. And, after a brief struggle, during which Lupin caught a glimpse of the man's bestial and contorted features, the two of them stood face to face, railing at each other like mortal enemies.

Then they stopped. Daubrecq sat down. There was mischief in his face, and sarcasm as well. And he began to talk again, with sharp taps on the table, as though he were dictating terms.

She no longer stirred. She sat haughtily in her chair and towered over him, absent-minded, with roaming eyes. Lupin, captivated by that powerful and sorrowful countenance, continued to watch her; and he was vainly seeking to remember of what or of whom she reminded him, when he noticed that she had turned her head slightly and that she was imperceptibly moving her arm.

Her arm strayed farther and farther and her hand crept along the table and Lupin saw that, at the end of the table, there stood a water bottle with a gold-topped stopper. The hand reached the water bottle, felt it, rose gently and seized the stopper. A quick movement of the head, a glance, and the stopper was put back in its place.

Obviously, it was not what the woman hoped to find.

"Dash it!" said Lupin. "She's after the crystal stopper too! The matter is becoming more complicated daily; there's no doubt about it."

But, on renewing his observation of the visitor, he was astounded to note the sudden and unexpected expression of her countenance, a terrible, implacable, ferocious expression. And he saw that her hand was continuing its stealthy progress round the table and that, with an uninterrupted and crafty sliding movement, it was pushing back books and, slowly and surely, approaching a dagger whose blade gleamed among the scattered papers.

It gripped the handle.

Daubrecq went on talking. Behind his back, the hand rose steadily, little by little; and Lupin saw the woman's desperate and furious eyes fixed upon the spot in the neck where she intended to plant the knife:

"You're doing a very silly thing, fair lady," thought Lupin.

And he already began to turn over in his mind the best means of escaping and of taking Victoire with him.

She hesitated, however, with uplifted arm. But it was only a momentary weakness. She clenched her teeth. Her whole face, contracted with hatred, became yet further convulsed. And she made the dread movement.

At the same instant Daubrecq crouched and, springing from his seat, turned and seized the woman's frail wrist in mid-air.

Oddly enough, he addressed no reproach to her, as though the deed which she had attempted surprised him no more than any ordinary, very natural and simple act.

He shrugged his shoulders, like a man accustomed to that sort of danger, and strode up and down in silence.

She had dropped the weapon and was now crying, holding her head between her hands, with sobs that shook her whole frame.

He next came up to her and said a few words, once more tapping the table as he spoke.

She made a sign in the negative and, when he insisted, she, in her turn, stamped her foot on the floor and exclaimed, loud enough for Lupin to hear:

"Never! Never!"

Thereupon, without another word, Daubrecq fetched the fur cloak which she had brought with her and hung it over the woman's shoulders, while she shrouded her face in a lace wrap.

And he showed her out.

Two minutes later, the garden gate was locked again. "Pity I can't run after that strange person," thought Lupin, "and have a chat with her about the Daubrecq bird. Seems to me that we two could do a good stroke of business together."

In any case, there was one point to be cleared up: Daubrecq the deputy, whose life was so orderly, so apparently respectable, was in the habit of receiving visits at night, when his house was no longer watched by the police.

He sent Victoire to arrange with two members of his gang to keep watch for several days. And he himself remained awake next night.

As on the previous morning, he heard a noise at four o'clock. As on the previous morning, the deputy let someone in.

Lupin ran down his ladder and, when he came to the free space above the shutters, saw a man crawling at Daubrecq's feet, flinging his arms round Daubrecq's knees in frenzied despair and weeping, weeping convulsively.

Daubrecq, laughing, pushed him away repeatedly, but the man clung to him. He behaved almost like one out of his mind and, at last, in a genuine fit of madness, half rose to his feet, took the deputy by the throat and flung him back in a chair. Daubrecq struggled, powerless at first, while his veins swelled in his temples. But soon, with a strength far beyond the ordinary, he regained the mastery and deprived his adversary of all power of movement. Then, holding him with one hand, with the other he gave him two great smacks in the face.

The man got up, slowly. He was livid and could hardly stand on his legs. He waited for a moment, as though to recover his self-possession. Then, with a terrifying calmness, he drew a revolver from his pocket and levelled it at Daubrecq.

Daubrecq did not flinch. He even smiled, with a defiant air and without displaying more excitement than if he had been aimed at with a toy pistol.

The man stood for perhaps fifteen or twenty seconds, facing his enemy, with outstretched arm. Then, with the same deliberate slowness, revealing a self-control which was all the more impressive because it followed upon a fit of extreme excitement, he put up his revolver and, from another pocket, produced his note-case.

Daubrecq took a step forwards.

The man opened the pocketbook. A sheaf of banknotes appeared in sight.

Daubrecq seized and counted them. They were thousand-franc notes, and there were thirty of them.

The man looked on, without a movement of revolt, without a protest. He obviously understood the futility of words. Daubrecq was one of those who do not relent. Why should his visitor waste time in beseeching him or even in revenging himself upon him by uttering vain threats and insults? He had no hope of striking that unassailable enemy. Even Daubrecq's death would not deliver him from Daubrecq.

He took his hat and went away.

At eleven o'clock in the morning Victoire, on returning from her shopping, handed Lupin a note from his accomplices.

He opened it and read:

"The man who came to see Daubrecq last night is Langeroux the deputy, leader of the independent left. A poor man, with a large family."

"Come," said Lupin, "Daubrecq is nothing more nor less than a blackmailer; but, by Jupiter, he has jolly effective ways of going to work!"

Events tended to confirm Lupin's supposition. Three days later he saw another visitor hand Daubrecq an important sum of money. And, two days after that, one came and left a pearl necklace behind him.

The first was called Dachaumont, a senator and ex-cabinet-minister. The second was the Marquis d'Albufex, a Bonapartist deputy, formerly chief political agent in France of Prince Napoleon.

The scene, in each of these cases, was very similar to Langeroux the deputy's interview, a violent tragic scene, ending in Daubrecq's victory.

"And so on and so forth," thought Lupin, when he received these particulars. "I have been present at four visits. I shall know no more if there are ten, or twenty, or thirty ... It is enough for me to learn the names of the visitors from my friends on sentry outside. Shall I go and call on them? What for? They have no reason to confide in me ... On the other hand, am I to stay on here, delayed by investigations which lead to nothing and which Victoire can continue just as well without me?"

He was very much perplexed. The news of the inquiry into the case of Gilbert and Vaucheray was becoming worse and worse, the days were slipping by, and not an hour passed without his asking himself, in anguish, whether all his efforts – granting that he succeeded – would not end in farcical results, absolutely foreign to the aim which he was pursuing.

For, after all, supposing that he did fathom Daubrecq's underhand dealings, would that give him the means of rescuing Gilbert and Vaucheray?

That day an incident occurred which put an end to his indecision. After lunch Victoire heard snatches of a conversation which Daubrecq held with someone on the telephone. Lupin gathered, from what Victoire reported, that the deputy had an appointment with a lady for half-past eight and that he was going to take her to a theatre:

"I shall get a pit-tier box, like the one we had six weeks ago," Daubrecq had said. And he added, with a laugh, "I hope that I shall not have the burglars in during that time."

There was not a doubt in Lupin's mind. Daubrecq was about to spend his evening in the same manner in which he had spent the evening six weeks ago, while they were breaking into his villa at Enghien. To know the person whom he was to meet and perhaps thus to discover how Gilbert and Vaucheray had learnt that Daubrecq would be away from eight o'clock in the evening until one o'clock in the morning: these were matters of the utmost importance.

Lupin left the house in the afternoon, with Victoire's assistance. He knew through her that Daubrecq was coming home for dinner earlier than usual.

He went to his flat in the rue Chateaubriand, telephoned for three of his friends, dressed and made himself up in his favourite character of a Russian prince, with fair hair and moustache and short-cut whiskers.

The accomplices arrived in a motor car.

At that moment, Achille, his man, brought him a telegram, addressed to Monsieur Michel Beaumont, rue Chateaubriand, which ran:

Do not come to theatre this evening. Danger of your intervention spoiling everything.

There was a flower vase on the chimney piece beside him. Lupin took it and smashed it to pieces.

"That's it, that's it," he snarled. "They are playing with me as I usually play with others. Same behaviour. Same tricks. Only there's this difference ..."

What difference? He hardly knew. The truth was that he too was baffled and disconcerted to the inmost recesses of his being and that he was continuing to act only from obstinacy, from a sense of duty, so to speak, and without putting his ordinary good humour and high spirits into the work.

"Come along," he said to his accomplices.

By his instructions, the chauffeur set them down near the Square Lamartine, but kept the motor going. Lupin foresaw that Daubrecq, in order to escape the detectives watching the house, would jump into the first taxi; and he did not intend to be outdistanced.

He had not allowed for Daubrecq's cleverness.

At half-past seven both leaves of the garden gate were flung open, a bright light flashed and a motorcycle darted across the road, skirted the square, turned in front of the motor car and shot away towards the Bois at a speed so great that they would have been mad to go in pursuit of it.

"Goodbye, Daisy!" said Lupin, trying to jest, but really overcome with rage.

He eyed his accomplices in the hope that one of them would venture to give a mocking smile. How pleased he would have been to vent his nerves on them!

"Let's go home," he said to his companions.

He gave them some dinner; then he smoked a cigar and they set off again in the car and went the round of the theatres, beginning with those which were giving light operas and musical comedies, for which he presumed that Daubrecq and his lady would have a preference. He took a stall, inspected the lower-tier boxes and went away again.

He next drove to the more serious theatres: the Renaissance, the Gymnase.

At last, at ten o'clock in the evening, he saw a pit-tier box at the Vaudeville almost entirely protected from inspection by its two screens; and, on tipping the box keeper, was told that it contained a short, stout, elderly gentleman and a lady who was wearing a thick lace veil.

The next box was free. He took it, went back to his friends to give them their instructions and sat down near the couple.

During the interval, when the lights went up, he perceived Daubrecq's profile. The lady remained at the back of the box, invisible. The two were speaking in a low voice; and, when the curtain rose again, they went on speaking, but in such a way that Lupin could not distinguish a word.

Ten minutes passed. Someone tapped at their door. It was one of the men from the box office.

"Are you Monsieur le député Daubrecq, sir?" he asked.

"Yes," said Daubrecq, in a voice of surprise. "But how do you know my name?"

"There's a gentleman asking for you on the telephone. He told me to go to Box 22."

"But who is it?"

"Monsieur le Marquis d'Albufex."

"Eh?"

"What am I to say, sir?"

"I'm coming ... I'm coming ..."

Daubrecq rose hurriedly from his seat and followed the clerk to the box-office.

He was not yet out of sight when Lupin sprang from his box, worked the lock of the next door and sat down beside the lady.

She gave a stifled cry.

"Hush!" he said. "I have to speak to you. It is most important."

"Ah!" she said, between her teeth. "Arsène Lupin!" He was dumbfounded. For a moment he sat quiet, open-mouthed. The woman knew him! And not only did she know him, but she had recognised him through his disguise! Accustomed though he was to the most extraordinary and unusual events, this disconcerted him.

He did not even dream of protesting and stammered:

"So you know …? So you know?"

He snatched at the lady's veil and pulled it aside before she had time to defend herself:

"What!" he muttered, with increased amazement. "Is it possible?"

It was the woman whom he had seen at Daubrecq's a few days earlier, the woman who had raised her dagger against Daubrecq and who had intended to stab him with all the strength of her hatred.

It was her turn to be taken aback:

"What! Have you seen me before?"

"Yes, the other night, at his house – I saw what you tried to do …"

She made a movement to escape. He held her back and, speaking with great eagerness:

"I must know who you are," he said. "That was why I had Daubrecq telephoned for."

She looked aghast:

"Do you mean to say it was not the Marquis d'Albufex?"

"No, it was one of my assistants."

"Then Daubrecq will come back?"

"Yes, but we have time ... Listen to me ... We must meet again ... He is your enemy ... I will save you from him ..."

"Why should you? What is your object?"

"Do not distrust me ... it is quite certain that our interests are identical ... Where can I see you? Tomorrow, surely? At what time? And where?"

"Well ..."

She looked at him with obvious hesitation, not knowing what to do, on the point of speaking and yet full of uneasiness and doubt.

He pressed her:

"Oh, I entreat you ... answer me just one word ... and at once ... It would be a pity for him to find me here ... I entreat you ..."

She answered sharply:

"My name doesn't matter ... We will see each other first and you shall explain to me ... Yes, we will meet ... Listen, tomorrow, at three o'clock, at the corner of the boulevard ..."

At that exact moment, the door of the box opened, so to speak, with a bang, and Daubrecq appeared.

"Rats!" Lupin mumbled, under his breath, furious at being caught before obtaining what he wanted.

Daubrecq gave a chuckle:

"So that's it ... I thought something was up ... Ah, the telephone-trick: a little out of date, sir! I had not gone halfway when I turned back."

He pushed Lupin to the front of the box and, sitting down beside the lady, said:

"And, now my lord, who are we? A servant at the police office, probably? There's a professional look about that mug of yours."

He stared hard at Lupin, who did not move a muscle, and tried to put a name to the face, but failed to recognise the man whom he had called Polonius.

Lupin, without taking his eyes from Daubrecq either, reflected. He would not for anything in the world have thrown up the game at that point or neglected this favourable opportunity of coming to an understanding with his mortal enemy.

The woman sat in her corner, motionless, and watched them both.

Lupin said:

"Let us go outside, sir. That will make our interview easier."

"No, my lord, here," grinned the deputy. "It will take place here, presently, during the interval. Then we shall not be disturbing anybody."

"But ..."

"Save your breath, my man; you shan't budge."

And he took Lupin by the coat collar, with the obvious intention of not letting go of him before the interval.

A rash move! Was it likely that Lupin would consent to remain in such an attitude, especially before a woman, a woman to whom he had offered his alliance, a woman – and he now thought of it for the first time – who was distinctly good-looking and whose grave beauty attracted him. His whole pride as a man rose at the thought.

However, he said nothing. He accepted the heavy weight of the hand on his shoulder and even sat bent in two, as though beaten, powerless, almost frightened.

"Eh, clever!" said the deputy, scoffingly. "We don't seem to be swaggering quite so much."

The stage was full of actors who were arguing and making a noise.

Daubrecq had loosened his grasp slightly and Lupin felt that the moment had come. With the edge of his hand, he gave him a violent blow in the hollow of the arm, as he might have done with a hatchet.

The pain took Daubrecq off his guard. Lupin now released himself entirely and sprang at the other to clutch him by the throat. But Daubrecq had at once put himself on the defensive and stepped back and their four hands seized one another.

They gripped with superhuman energy, the whole force of the two adversaries concentrating in those hands. Daubrecq's were of monstrous size; and Lupin, caught in that iron vice, felt as though he were fighting not with a man, but with some terrible beast, a huge gorilla.

They held each other against the door, bending low, like a pair of wrestlers groping and trying to lay hold of each other. Their bones creaked. Whichever gave way first was bound to be caught by the throat and strangled. And all this happened amid a sudden silence, for the actors on the stage were now listening to one of their number, who was speaking in a low voice.

The woman stood back flat against the partition, looking at them in terror. Had she taken sides with either of them, with a single movement, the victory would at once have been decided in that one's favour. But which of them should she assist? What could Lupin represent in her eyes? A friend? An enemy?

She briskly made for the front of the box, forced back the screen and, leaning forwards, seemed to give a signal.

Then she returned and tried to slip to the door.

Lupin, as though wishing to help her, said:

"Why don't you move the chair?"

He was speaking of a heavy chair which had fallen down between him and Daubrecq and across which they were struggling.

The woman stooped and pulled away the chair. That was what Lupin was waiting for. Once rid of the obstacle, he caught Daubrecq a smart kick on the shin with the tip of his patent-leather boot. The result was the same as with the blow which he had given him on the arm. The pain caused a second's apprehension and distraction, of which he at once took advantage to beat down Daubrecq's outstretched hands and to dig his ten fingers into his adversary's throat and neck.

Daubrecq struggled. Daubrecq tried to pull away the hands that were throttling him; but he was beginning to choke and felt his strength decreasing.

"Aha, you old monkey!" growled Lupin, forcing him to the floor. "Why don't you shout for help? How frightened you must be of a scandal!"

At the sound of the fall there came a knocking at the partition, on the other side.

"Knock away, knock away," said Lupin, under his breath. "The play is on the stage. This is my business and, until I've mastered this gorilla ..."

It did not take him long. The deputy was choking. Lupin stunned him with a blow on the jaw; and all that remained for him to do was to take the woman away and make his escape with her before the alarm was given.

But, when he turned round, he saw that the woman was gone.

She could not be far. Darting from the box, he set off at a run, regardless of the programme sellers and check takers.

On reaching the entrance lobby, he saw her through an open door, crossing the pavement of the Chaussee d'Antin.

She was stepping into a motor car when he came up with her.

The door closed behind her.

He seized the handle and tried to pull at it.

But a man jumped up inside and sent his fist flying into Lupin's face, with less skill but no less force than Lupin had sent his into Daubrecq's face.

Stunned though he was by the blow, he nevertheless had ample time to recognise the man, in a sudden, startled vision, and also to recognise, under his chauffeur's disguise, the man who was driving the car. It was the Growler and the Masher, the two men in charge of the boats on the Enghien night, two friends of Gilbert and Vaucheray: in short, two of Lupin's own accomplices.

When he reached his rooms in the rue Chateaubriand, Lupin, after washing the blood from his face, sat for over an hour in a chair, as though overwhelmed. For the first time in his life he was experiencing the pain of treachery. For the first time his comrades in the fight were turning against their chief.

Mechanically, to divert his thoughts, he turned to his correspondence and tore the wrapper from an evening paper. Among the late news he found the following paragraphs:

THE VILLA MARIE-THERESE CASE

The real identity of Vaucheray, one of the alleged murderers of Leonard the valet, has at last been ascertained. He is a miscreant of the worst type, a hardened criminal who has already twice been sentenced for murder, in default, under another name. No doubt, the police will end by also discovering the real name of his accomplice, Gilbert. In any event, the examining magistrate is determined to commit the prisoners for trial as soon as possible. The public will have no reason to complain of the delays of the law.

In between other newspapers and prospectuses lay a letter. Lupin jumped when he saw it. It was addressed:

Monsieur de Beaumont, Michel.

"Oh," he gasped, "a letter from Gilbert!"
It contained these few words:

Help, governor! I am frightened. I am frightened …

Once again, Lupin spent a night alternating between sleeplessness and nightmares. Once again, he was tormented by atrocious and terrifying visions.

THE CHIEF OF THE ENEMIES

"Poor boy!" murmured Lupin, when his eyes fell on Gilbert's letter next morning. "How he must feel it!"

On the very first day when he saw him, he had taken a liking to that well-set-up youngster, so careless, gay and fond of life. Gilbert was devoted to him, would have accepted death at a sign from his master. And Lupin also loved his frankness, his good humour, his simplicity, his bright, open face.

"Gilbert," he often used to say, "you are an honest man. Do you know, if I were you, I should chuck the business and become an honest man for good."

"After you, governor," Gilbert would reply, with a laugh.

"Won't you, though?"

"No, governor. An honest man is a chap who works and grinds. It's a taste which I may have had as a nipper; but they've made me lose it since."

"Who's they?"

Gilbert was silent. He was always silent when questioned about his early life; and all that Lupin knew was that he had been an orphan since childhood and that he had lived all over the place, changing his name and taking up the queerest jobs. The whole thing was a mystery which no one had been able to fathom; and it did not look as though the police would make much of it either.

Nor, on the other hand, did it look as though the police would consider that mystery a reason for delaying proceedings. They would send Vaucheray's accomplice for trial – under his name of Gilbert or any other name – and visit him with the same inevitable punishment.

"Poor boy!" repeated Lupin. "They're persecuting him like this only because of me. They are afraid of his escaping and they are in a hurry to finish the business: the verdict first and then ... the execution.

"Oh, the butchers! A lad of twenty, who has committed no murder, who is not even an accomplice in the murder ..."

Alas, Lupin well knew that this was a thing impossible to prove and that he must concentrate his efforts upon another point. But upon which? Was he to abandon the trail of the crystal stopper?

He could not make up his mind to that. His one and only diversion from the search was to go to Enghien, where the Growler and the Masher lived, and make sure that nothing had been seen of them since the murder at the Villa Marie-Therese. Apart from this, he applied himself to the question of Daubrecq and nothing else.

He refused even to trouble his head about the problems set before him: the treachery of the Growler and the Masher; their connection with the grey-haired lady; the spying of which he himself was the object.

"Steady, Lupin," he said. "One only argues falsely in a fever. So hold your tongue. No inferences, above all things! Nothing is more foolish than to infer one fact from another before finding a certain starting point. That's where you get up a tree. Listen to your instinct. Act according to your instinct. And as you are persuaded, outside all argument, outside all logic, one might say, that this business turns upon that confounded stopper, go for it boldly. Have at Daubrecq and his bit of crystal!"

Lupin did not wait to arrive at these conclusions before settling his actions accordingly. At the moment when he was stating them in his mind, three days after the scene at the Vaudeville, he was sitting, dressed like a retired tradesman, in an old overcoat, with a muffler round his neck, on a bench in the avenue Victor-Hugo, at some distance from the Square Lamartine. Victoire had his instructions to pass by that bench at the same hour every morning.

"Yes," he repeated to himself, "the crystal stopper: everything turns on that ... Once I get hold of it ..."

Victoire arrived, with her shopping basket on her arm. He at once noticed her extraordinary agitation and pallor:

"What's the matter?" asked Lupin, walking beside his old nurse.

She went into a big grocer's, which was crowded with people, and, turning to him:

"Here," she said, in a voice torn with excitement. "Here's what you've been hunting for."

And, taking something from her basket, she gave it to him.

Lupin stood astounded: in his hand lay the crystal stopper.

"Can it be true? Can it be true?" he muttered, as though the ease of the solution had thrown him off his balance.

But the fact remained, visible and palpable. He recognised by its shape, by its size, by the worn gilding of its facets, recognised beyond any possible doubt the crystal stopper which he had seen before. He even remarked a tiny, hardly noticeable little scratch on the stem which he remembered perfectly.

However, while the thing presented all the same characteristics, it possessed no other that seemed out of the way. It was a crystal stopper, that was all. There was no really special mark to distinguish it from other stoppers. There was no sign upon it, no stamp; and, being cut from a single piece, it contained no foreign object.

"What then?"

And Lupin received a quick insight into the depth of his mistake. What good could the possession of that crystal stopper do him so long as he was ignorant of its value? That bit of glass had no existence in itself; it counted only through the meaning that attached to it. Before taking it, the thing was to be certain. And how could he tell that, in taking it, in robbing Daubrecq of it, he was not committing an act of folly?

It was a question which was impossible of solution, but which forced itself upon him with singular directness.

"No blunders!" he said to himself, as he pocketed the stopper. "In this confounded business, blunders are fatal."

He had not taken his eyes off Victoire. Accompanied

by a shopman, she went from counter to counter, among the throng of customers. She next stood for some little while at the pay desk and passed in front of Lupin.

He whispered her instructions:

"Meet me behind the Lycée Janson."

She joined him in an unfrequented street:

"And suppose I'm followed?" she said.

"No," he declared. "I looked carefully. Listen to me. Where did you find the stopper?"

"In the drawer of the table by his bed."

"But we had felt there already."

"Yes; and I did so again this morning. I expect he put it there last night."

"And I expect he'll want to take it from there again," said Lupin.

"Very likely."

"And suppose he finds it gone?"

Victoire looked frightened.

"Answer me," said Lupin. "If he finds it gone, he'll accuse you of taking it, won't he?"

"Certainly."

"Then go and put it back, as fast as you can."

"Oh dear, oh dear!" she moaned. "I hope he won't have had time to find out. Give it to me, quick."

"Here you are," said Lupin.

He felt in the pocket of his overcoat.

"Well?" said Victoire, holding out her hand.

"Well," he said, after a moment, "it's gone."

"What!"

"Yes, upon my word, it's gone ... somebody's taken it from me."

He burst into a peal of laughter, a laughter which,this time, was free from all bitterness.

Victoire flew out at him:

"Laugh away! Putting me in such a predicament!"

"How can I help laughing? You must confess that it's funny. It's no longer a tragedy that we're acting, but a fairy tale, as much a fairy tale as Puss in Boots or Jack and the Beanstalk. I must write it when I get a few weeks to myself: The Magic Stopper; or, The Mishaps of Poor Arsène."

"Well ... who has taken it from you?"

"What are you talking about? It has flown away ... vanished from my pocket: hey presto, begone!"

He gave the old servant a gentle push and, in a more serious tone:

"Go home, Victoire, and don't upset yourself. Of course, someone saw you give me the stopper and took advantage of the crowd in the shop to pick my pocket of it. That only shows that we are watched more closely than I thought and by adversaries of the first rank. But, once more, be easy. Honest men always come by their own ... Have you anything else to tell me?"

"Yes. Someone came yesterday evening, while Monsieur Daubrecq was out. I saw lights reflected upon the trees in the garden."

"The portress' bedroom?"

"The portress was up."

"Then it was some of those detective fellows; they are still hunting. I'll see you later, Victoire. You must let me in again."

"What! You want to ..."

"What do I risk? Your room is on the third floor.

Daubrecq suspects nothing."

"But the others!"

"The others? If it was to their interest to play me a trick, they'd have tried before now. I'm in their way, that's all. They're not afraid of me. So till later, Victoire, at five o'clock exactly."

One further surprise awaited Lupin. In the evening his old nurse told him that, having opened the drawer of the bedside table from curiosity, she had found the crystal stopper there again.

Lupin was no longer to be excited by these miraculous incidents. He simply said to himself:

"So it's been brought back. And the person who brought it back and who enters this house by some unexplained means considered, as I did, that the stopper ought not to disappear. And yet Daubrecq, who knows that he is being spied upon to his very bedroom, has once more left the stopper in a drawer, as though he attached no importance to it at all! Now what is one to make of that?"

Though Lupin did not make anything of it, nevertheless he could not escape certain arguments, certain associations of ideas that gave him the same vague foretaste of light which one receives on approaching the outlet of a tunnel.

"It is inevitable, as the case stands," he thought, "that there must soon be an encounter between myself and the others. From that moment I shall be master of the situation."

Five days passed, during which Lupin did not glean the slightest particular. On the sixth day Daubrecq received a visit, in the small hours, from a gentleman, Laybach the deputy, who, like his colleagues, dragged himself at his feet in despair and, when all was done, handed him twenty thousand francs.

Two more days; and then, one night, posted on the landing of the second floor, Lupin heard the creaking of a door, the front door, as he perceived, which led from the hall into the garden. In the darkness he distinguished, or rather divined, the presence of two persons, who climbed the stairs and stopped on the first floor, outside Daubrecq's bedroom.

What were they doing there? It was not possible to enter the room, because Daubrecq bolted his door every night. Then what were they hoping?

Manifestly, handiwork of some kind was being performed, as Lupin discovered from the dull sounds of rubbing against the door. Then words, uttered almost beneath a whisper, reached him:

"Is it all right?"

"Yes, quite, but, all the same, we'd better put it off till tomorrow, because ..."

Lupin did not hear the end of the sentence. The men were already groping their way downstairs. The hall door was closed, very gently, and then the gate.

"It's curious, say what one likes," thought Lupin. "Here is a house in which Daubrecq carefully conceals his rascalities and is on his guard, not without good reason, against spies; and everybody walks in and out as in a booth at a fair. Victoire lets me in, the portress admits the emissaries of the police: that's well and good; but who is playing false in these people's favour? Are we to suppose that they are acting alone? But what fearlessness! And how well they know their way about!"

In the afternoon, during Daubrecq's absence, he examined the door of the first-floor bedroom. And, at the first glance, he understood: one of the lower panels had been skilfully cut out and was only held in place by invisible tacks. The people, therefore, who had done this work were the same who had acted at his two places, in the rue Matignon and the rue Chateaubriand.

He also found that the work dated back to an earlier period and that, as in his case, the opening had been prepared beforehand, in anticipation of favourable circumstances or of some immediate need.

The day did not seem long to Lupin. Knowledge was at hand. Not only would he discover the manner in which his adversaries employed those little openings, which were apparently unemployable, since they did not allow a person to reach the upper bolts, but he would learn who the ingenious and energetic adversaries were with whom he repeatedly and inevitably found himself confronted.

One incident annoyed him. In the evening Daubrecq, who had complained of feeling tired at dinner, came home at ten o'clock and, contrary to his usual custom, pushed the bolts of the hall door. In that case, how would the others be able to carry out their plan and go to Daubrecq's room? Lupin waited for an hour after Daubrecq put out his light. Then he went down to the deputy's study, opened one of the windows ajar and returned to the third floor and fixed his rope ladder so that, in case of need, he could reach the study without passing though the house. Lastly, he resumed his post on the second-floor landing.

He did not have to wait long. An hour earlier than on the previous night someone tried to open the hall door. When the attempt failed, a few minutes of absolute silence followed. And Lupin was beginning to think that the men had abandoned the idea, when he gave a sudden start. Someone had passed, without the least sound to interrupt the silence. He would not have known it, so utterly were the thing's steps deadened by the stair carpet, if the baluster-rail, which he himself held in his hand, had not shaken slightly. Someone was coming upstairs.

And, as the ascent continued, Lupin became aware of the uncanny feeling that he heard nothing more than before. He knew, because of the rail, that a thing was coming and he could count the number of steps climbed by noting each vibration of the rail; but no other indication gave him that dim sensation of presence which we feel in distinguishing movements which we do not see, in perceiving sounds which we do not hear. And yet a blacker darkness ought to have taken shape within the darkness and something ought, at least, to modify the quality of the silence. No, he might well have believed that there was no one there.

And Lupin, in spite of himself and against the evidence of his reason, ended by believing it, for the rail no longer moved and he thought that he might have been the sport of an illusion.

And this lasted a long time. He hesitated, not knowing what to do, not knowing what to suppose. But an odd circumstance impressed him. A clock struck two. He recognised the chime of Daubrecq's clock. And the chime was that of a clock from which one is not separated by the obstacle of a door.

Lupin slipped down the stairs and went to the door. It was closed, but there was a space on the left, at the bottom, a space left by the removal of the little panel.

He listened. Daubrecq, at that moment, turned in his bed; and his breathing was resumed, evenly and a little stertorously. And Lupin plainly heard the sound of rumpling garments. Beyond a doubt, the thing was there, fumbling and feeling through the clothes which Daubrecq had laid beside his bed.

"Now," thought Lupin, "we shall learn something. But how the deuce did the beggar get in? Has he managed to draw the bolts and open the door? But, if so, why did he make the mistake of shutting it again?"

Not for a second – a curious anomaly in a man like Lupin, an anomaly to be explained only by the uncanny feeling which the whole adventure produced in him – not for a second did he suspect the very simple truth which was about to be revealed to him. Continuing his way down, he crouched on one of the bottom steps of the staircase, thus placing himself between the door of the bedroom and the hall door, on the road which Daubrecq's enemy must inevitably take in order to join his accomplices.

He questioned the darkness with an unspeakable anguish. He was on the point of unmasking that enemy of Daubrecq's, who was also his own adversary. He would thwart his plans. And the booty captured from Daubrecq he would capture in his turn, while Daubrecq slept and while the accomplices lurking behind the hall door or outside the garden gate vainly awaited their leader's return.

And that return took place. Lupin knew it by the renewed vibration of the balusters. And, once more, with every sense strained and every nerve on edge, he strove to discern the mysterious thing that was coming towards him. He suddenly realised it when only a few yards away. He himself, hidden in a still darker recess, could not be seen. And what he saw – in the very vaguest manner – was approaching stair by stair, with infinite precautions, holding on to each separate baluster.

"Whom the devil have I to do with?" said Lupin to himself, while his heart thumped inside his chest.

The catastrophe was hastened. A careless movement on Lupin's part was observed by the stranger, who stopped short. Lupin was afraid lest the other should turn back and take to flight. He sprang at the adversary and was stupefied at encountering nothing but space and knocking against the rail without seizing the form which he saw. But he at once rushed forwards, crossed the best part of the hall and caught up his antagonist just as he was reaching the door opening on the garden.

There was a cry of fright, answered by other cries on the further side of the door.

"Oh, hang it, what's this?" muttered Lupin, whose arms had closed, in the dark, around a little, tiny, trembling, whimpering thing.

Suddenly understanding, he stood for a moment motionless and dismayed, at a loss what to do with his conquered prey. But the others were shouting and stamping outside the door. Thereupon, dreading lest Daubrecq should wake up, he slipped the little thing under his jacket, against his chest, stopped the crying with his handkerchief rolled into a ball and hurried up the three flights of stairs.

"Here," he said to Victoire, who woke with a start. "I've brought you the indomitable chief of our enemies, the Hercules of the gang. Have you a feeding-bottle about you?"

He put down in the easy-chair a child of six or seven years of age, the tiniest little fellow in a grey jersey and a knitted woollen cap, whose pale and exquisitely pretty features were streaked with the tears that streamed from the terrified eyes.

"Where did you pick that up?" asked Victoire, aghast.

"At the foot of the stairs, as it was coming out of Daubrecq's bedroom," replied Lupin, feeling the jersey in the hope that the child had brought booty of some kind from that room.

Victoire was stirred to pity:

"Poor little dear! Look, he's trying not to cry! Oh, saints above, his hands are like ice! Don't be afraid, sonny, we shan't hurt you: the gentleman's all right."

"Yes," said Lupin, "the gentleman's quite all right, but there's another very wicked gentleman who'll wake up if they go on making such a rumpus outside the hall door. Do you hear them, Victoire?"

"Who is it?"

"The satellites of our young Hercules, the indomitable leader's gang."

"Well ...?" stammered Victoire, utterly unnerved.

"Well, as I don't want to be caught in the trap, I shall start by clearing out. Are you coming, Hercules?"

He rolled the child in a blanket, so that only its head remained outside, gagged its mouth as gently as possible and made Victoire fasten it to his shoulders:

"See, Hercules? We're having a game. You never thought you'd find gentlemen to play piggy back with you at three o'clock in the morning! Come, whoosh, let's fly away! You don't get giddy, I hope?"

He stepped across the window ledge and set foot on one of the rungs of the ladder. He was in the garden in a minute.

He had never ceased hearing and now heard more plainly still the blows that were being struck upon the front door. He was astounded that Daubrecq was not awakened by so violent a din:

"If I don't put a stop to this, they'll spoil everything," he said to himself.

He stood in an angle of the house, invisible in the darkness, and measured the distance between himself and the gate. The gate was open. To his right, he saw the steps, on the top of which the people were flinging themselves about; to his left, the building occupied by the portress.

The woman had come out of her lodge and was standing near the people, entreating them:

"Oh, do be quiet, do be quiet! He'll come!"

"Capital!" said Lupin. "The good woman is an accomplice as well. By Jingo, what a pluralist!"

He rushed across to her and, taking her by the scruff of the neck, hissed:

"Go and tell them I've got the child … They can come

and fetch it at my place, rue Chateaubriand."

A little way off, in the avenue, stood a taxi which Lupin presumed to be engaged by the gang. Speaking authoritatively, as though he were one of the accomplices, he stepped into the cab and told the man to drive him home.

"Well," he said to the child, "that wasn't much of a shake-up, was it? What do you say to going to sleep on the gentleman's bed?"

As his servant, Achille, was asleep, Lupin made the little chap comfortable and stroked his hair for him. The child seemed numbed. His poor face was as though petrified into a stiff expression made up, at one and the same time, of fear and the wish not to show fear, of the longing to scream and a pitiful effort not to scream.

"Cry, my pet, cry," said Lupin. "It'll do you good to cry."

The child did not cry, but the voice was so gentle and so kind that he relaxed his tense muscles; and, now that his eyes were calmer and his mouth less contorted, Lupin, who was examining him closely, found something that he recognised, an undoubted resemblance.

This again confirmed certain facts which he suspected and which he had for some time been linking in his mind. Indeed, unless he was mistaken, the position was becoming very different and he would soon assume the direction of events. After that ...

A ring at the bell followed, at once, by two others, sharp ones.

"Hullo!" said Lupin to the child. "Here's Mummy come to fetch you. Don't move."

He ran and opened the door.

A woman entered, wildly:

"My son!" she screamed. "My son! Where is he?"

"In my room," said Lupin.

Without asking more, thus proving that she knew the way, she rushed to the bedroom.

"As I thought," muttered Lupin. "The youngish woman with the grey hair: Daubrecq's friend and enemy."

He walked to the window and looked through the curtains. Two men were striding up and down the opposite pavement: the Growler and the Masher.

"And they're not even hiding themselves," he said to himself. "That's a good sign. They consider that they can't do without me any longer and that they've got to obey the governor. There remains the pretty lady with the grey hair. That will be more difficult. It's you and I now, Mummy."

He found the mother and the boy clasped in each other's arms; and the mother, in a great state of alarm, her eyes moist with tears, was saying:

"You're not hurt? You're sure? Oh, how frightened you must have been, my poor little Jacques!"

"A fine little fellow," said Lupin.

She did not reply. She was feeling the child's jersey, as Lupin had done, no doubt to see if he had succeeded in his nocturnal mission; and she questioned him in a whisper.

"No, Mummy," said the child. "No, really."

She kissed him fondly and petted him, until, in a little while, the child, worn out with fatigue and excitement, fell asleep. She remained leaning over him for a long time. She herself seemed very much worn out and in need of rest.

Lupin did not disturb her contemplation. He looked at her anxiously, with an attention which she did not perceive, and he noticed the wider rings round her eyes and the deeper marks of wrinkles. Yet he considered her handsomer than he had thought, with that touching beauty which habitual suffering gives to certain faces that are more human, more sensitive than others.

She wore so sad an expression that, in a burst of instinctive sympathy, he went up to her and said: "I do not know what your plans are, but, whatever they may be, you stand in need of help. You cannot succeed alone."

"I am not alone."

"The two men outside? I know them. They're no good. I beseech you, make use of me. You remember the other evening, at the theatre, in the private box? You were on the point of speaking. Do not hesitate today."

She turned her eyes on him, looked at him long and fixedly and, as though unable to escape that opposing will, she said:

"What do you know exactly? What do you know about me?"

"There are many things that I do not know. I do not know your name. But I know ..."

She interrupted him with a gesture; and, resolutely, in her turn, dominating the man who was compelling her to speak:

"It doesn't matter," she exclaimed. "What you know, after all, is not much and is of no importance. But what are your plans? You offer me your help: with what view? For what work? You have flung yourself headlong into this business; I have been unable to undertake anything without meeting you on my path: you must be contemplating some aim ... What aim?"

"What aim? Upon my word, it seems to me that my conduct ..."

"No, no," she said, emphatically, "no fine phrases! What you and I want is certainties; and, to achieve them, absolute frankness. I will give you an example. Monsieur Daubrecq possesses a thing of unparalleled value, not in itself, but for what it represents. That thing you know. You have twice held it in your hands. I have twice taken it from you. Well, I am entitled to believe that, when you tried to obtain possession of it, you meant to use the power which you attribute to it and to use it to your own advantage ..."

"What makes you say that?"

"Yes, you meant to use it to forward your schemes, in the interest of your own affairs, in accordance with your habits as a ..."

"As a burglar and a swindler," said Lupin, completing the sentence for her.

She did not protest. He tried to read her secret thoughts in the depths of her eyes. What did she want with him? What was she afraid of? If she mistrusted him, had he not also reasons to mistrust that woman who had twice taken the crystal stopper from him to restore it to Daubrecq? Mortal enemy of Daubrecq's though she were, up to what point did she remain subject to that man's will? By surrendering himself to her, did he not risk surrendering himself to Daubrecq? And yet he had never looked upon graver eyes nor a more honest face.

Without further hesitation, he stated:

"My object is simple enough. It is the release of my friends Gilbert and Vaucheray."

"Is that true? Is that true?" she exclaimed, quivering all over and questioning him with an anxious glance.

"If you knew me ..."

"I do know you ... I know who you are. For months, I have taken part in your life, without your suspecting it ... and yet, for certain reasons, I still doubt ..."

He said, in a more decisive tone:

"You do not know me. If you knew me, you would know that there can be no peace for me before my two companions have escaped the awful fate that awaits them."

She rushed at him, took him by the shoulders and positively distraught, said:

"What? What did you say? The awful fate? Then you believe ... you believe ..."

"I really believe," said Lupin, who felt how greatly this threat upset her, "I really believe that, if I am not in time, Gilbert and Vaucheray are done for."

"Be quiet! Be quiet!" she cried, clutching him fiercely. "Be quiet! You mustn't say that ... There is no reason ... It's just you who supposes ..."

"It's not only I, it's Gilbert as well ..."

"What? Gilbert? How do you know?"

"From himself?"

"From him?"

"Yes, from Gilbert, who has no hope left but in me; from Gilbert, who knows that only one man in the world can save him and who, a few days ago, sent me a despairing appeal from prison. Here is his letter."

She snatched the paper greedily and read in stammering accents:

"Help, governor! I am frightened! I am frightened …!"

She dropped the letter. Her hands fluttered in space. It was as though her staring eyes beheld the sinister vision which had already so often terrified Lupin. She gave a scream of horror, tried to rise and fainted.

THE
TWENTY-SEVEN

The child was sleeping peacefully on the bed. The mother did not move from the sofa on which Lupin had laid her; but her easier breathing and the blood which was now returning to her face announced her impending recovery from her swoon.

He observed that she wore a wedding ring. Seeing a locket hanging from her bodice, he stooped and, turning it, found a miniature photograph representing a man of about forty and a lad – a stripling rather – in a schoolboy's uniform. He studied the fresh, young face set in curly hair:

"It's as I thought," he said. "Ah, poor woman!"

The hand which he took between his grew warmer by degrees. The eyes opened, then closed again. She murmured:

"Jacques ..."

"Do not distress yourself ... it's all right he's asleep."

She recovered consciousness entirely. But, as she did not speak, Lupin put questions to her, to make her feel a gradual need of unburdening herself. And he said, pointing to the locket:

"The schoolboy is Gilbert, isn't he?"

"Yes," she said.

"And Gilbert is your son?"

She gave a shiver and whispered:

"Yes, Gilbert is my son, my eldest son."

So she was the mother of Gilbert, of Gilbert the prisoner at the Sante, relentlessly pursued by the authorities and now awaiting his trial for murder!

Lupin continued:

"And the other portrait?"

"My husband."

"Your husband?"

"Yes, he died three years ago."

She was now sitting up. Life quivered in her veins once more, together with the horror of living and the horror of all the ghastly things that threatened her. Lupin went on to ask:

"What was your husband's name?"

She hesitated a moment and answered:

"Mergy."

He exclaimed:

"Victorien Mergy the deputy?"

"Yes."

There was a long pause. Lupin remembered the incident and the stir which it had caused. Three years ago, Mergy the deputy had blown out his brains in the lobby of the Chamber, without leaving a word of explanation behind him; and no one had ever discovered the slightest reason for that suicide.

"Do you know the reason?" asked Lupin, completing his thought aloud.

"Yes, I know it."

"Gilbert, perhaps?"

"No, Gilbert had disappeared for some years, turned out of doors and cursed by my husband. It was a very great sorrow, but there was another motive."

"What was that?" asked Lupin.

But it was not necessary for Lupin to put further questions. Madame Mergy could keep silent no longer and, slowly at first, with all the anguish of that past which had to be called up, she told her story:

"Twenty-five years ago, when my name was Clarisse Darcel and my parents living, I knew three young men at Nice. Their names will at once give you an insight into the present tragedy: they were Alexis Daubrecq, Victorien Mergy and Louis Prasville. The three were old acquaintances, had gone to college in the same year and served in the same regiment. Prasville, at that time, was in love with a singer at the opera-house at Nice. The two others, Mergy and Daubrecq, were in love with me. I shall be brief as regards all this and, for the rest, as regards the whole story, for the facts tell their own tale. I fell in love with Victorien Mergy from the first. Perhaps I was wrong not to declare myself at once. But true love is always timid, hesitating and shy; and I did not announce my choice until I felt quite certain and quite free. Unfortunately, that period of waiting, so delightful for those who cherish a secret passion, had permitted Daubrecq to hope. His anger was something horrible."

Clarisse Mergy stopped for a few seconds and resumed, in a stifled voice:

"I shall never forget it. The three of us were in the drawing room. Oh, I can hear even now the terrible words of threat and hatred which he uttered! Victorien was absolutely astounded. He had never seen his friend like this, with that repugnant face, that bestial expression: yes, the expression of a wild beast. Daubrecq ground his teeth. He stamped his feet. His bloodshot eyes – he did not wear spectacles in those days – rolled in their sockets; and he kept on saying, 'I shall be revenged ... I shall be revenged ... Oh, you don't know what I am capable of! I shall wait ten years, twenty years, if necessary ... But it will come like a thunderbolt ... Ah, you don't know! To be revenged ... To do harm for harm's sake ... what joy! I was born to do harm ... And you will both beseech my mercy on your knees, on your knees, yes, on your knees ...' At that moment, my father entered the room; and, with his assistance and the footman's, Victorien Mergy flung the loathsome creature out of doors. Six weeks later, I married Victorien."

"And Daubrecq?" asked Lupin, interrupting her. "Did he not try ..."

"No, but on our wedding-day, Louis Prasville, who acted as my husband's best man in defiance of Danbrecq's opposition, went home to find the girl he loved, the opera-singer, dead, strangled ..."

"What!" said Lupin, with a start. "Had Daubrecq ..."

"It was known that Daubrecq had been persecuting her with his attentions for some days; but nothing more was known. It was impossible to discover who had gone in or out during Prasville's absence. There was not a trace found of any kind: nothing, absolutely nothing."

"But Prasville ..."

"There was no doubt of the truth in Prasville's mind or ours. Daubrecq had tried to run away with the girl, perhaps tried to force her, to hustle her and, in the course of the struggle, maddened, losing his head, caught her by the throat and killed her, perhaps without knowing what he was doing. But there was no evidence of all this; and Daubrecq was not even questioned."

"And what became of him next?"

"For some years we heard nothing of him. We knew only that he had lost all his money gambling and that he was travelling in America. And, in spite of myself, I forgot his anger and his threats and was only too ready to believe that he had ceased to love me and no longer harboured his schemes of revenge. Besides, I was so happy that I did not care to think of anything but my happiness, my love, my husband's political career, the health of my son Antoine."

"Antoine?"

"Yes, Antoine is Gilbert's real name. The unhappy boy has at least succeeded in concealing his identity."

Lupin asked, with some hesitation:

"At what period did ... Gilbert ... begin?"

"I cannot tell you exactly. Gilbert – I prefer to call him that and not to pronounce his real name – Gilbert, as a child, was what he is today: lovable, liked by everybody, charming, but lazy and unruly. When he was fifteen, we put him to a boarding school in one of the suburbs, with the deliberate object of not having him too much at home. After two years he was expelled from school and sent back to us."

"Why?"

"Because of his conduct. The masters had discovered that he used to slip out at night and also that he would disappear for weeks at a time, while pretending to be at home with us."

"What used he to do?"

"Amuse himself backing horses, spending his time in cafes and public dancing rooms."

"Then he had money?"

"Yes."

"Who gave it him?"

"The devil on his shoulder, the man who, secretly, unknown to his parents, enticed him away from school, the man who led him astray, who corrupted him, who took him from us, who taught him to lie, to waste his substance and to steal."

"Daubrecq?"

"Daubrecq."

Clarisse Mergy put her hands together to hide the redness of her face. She continued, in her tired voice:

"Daubrecq had taken his revenge. On the day after my husband turned our unhappy child out of the house, Daubrecq sent us a most cynical letter in which he revealed the odious part which he had played and the machinations by which he had succeeded in depraving our son. And he went on to say, 'The reformatory, one of these days … Later on, the assize court … And then, let us hope and trust, the scaffold!'"

Lupin exclaimed:

"What! Did Daubrecq plot the present business?"

"No, no, that is only an accident. The hateful prophecy was just a wish which he expressed. But oh, how it terrified me! I was ailing at the time; my other son, my little Jacques, had just been born. And every day we heard of some fresh misdeed of Gilbert's – forgeries, swindles – so much so that we spread the news, in our immediate surroundings, of his departure for abroad, followed by his death. Life was a misery; and it became still more so when the political storm, in which my husband was to meet his death burst."

"What do you mean?"

"A word will be enough: my husband's name was on the list of the twenty-seven."

"Ah!"

The veil was suddenly lifted from Lupin's eyes and he saw, as in a flash of lightning, a whole legion of things which, until then, had been hidden in the darkness.

Clarisse Mergy continued, in a firmer voice:

"Yes, his name was on it, but by mistake, by a piece of incredible ill-luck of which he was the victim. It is true that Victorien Mergy was a member of the committee appointed to consider the question of the Two-Seas Canal. It is true that he voted with the members who were in favour of the company's scheme. He was even paid – yes, I tell you so plainly and I will mention the sum – he was paid fifteen thousand francs. But he was paid on behalf of another, of one of his political friends, a man in whom he had absolute confidence and of whom he was the blind, unconscious tool. He thought he was showing his friend a kindness; and it proved his own undoing. It was not until the day after the suicide of the chairman of the company and the disappearance of the secretary, the day on which the affair of the canal was published in the papers, with its whole series of swindles and abominations, that my husband knew that a number of his fellow members had been bribed and learnt that the mysterious list, of which people suddenly began to speak, mentioned his name with theirs and with the names of other deputies, leaders of parties and influential politicians. Oh, what awful days those were! Would the list be published? Would his name come out? The torture of it! You remember the mad excitement in the Chamber, the atmosphere of terror and denunciation that prevailed. Who owned the list? Nobody could say. It was known to be in existence and that was all. Two names were sacrificed to public odium. Two men were swept away by the storm. And it remained unknown where the denunciation came from and in whose hands the incriminating documents were."

"Daubrecq," suggested Lupin.

"No, no!" cried Madame Mergy. "Daubrecq was nothing at that time: he had not yet appeared upon the scene. No, don't you remember, the truth came out suddenly through the very man who was keeping it back: Germineaux, the ex-minister of justice, a cousin of the chairman of the Canal Company. As he lay dying of consumption, he wrote from his sick-bed to the chief of police, bequeathing him that list of names, which, he said, would be found, after his death, in an iron chest in the corner of his room. The house was surrounded by police and the prefect took up his quarters by the sick man's bedside. Germineaux died. The chest was opened and found to be empty."

"Daubrecq, this time," Lupin declared.

"Yes, Daubrecq," said Madame Mergy, whose excitement was momentarily increasing. "Alexis Daubrecq, who, for six months, disguised beyond recognition, had acted as Germineaux's secretary. It does not matter how he discovered that Germineaux was the possessor of the paper in question. The fact remains that he broke open the chest on the night before the death. So much was proved at the inquiry; and Daubrecq's identity was established."

"But he was not arrested?"

"What would have been the use? They knew well enough that he must have deposited the list in a place of safety. His arrest would have involved a scandal, the reopening of the whole case ..."

"So ..."

"So they negotiated terms."

Lupin laughed:

"That's funny, negotiating terms with Daubrecq!"

"Yes, very funny," said Madame Mergy, bitterly. "During this time he acted and without delay, shamelessly, making straight for the goal. A week after the theft, he went to the Chamber of Deputies, asked for my husband and bluntly demanded thirty thousand francs of him, to be paid within twenty-four hours. If not, he threatened him with exposure and disgrace. My husband knew the man he was dealing with, knew him to be implacable and filled with relentless hatred. He lost his head and shot himself."

"How absurd!" Lupin could not help saying. "How absurd! Daubrecq possesses a list of twenty-seven names. To give up any one of those names he is obliged, if he would have his accusation believed, to publish the list itself – that is to say, to part with the document, or at least a photograph of it. Well, in so doing, he creates a scandal, it is true, but he deprives himself, at the same time, of all further means of levying blackmail."

"Yes and no," she said.

"How do you know?"

"Through Daubrecq himself. The villain came to see me and cynically told me of his interview with my husband and the words that had passed between them. Well, there is more than that list, more than that famous bit of paper on which the secretary put down the names and the amounts paid and to which, you will remember, the chairman of the company, before dying, affixed his signature in letters of blood. There is more than that. There is certain less positive proof, which the people interested do not know of: the correspondence between the chairman and the secretary, between the chairman and his counsel, and so on. Of course, the list scribbled on the bit of paper is the only evidence that counts; it is the one incontestable proof which it would be no good copying or even photographing, for its genuineness can be tested most absolutely. But, all the same, the rest of the proof is dangerous. It has already been enough to do away with two deputies. And Daubrecq is marvelously clever at turning this fact to account. He selects his victim, frightens him out of his senses, points out to him the inevitable scandal; and the victim pays the required sum. Or else he kills himself, as my husband did. Do you understand now?"

"Yes," said Lupin.

And, in the silence that followed, he drew a mental picture of Daubrecq's life. He saw him the owner of that list, using his power, gradually emerging from the shadow, lavishly squandering the money which he extorted from his victims, securing his election as a district councillor and deputy, holding sway by dint of threats and terror, unpunished, invulnerable, unattackable, feared by the government, which would rather submit to his orders than declare war upon him, respected by the judicial authorities: so powerful, in a word, that Prasville had been appointed secretary general of police, over the heads of all who had prior claims, for the sole reason that he hated Daubrecq with a personal hatred.

"And you saw him again?" he asked.

"I saw him again. I had to. My husband was dead, but his honour remained untouched. Nobody suspected the truth. In order at least to defend the name which he left me, I accepted my first interview with Daubrecq."

"Your first, yes, for there have been others."

"Many others," she said, in a strained voice, "yes, many others ... at the theatre ... or in the evening, at Enghien ... or else in Paris, at night ... for I was ashamed to meet that man and I did not want people to know it... But it was necessary ... A duty more imperative than any other commanded it: the duty of avenging my husband ..."

She bent over Lupin and, eagerly:

"Yes, revenge has been the motive of my conduct and the sole preoccupation of my life. To avenge my husband, to avenge my ruined son, to avenge myself for all the harm that he has done me: I had no other dream, no other object in life. That is what I wanted: to see that man crushed, reduced to poverty, to tears – as though he still knew how to cry! – sobbing in the throes of despair ..."

"You wanted his death," said Lupin, remembering the scene between them in Daubrecq's study.

"No, not his death. I have often thought of it, I have even raised my arm to strike him, but what would have been the good? He must have taken his precautions. The paper would remain. And then there is no revenge in killing a man ... My hatred went further than that ... It demanded his ruin, his downfall; and, to achieve that, there was but one way: to cut his claws. Daubrecq, deprived of the document that gives him his immense power, ceases to exist. It means immediate bankruptcy and disaster ... under the most wretched conditions. That is what I have sought."

"But Daubrecq must have been aware of your intentions?"

"Certainly. And, I assure you, those were strange meetings of ours: I watching him closely, trying to guess his secret behind his actions and his words, and he ... he ..."

"And he," said Lupin, finishing Clarisse's thought, "lying in wait for the prey which he desires ... for the woman whom he has never ceased to love ... whom he loves ... and whom he covets with all his might and with all his furious passion ..."

She lowered her head and said, simply:

"Yes."

A strange duel indeed was that which brought face to face those two beings separated by so many implacable things! How unbridled must Daubrecq's passion be for him to risk that perpetual threat of death and to introduce to the privacy of his house this woman whose life he had shattered! But also how absolutely safe he must feel himself!

"And your search ended ... how?" asked Lupin.

"My search," she replied, "long remained without fruit. You know the methods of investigation which you have followed and which the police have followed on their side. Well, I myself employed them, years before either of you did, and in vain. I was beginning to despair. Then, one day, when I had gone to see Daubrecq in his villa at Enghien, I picked up under his writing table a letter which he had begun to write, crumpled up and thrown into the wastepaper-basket. It consisted of a few lines in bad English; and I was able to read this: 'Empty the crystal within, so as to leave a void which it is impossible to suspect.' Perhaps I should not have attached to this sentence all the importance which it deserved, if Daubrecq, who was out in the garden, had not come running in and begun to turn out the wastepaper-basket, with an eagerness which was very significant. He gave me a suspicious look: 'There was a letter there,' he said. I pretended not to understand. He did not insist, but his agitation did not escape me; and I continued my quest in this direction. A month later, I discovered, among the ashes in the drawing-room fireplace, the torn half of an English invoice. I gathered that a Stourbridge glassblower, of the name of John Howard, had supplied Daubrecq with a crystal bottle made after a model. The word 'crystal' struck me at once. I went to Stourbridge, got round the foreman of the glass-works and learnt that the stopper of this bottle had been hollowed out inside, in accordance with the instruction in the order, so as to leave a cavity, the existence of which would escape observation."

Lupin nodded his head:

"The thing tallies beyond a doubt. Nevertheless, it did not seem to me, that, even under the gilt layer ... And then the hiding place would be very tiny!"

"Tiny, but large enough," she said. "On my return from England, I went to the police office to see Prasville, whose friendship for me had remained unchanged. I did not hesitate to tell him, first, the reasons which had driven my husband to suicide and, secondly, the object of revenge which I was pursuing. When I informed him of my discoveries, he jumped for joy; and I felt that his hatred for Daubrecq was as strong as ever. I learnt from him that the list was written on a slip of exceedingly thin foreign-post paper, which, when rolled up into a sort of pellet, would easily fit into an exceedingly limited space. Neither he nor I had the least hesitation. We knew the hiding place. We agreed to act independently of each other, while continuing to correspond in secret. I put him in touch with Clemence, the portress in the Square Lamartine, who was entirely devoted to me ..."

"But less so to Prasville," said Lupin, "for I can prove that she betrays him."

"Now perhaps, but not at the start; and the police searches were numerous. It was at that time, ten months ago, that Gilbert came into my life again. A mother never loses her love for her son, whatever he may do, whatever he may have done. And then Gilbert has such a way with him ... well, you know him. He cried, kissed my little Jacques, his brother and I forgave him."

She stopped and, weary-voiced, with her eyes fixed on the floor, continued:

"Would to Heaven that I had not forgiven him! Ah, if that hour could but return, how readily I should find the horrible courage to turn him away! My poor child ... it was I who ruined him!" And, pensively, "I should have had that or any sort of courage, if he had been as I pictured him to myself and as he himself told me that he had long been: bearing the marks of vice and dissipation, coarse, deteriorated.

"But, though he was utterly changed in appearance, so much so that I could hardly recognise him, there was, from the point of view of – how shall I put it? – from the moral point of view, an undoubted improvement. You had helped him, lifted him; and, though his mode of life was hateful to me, nevertheless he retained a certain self-respect ... a sort of underlying decency that showed itself on the surface once more. He was gay, careless, happy ... and he used to talk of you with such affection!"

She picked her words, betraying her embarrassment, not daring, in Lupin's presence, to condemn the line of life which Gilbert had selected and yet unable to speak in favour of it.

"What happened next?" asked Lupin.

"I saw him very often. He would come to me by stealth, or else I went to him and we would go for walks in the country. In this way, I was gradually induced to tell him our story, of his father's suicide and the object which I was pursuing. He at once took fire. He too wanted to avenge his father and, by stealing the crystal stopper, to avenge himself on Daubrecq for the harm which he had done him. His first idea – from which, I am bound to tell you, he never swerved – was to arrange with you."

"Well, then," cried Lupin, "he ought to have ...!"

"Yes, I know ... and I was of the same opinion. Unfortunately, my poor Gilbert – you know how weak he is! – was under the influence of one of his comrades."

"Vaucheray?"

"Yes, Vaucheray, a saturnine spirit, full of bitterness and envy, an ambitious, unscrupulous, gloomy, crafty man, who had acquired a great influence over my son. Gilbert made the mistake of confiding in him and asking his advice. That was the origin of all the mischief. Vaucheray convinced him and convinced me as well that it would be better if we acted by ourselves. He studied the business, took the lead and finally organised the Enghien expedition and, under your direction, the burglary at the Villa Marie-Therese, which Prasville and his detectives had been unable to search thoroughly, because of the active watch maintained by Leonard the valet. It was a mad scheme. We ought either to have trusted in your experience entirely, or else to have left you out altogether, taking the risk of fatal mistakes and dangerous hesitations. But we could not help ourselves. Vaucheray ruled us. I agreed to meet Daubrecq at the theatre. During this time the thing took place. When I came home, at twelve o'clock at night, I heard the terrible result: Leonard murdered, my son arrested. I at once received an intuition of the future. Daubrecq's appalling prophecy was being realised: it meant trial and sentence. And this through my fault, through the fault of me, the mother, who had driven my son towards the abyss from which nothing could extricate him now."

Clarisse wrung her hands and shivered from head to foot. What suffering can compare with that of a mother trembling for the head of her son? Stirred with pity, Lupin said:

"We shall save him. Of that there is not the shadow of a doubt. But, it is necessary that I should know all the details. Finish your story, please. How did you know, on the same night, what had happened at Enghien?"

She mastered herself and, with a face wrung with fevered anguish, replied:

"Through two of your accomplices, or rather two accomplices of Vaucheray, to whom they were wholly devoted and who had chosen them to row the boats."

"The two men outside: the Growler and the Masher?"

"Yes. On your return from the villa, when you landed after being pursued on the lake by the commissary of police, you said a few words to them, by way of explanation, as you went to your car. Mad with fright, they rushed to my place, where they had been before, and told me the hideous news. Gilbert was in prison! Oh, what an awful night! What was I to do? Look for you? Certainly; and implore your assistance. But where was I to find you? It was then that the two whom you call the Growler and the Masher, driven into a corner by circumstances, decided to tell me of the part played by Vaucheray, his ambitions, his plan, which had long been ripening ..."

"To get rid of me, I suppose?" said Lupin, with a grin.

"Yes. As Gilbert possessed your complete confidence,

Vaucheray watched him and, in this way, got to know all the places which you live at. A few days more and, owning the crystal stopper, holding the list of the twenty-seven, inheriting all Daubrecq's power, he would have delivered you to the police, without compromising a single member of your gang, which he looked upon as thenceforth his."

"The ass!" muttered Lupin. "A muddler like that!" And he added, "So the panels of the doors ..."

"Were cut out by his instructions, in anticipation of the contest on which he was embarking against you and against Daubrecq, at whose house he did the same thing. He had under his orders a sort of acrobat, an extraordinarily thin dwarf, who was able to wriggle through those apertures and who thus detected all your correspondence and all your secrets. That is what his two friends revealed to me. I at once conceived the idea of saving my elder son by making use of his brother, my little Jacques, who is himself so slight and so intelligent, so plucky, as you have seen. We set out that night. Acting on the information of my companions, I went to Gilbert's rooms and found the keys of your flat in the rue Matignon, where it appeared that you were to sleep. Unfortunately, I changed my mind on the way and thought much less of asking for your help than of recovering the crystal stopper, which, if it had been discovered at Enghien, must obviously be at your flat. I was right in my calculations. In a few minutes, my little Jacques, who had slipped into your bedroom, brought it to me. I went away quivering with hope. Mistress in my turn of the talisman, keeping it to myself, without telling Prasville, I had absolute power over Daubrecq. I could make him do all that I wanted; he would become the slave of my will and, instructed by me, would take every step in Gilbert's favour and obtain that he should be given the means of escape or else that he should not be sentenced. It meant my boy's safety."

"Well?"

Clarisse rose from her seat, with a passionate movement of her whole being, leant over Lupin and said, in a hollow voice:

"There was nothing in that piece of crystal, nothing, do you understand? No paper, no hiding place! The whole expedition to Enghien was futile! The murder of Leonard was useless! The arrest of my son was useless! All my efforts were useless!"

"But why? Why?"

"Why? Because what you stole from Daubrecq was not the stopper made by his instructions, but the stopper which was sent to John Howard, the Stourbridge glassworker, to serve as a model."

If Lupin had not been in the presence of so deep a grief, he could not have refrained from one of those satirical outbursts with which the mischievous tricks of fate are wont to inspire him. As it was, he muttered between his teeth:

"How stupid! And still more stupid as Daubrecq had been given the warning."

"No," she said. "I went to Enghien on the same day. In all that business Daubrecq saw and sees nothing but an ordinary burglary, an annexation of his treasures. The fact that you took part in it put him off the scent."

"Still, the disappearance of the stopper …"

"To begin with, the thing can have had but a secondary importance for him, as it is only the model."

"How do you know?"

"There is a scratch at the bottom of the stem; and I have made enquiries in England since."

"Very well; but why did the key of the cupboard from which it was stolen never leave the manservant's possession? And why, in the second place, was it found afterward in the drawer of a table in Daubrecq's house in Paris?"

"Of course, Daubrecq takes care of it and clings to it in the way in which one clings to the model of any valuable thing. And that is why I replaced the stopper in the cupboard before its absence was noticed. And that also is why, on the second occasion, I made my little Jacques take the stopper from your overcoat pocket and told the portress to put it back in the drawer."

"Then he suspects nothing?"

"Nothing. He knows that the list is being looked for, but he does not know that Prasville and I are aware of the thing in which he hides it."

Lupin had risen from his seat and was walking up and down the room, thinking. Then he stood still beside Clarisse and asked:

"When all is said, since the Enghien incident, you have not advanced a single step?"

"Not one. I have acted from day to day, led by those two men or leading them, without any definite plan."

"Or, at least," he said, "without any other plan than that of getting the list of the twenty-seven from Daubrecq."

"Yes, but how? Besides, your tactics made things more difficult for me. It did not take us long to recognise your old servant Victoire in Daubrecq's new cook and to discover, from what the portress told us, that Victoire was putting you up in her room; and I was afraid of your schemes."

"It was you, was it not, who wrote to me to retire from the contest?"

"Yes."

"You also asked me not to go to the theatre on the Vaudeville night?"

"Yes, the portress caught Victoire listening to Daubrecq's conversation with me on the telephone; and the Masher, who was watching the house, saw you go out. I suspected, therefore, that you would follow Daubrecq that evening."

"And the woman who came here, late one afternoon ..."

"Was myself. I felt disheartened and wanted to see you."

"And you intercepted Gilbert's letter?"

"Yes, I recognised his writing on the envelope."

"But your little Jacques was not with you?"

"No, he was outside, in a motor car, with the Masher, who lifted him up to me through the drawing-room window; and he slipped into your bedroom through the opening in the panel."

"What was in the letter?"

"As ill-luck would have it, reproaches. Gilbert accused you of forsaking him, of taking over the business on your own account. In short, it confirmed me in my distrust; and I ran away."

Lupin shrugged his shoulders with irritation:

"What a shocking waste of time! And what a fatality that we were not able to come to an understanding earlier! You and I have been playing at hide-and-seek, laying absurd traps for each other, while the days were passing, precious days beyond repair."

"You see, you see," she said, shivering, "you too are afraid of the future!"

"No, I am not afraid," cried Lupin. "But I am thinking of all the useful work that we could have done by this time, if we had united our efforts. I am thinking of all the mistakes and all the acts of imprudence which we should have been saved, if we had been working together. I am thinking that your attempt tonight to search the clothes which Daubrecq was wearing was as vain as the others and that, at this moment, thanks to our foolish duel, thanks to the din which we raised in his house, Daubrecq is warned and will be more on his guard than ever."

Clarisse Mergy shook her head:

"No, no, I don't think that; the noise will not have roused him, for we postponed the attempt for twenty-four hours so that the portress might put a narcotic in his wine." And she added, slowly, "And then, you see, nothing can make Daubrecq be more on his guard than he is already. His life is nothing but one mass of precautions against danger. He leaves nothing to chance ... Besides, has he not all the trumps in his hand?"

Lupin went up to her and asked:

"What do you mean to convey? According to you, is there nothing to hope for on that side? Is there not a single means of attaining our end?"

"Yes," she murmured, "there is one, one only ..."

He noticed her pallor before she had time to hide her face between her hands again. And again a feverish shiver shook her frame.

He seemed to understand the reason of her dismay; and, bending towards her, touched by her grief:

"Please," he said, "please answer me openly and frankly. It's for Gilbert's sake, is it not? Though the police, fortunately, have not been able to solve the riddle of his past, though the real name of Vaucheray's accomplice has not leaked out, there is one man, at least, who knows it: isn't that so? Daubrecq has recognised your son Antoine, through the alias of Gilbert, has he not?"

"Yes, yes ..."

"And he promises to save him, doesn't he? He offers you his freedom, his release, his escape, his life: that was what he offered you, was it not, on the night in his study, when you tried to stab him?"

"Yes ... yes ... that was it ..."

"And he makes one condition, does he not? An abominable condition, such as would suggest itself to a wretch like that? I am right, am I not?"

Clarisse did not reply. She seemed exhausted by her protracted struggle with a man who was gaining ground daily and against whom it was impossible for her to fight. Lupin saw in her the prey conquered in advance, delivered to the victor's whim. Clarisse Mergy, the loving wife of that Mergy whom Daubrecq had really murdered, the terrified mother of that Gilbert whom Daubrecq had led astray, Clarisse Mergy, to save her son from the scaffold, must, come what may and however ignominious the position, yield to Daubrecq's wishes. She would be the mistress, the wife, the obedient slave of Daubrecq, of that monster with the appearance and the ways of a wild beast, that unspeakable person of whom Lupin could not think without revulsion and disgust.

Sitting down beside her, gently, with gestures of pity, he made her lift her head and, with his eyes on hers, said:

"Listen to me. I swear that I will save your son: I swear it ... Your son shall not die, do you understand? There is not a power on earth that can allow your son's head to be touched as long as I am alive."

"I believe you ... I trust your word."

"Do. It is the word of a man who does not know defeat. I shall succeed. Only, I entreat you to make me an irrevocable promise."

"What is that?"

"You must not see Daubrecq again."

"I swear it."

"You must put from your mind any idea, any fear, however obscure, of an understanding between yourself and him ... of any sort of bargain ..."

"I swear it."

She looked at him with an expression of absolute security and reliance; and he, under her gaze, felt the joy of devotion and an ardent longing to restore that woman's happiness, or, at least, to give her the peace and oblivion that heal the worst wounds:

"Come," he said, in a cheerful tone, rising from his chair, "all will yet be well. We have two months, three months before us. It is more than I need ... on condition, of course, that I am unhampered in my movements. And, for that, you will have to withdraw from the contest, you know."

"How do you mean?"

"Yes, you must disappear for a time; go and live in the country. Have you no pity for your little Jacques? This sort of thing would end by shattering the poor little man's nerves ... And he has certainly earned his rest, haven't you, Hercules?"

The next day Clarisse Mergy, who was nearly breaking down under the strain of events and who herself needed repose, lest she should fall seriously ill, went, with her son, to board with a friend who had a house on the skirt of the Forest of Saint-Germain. She felt very weak, her brain was haunted by visions and her nerves were upset by troubles which the least excitement aggravated. She lived there for some days in a state of physical and mental inertia, thinking of nothing and forbidden to see the papers.

One afternoon, while Lupin, changing his tactics, was working out a scheme for kidnapping and confining Daubrecq; while the Growler and the Masher, whom he had promised to forgive if he succeeded, were watching the enemy's movements; while the newspapers were announcing the forthcoming trial for murder of Arsène Lupin's two accomplices, one afternoon, at four o'clock, the telephone bell rang suddenly in the flat in the rue Chateaubriand.

Lupin took down the receiver:

"Hullo!"

A woman's voice, a breathless voice, said:

"Monsieur Michel Beaumont?"

"You are speaking to him, Madame. To whom have I the honour ..."

"Quick, Monsieur, come at once; Madame Mergy has taken poison."

Lupin did not wait to hear details. He rushed out, sprang into his motor car and drove to Saint-Germain.

Clarisse's friend was waiting for him at the door of the bedroom.

"Dead?" he asked.

"No," she replied, "she did not take enough. The doctor has just gone. He says she will get over it."

"And why did she make the attempt?"

"Her son Jacques has disappeared."

"Carried off?"

"Yes, he was playing just inside the forest. A motor car was seen pulling up. Then there were screams. Clarisse tried to run, but her strength failed and she fell to the ground, moaning, 'It's he ... it's that man ... all is lost!' She looked like a madwoman."

"Suddenly, she put a little bottle to her lips and swallowed the contents."

"What happened next?"

"My husband and I carried her to her room. She was in great pain."

"How did you know my address, my name?"

"From herself, while the doctor was attending to her. Then I telephoned you."

"Has anyone else been told?"

"No, nobody. I know that Clarisse has had terrible things to bear ... and that she prefers not to be talked about."

"Can I see her?"

"She is asleep just now. And the doctor has forbidden all excitement."

"Is the doctor anxious about her?"

"He is afraid of a fit of fever, any nervous strain, an attack of some kind which might cause her to make a fresh attempt on her life. And that would be ..."

"What is needed to avoid it?"

"A week or a fortnight of absolute quiet, which is impossible as long as her little Jacques ..."

Lupin interrupted her:

"You think that, if she got her son back ..."

"Oh, certainly, there would be nothing more to fear!"

"You're sure? You're sure? Yes, of course you are ...! Well, when Madame Mergy wakes, tell her from me that I will bring her back her son this evening, before midnight. This evening, before midnight: it's a solemn promise."

With these words, Lupin hurried out of the house and, stepping into his car, shouted to the driver:

"Go to Paris, Square Lamartine, Daubrecq the deputy's!"

THE DEATH SENTENCE

Lupin's motor car was not only an office, a writing room furnished with books, stationery, pens and ink, but also a regular actor's dressing room, containing a complete make-up box, a trunk filled with every variety of wearing apparel, another crammed with 'properties' – umbrellas, walking sticks, scarves, eyeglasses and so on – in short, a complete set of paraphernalia which enabled him to alter his appearance from top to toe in the course of a drive.

The man who rang at Daubrecq the deputy's gate, at six o'clock that evening, was a stout, elderly gentleman, in a black frock coat, a bowler hat, spectacles and whiskers.

The portress took him to the front door of the house and rang the bell. Victoire appeared.

Lupin asked:

"Can Monsieur Daubrecq see Dr. Vernes?"

"Monsieur Daubrecq is in his bedroom; and it is rather late ..."

"Give him my card, please."

He wrote the words, 'From Madame Mergy', in the margin and added:

"There, he is sure to see me."

"But ..." Victoire began.

"Oh, drop your buts, old dear, do as I say, and don't make such a fuss about it!"

She was utterly taken aback and stammered:

"You ... is it you?"

"No, it's Louis XIV!" And, pushing her into a corner of the hall, "Listen ... The moment I'm done with him, go up to your room, put your things together anyhow and clear out."

"What!"

"Do as I tell you. You'll find my car waiting down the avenue. Come, stir your stumps! Announce me. I'll wait in the study."

"But it's dark in there."

"Turn on the light."

She switched on the electric light and left Lupin alone.

"It's here," he reflected, as he took a seat, "it's here that the crystal stopper lives ... Unless Daubrecq always keeps it by him ... But no, when people have a good hiding place, they make use of it. And this is a capital one; for none of us ... so far ..."

Concentrating all his attention, he examined the objects in the room; and he remembered the note which Daubrecq had written to Prasville:

Within reach of your hand, my dear Prasville! You touched it! A little more and the trick was done ...

Nothing seemed to have moved since that day. The same things were lying about on the desk: books, account books, a bottle of ink, a stamp box, pipes, tobacco, things that had been searched and probed over and over again.

"The bounder!" thought Lupin. "He's organised his business jolly cleverly. It's all dovetailed like a well-made play."

In his heart of hearts, though he knew exactly what he had come to do and how he meant to act, Lupin was thoroughly aware of the danger and uncertainty attending his visit to so powerful an adversary. It was quite within the bounds of possibility that Daubrecq, armed as he was, would remain master of the field and that the conversation would take an absolutely different turn from that which Lupin anticipated.

And this prospect angered him somewhat.

He drew himself up, as he heard a sound of footsteps approaching.

Daubrecq entered.

He entered without a word, made a sign to Lupin, who had risen from his chair, to resume his seat and himself sat down at the writing desk. Glancing at the card which he held in his hand:

"Dr. Vernes?"

"Yes, Monsieur le député, Dr. Vernes, of Saint-Germain."

"And I see that you come from Madame Mergy. A patient of yours?"

"A recent patient. I did not know her until I was called in to see her, the other day, in particularly tragic circumstances."

"Is she ill?"

"Madame Mergy has taken poison."

"What!"

Daubrecq gave a start and he continued, without concealing his distress:

"What's that you say? Poison! Is she dead?"

"No, the dose was not large enough. If no complications ensue, I consider that Madame Mergy's life is saved."

Daubrecq said nothing and sat silent, with his head turned to Lupin.

"Is he looking at me? Are his eyes open or shut?" Lupin asked himself.

It worried Lupin terribly not to see his adversary's eyes, those eyes hidden by the double obstacle of spectacles and black glasses: weak, bloodshot eyes, Madame Mergy had told him. How could he follow the secret train of the man's thought without seeing the expression of his face? It was almost like fighting an enemy who wielded an invisible sword.

Presently, Daubrecq spoke:

"So Madame Mergy's life is saved ... And she has sent you to me ... I don't quite understand ... I hardly know the lady."

"Now for the ticklish moment," thought Lupin. "Have at him!"

And, in a genial, good-natured and rather shy tone, he said:

"No, Monsieur le député, there are cases in which a doctor's duty becomes very complex ... very puzzling ... And you may think that, in taking this step ... However, to cut a long story short, while I was attending Madame Mergy, she made a second attempt to poison herself ... Yes; the bottle, unfortunately, had been left within her reach. I snatched it from her. We had a struggle. And, railing in her fever, she said to me, in broken words, 'He's the man ... He's the man ... Daubrecq the deputy ... Make him give me back my son. Tell him to ... or else I would rather die ... Yes, now, tonight ... I would rather die.' That's what she said, Monsieur le député ... So I thought that I ought to let you know. It is quite certain that, in the lady's highly nervous state of mind ... Of course, I don't know the exact meaning of her words – I asked no questions of anybody – obeyed a spontaneous impulse and came straight to you."

Daubrecq reflected for a little while and said:

"It amounts to this, doctor, that you have come to ask me if I know the whereabouts of this child whom I presume to have disappeared. Is that it?"

"Yes."

"And, if I did happen to know, you would take him back to his mother?"

There was a longer pause. Lupin asked himself:

"Can he by chance have swallowed the story? Is the threat of that death enough? Oh, nonsense it's out of the question! And yet ... and yet ... he seems to be hesitating."

"Will you excuse me?" asked Daubrecq, drawing the telephone, on his writing desk, towards him. "I have an urgent message."

"Certainly, Monsieur le député."

Daubrecq called out:

"Hullo! 822 19, please, 822 19."

Having repeated the number, he sat without moving.

Lupin smiled:

"The headquarters of police, isn't it? The secretary general's office ..."

"Yes, doctor ... How do you know?"

"Oh, as a divisional surgeon, I sometimes have to ring them up."

And, within himself, Lupin asked:

"What the devil does all this mean? The secretary general is Prasville ... Then, what?"

Daubrecq put both receivers to his ears and said:

"Are you 822 19? I want to speak to Monsieur Prasville, the secretary general ... Do you say he's not there ...? Yes, yes, he is: he's always in his office at this time... Tell him it's Monsieur Daubrecq ... Monsieur Daubrecq the deputy ... a most important communication."

"Perhaps I'm in the way?" Lupin suggested.

"Not at all, doctor, not at all," said Daubrecq. "Besides, what I have to say has a certain bearing on your errand." And, into the telephone, "Hullo! Monsieur Prasville ... Ah, it's you, Prasville, old cock ... Why, you seem quite staggered! Yes, you're right, it's an age since you and I met. But, after all, we've never been far away in thought ... And I've had plenty of visits from you and your henchmen ... In my absence, it's true. Hullo ... What? Oh, you're in a hurry? I beg your pardon ... So am I, for that matter ... Well, to come to the point, there's a little service I want to do you ... Wait, can't you, you brute? You won't regret it ... It concerns your renown ... Hullo! ... Are you listening? ... Well, take half-a-dozen men with you ... plain-clothes detectives, by preference: you'll find them at the night office ... Jump into a taxi, two taxis, and come along here as fast as you can ... I've got a rare quarry for you, old chap. One of the upper ten ... a lord, a marquis Napoleon himself ... in a word, Arsène Lupin!"

Lupin sprang to his feet. He was prepared for everything but this. Yet something within him stronger than astonishment, an impulse of his whole nature, made him say, with a laugh:

"Oh, well done, well done!"

Daubrecq bowed his head, by way of thanks, and muttered:

"I haven't quite finished ... A little patience, if you don't mind." And he continued, "Hullo! Prasville! No, no, old chap, I'm not humbugging ... You'll find Lupin here, with me, in my study ... Lupin, who's worrying me like the rest of you ... Oh, one more or less makes no difference to me! But, all the same, this one's pushing it a little much. And I am appealing to your sense of kindness. Rid me of the fellow, do ... Half-a-dozen of your satellites and the two who are pacing up and down outside my house will be enough ... Oh, while you're about it, go up to the third floor and rope in my cook as well ... She's the famous Victoire: you know, Master Lupin's old nurse ... And, look here, one more tip, to show you how I love you: send a squad of men to the rue Chateaubriand, at the corner of the rue Balzac ... That's where our national hero lives, under the name of Michel Beaumont ... Do you twig, old cockalorum? And now to business. Hustle!"

When Daubrecq turned his head, Lupin was standing up, with clenched fists. His burst of admiration had not survived the rest of the speech and the revelations which Daubrecq had made about Victoire and the flat in the rue Chateaubriand. The humiliation was too great; and Lupin no longer bothered to play the part of the small general practitioner. He had but one idea in his head: not to give way to the tremendous fit of rage that was urging him to rush at Daubrecq like a bull.

Daubrecq gave the sort of little cluck which, for him, did duty for a laugh. He came waddling up, with his hands in his trouser-pockets, and said, incisively:

"Don't you think that this is all for the best? I've cleared the ground, relieved the situation ... At least, we now know where we stand. Lupin versus Daubrecq; and that's all about it. Besides, think of the time saved! Dr. Vernes, the divisional surgeon, would have taken two hours to spin his yarn! Whereas, like this, Master Lupin will be compelled to get his little story told in thirty minutes ... unless he wants to get himself collared and his accomplices nabbed. What a shock! What a bolt from the blue! Thirty minutes and not a minute more. In thirty minutes from now, you'll have to clear out, scud away like a hare and beat a disordered retreat. Ha, ha, ha, what fun! I say, Polonius, you really are unlucky, each time you come up against Bibi Daubrecq! For it was you who were hiding behind that curtain, wasn't it, my ill-starred Polonius?"

Lupin did not stir a muscle. The one and only solution that would have calmed his feelings, that is to say, for him to throttle his adversary then and there, was so absurd that he preferred to accept Daubrecq's gibes without attempting to retort, though each of them cut him like the lash of a whip. It was the second time, in the same room and in similar circumstances, that he had to bow before that Daubrecq of misfortune and maintain the most ridiculous attitude in silence. And he felt convinced in his innermost being that, if he opened his mouth, it would be to spit words of anger and insult in his victor's face. What was the good? Was it not essential that he should keep cool and do the things which the new situation called for?

"Well, Monsieur Lupin, well?" resumed the deputy. "You look as if your nose were out of joint. Come, console yourself and admit that one sometimes comes across a joker who's not quite such a mug as his fellows. So you thought that, because I wear spectacles and eyeglasses, I was blind? Bless my soul, I don't say that I at once suspected Lupin behind Polonius and Polonius behind the gentleman who came and bored me in the box at the Vaudeville. No, no! But, all the same, it worried me. I could see that, between the police and Madame Mergy, there was a third bounder trying to get a finger in the pie. And, gradually, what with the words let fall by the portress, what with watching the movements of my cook and making inquiries about her in the proper quarter, I began to understand. Then, the other night, came the lightning-flash. I heard the row in the house, in spite of my being asleep. I managed to reconstruct the incident, to follow up Madame Mergy's traces, first, to the rue Chateaubriand and, afterward, to Saint-Germain ... And then ... what then? I put different facts together: the Enghien burglary ... Gilbert's arrest ...

the inevitable treaty of alliance between the weeping mother and the leader of the gang ... the old nurse installed as cook ... all these people entering my house through the doors or through the windows ... And I knew what I had to do. Master Lupin was sniffing at the secret. The scent of the twenty-seven attracted him. I had only to wait for his visit. The hour has arrived. Good evening, Master Lupin."

Daubrecq paused. He had delivered his speech with the evident satisfaction of a man entitled to claim the appreciation of the most captious critics.

As Lupin did not speak, he took out his watch: "I say! Only twenty-three minutes! How time flies! At this rate, we shan't have time to come to an explanation." And, stepping still closer to Lupin, "I'm bound to say, I'm disappointed. I thought that Lupin was a different sort of gentleman. So, the moment he meets a more or less serious adversary, the colossus falls to pieces? Poor young man! Have a glass of water, to bring you round!" Lupin did not utter a word, did not betray a gesture of irritation. With absolute composure, with a precision of movement that showed his perfect self-control and the clear plan of conduct which he had adopted, he gently pushed Daubrecq aside, went to the table and, in his turn, took down the receiver of the telephone:

"I want 565 34, please," he said.

He waited until he was through; and then, speaking in a slow voice and picking out every syllable, he said:

"Hullo ... rue Chateaubriand ...? Is that you, Achille ...? Yes, it's the governor. Listen to me carefully, Achille ... You must leave the flat! Hullo ...! Yes, at once. The police are coming in a few minutes. No, no, don't lose your head ...

You've got time. Only, do what I tell you. Is your bag still packed ...? Good. And is one of the sides empty, as I told you ...? Good. Well, go to my bedroom and stand with your face to the mantelpiece. Press with your left hand on the little carved rosette in front of the marble slab, in the middle, and with your right hand on the top of the mantel-shelf. You'll see a sort of drawer, with two little boxes in it. Be careful. One of them contains all our papers; the other, banknotes and jewellery. Put them both in the empty compartment of the bag. Take the bag in your hand and go as fast as you can, on foot, to the corner of the avenue Victor-Hugo and the avenue de Montespan. You'll find the car waiting, with Victoire. I'll join you there ... What ...? My clothes? My knick-knacks ...? Never mind about all that ... You be off. See you presently."

Lupin quietly pushed away the telephone. Then, taking Daubrecq by the arm, he made him sit in a chair by his side and said:

"And now listen to me, Daubrecq."

"Oho!" grinned the deputy. "Calling each other by our surnames, are we?"

"Yes," said Lupin, "I allowed you to." And, when Daubrecq released his arm with a certain misgiving, he said, "No, don't be afraid. We shan't come to blows. Neither of us has anything to gain by doing away with the other. A stab with a knife? What's the good? No, sir! Words, nothing but words. Words that strike home, though. Here are mine: they are plain and to the point. Answer me in the same way, without reflecting: that's far better. The boy?"

"I have him."

"Give him back."

"No."

"Madame Mergy will kill herself."

"No, she won't."

"I tell you she will."

"And I tell you she will not."

"But she's tried to, once."

"That's just the reason why she won't try again."

"Well, then ..."

"No."

Lupin, after a moment, went on:

"I expected that. Also, I thought, on my way here, that you would hardly tumble to the story of Dr. Vernes and that I should have to use other methods."

"Lupin's methods."

"As you say. I had made up my mind to throw off the mask. You pulled it off for me. Well done you! But that doesn't change my plans."

"Speak."

Lupin took from a pocketbook a double sheet of foolscap paper, unfolded it and handed it to Daubrecq, saying:

"Here is an exact, detailed inventory, with consecutive numbers, of the things removed by my friends and myself from your Villa Marie-Therese on the Lac d'Enghien. As you see, there are one hundred and thirteen items. Of those one hundred and thirteen items, sixty-eight, which have a red cross against them, have been sold and sent to America. The remainder, numbering forty-five, are in my possession ... until further orders. They happen to be the pick of the bunch. I offer you them in return for the immediate surrender of the child."

Daubrecq could not suppress a movement of surprise:

"Oho!" he said. "You seem very much bent upon it."

"Infinitely," said Lupin, "for I am persuaded that a longer separation from her son will mean death to Madame Mergy."

"And that upsets you, does it ... Lothario?"

"What!"

Lupin planted himself in front of the other and repeated:

"What! What do you mean?"

"Nothing ... Nothing ... Something that crossed my mind ... Clarisse Mergy is a young woman still and a pretty woman at that."

Lupin shrugged his shoulders:

"You brute!" he mumbled. "You imagine that everybody is like yourself, heartless and pitiless. It takes your breath away, what, to think that a shark like me can waste his time playing the Don Quixote? And you wonder what dirty motive I can have? Don't try to find out: it's beyond your powers of perception. Answer me, instead: do you accept?"

"So you're serious?" asked Daubrecq, who seemed but little disturbed by Lupin's contemptuous tone.

"Absolutely. The forty-five pieces are in a shed, of which I will give you the address, and they will be handed over to you, if you call there, at nine o'clock this evening, with the child."

There was no doubt about Daubrecq's reply. To him, the kidnapping of little Jacques had represented only a means of working upon Clarisse Mergy's feelings and perhaps also a warning for her to cease the contest upon which she had engaged. But the threat of a suicide must needs show Daubrecq that he was on the wrong track. That being so, why refuse the favourable bargain which Arsène Lupin was now offering him?

"I accept," he said.

"Here's the address of my shed: 99, rue Charles-Lafitte, Neuilly. You have only to ring the bell."

"And suppose I send Prasville, the secretary general, instead?"

"If you send Prasville," Lupin declared, "the place is so arranged that I shall see him coming and that I shall have time to escape, after setting fire to the trusses of hay and straw which surround and conceal your credence-tables, clocks and Gothic virgins."

"But your shed will be burnt down ..."

"I don't mind that: the police have their eye on it already. I am leaving it in any case."

"And how am I to know that this is not a trap?"

"Begin by receiving the goods and don't give up the child till afterward. I trust you, you see."

"Good," said Daubrecq; "you've foreseen everything. Very well, you shall have the nipper; the fair Clarisse shall live; and we will all be happy. And now, if I may give you a word of advice, it is to pack off as fast as you can."

"Not yet."

"Eh?"

"I said, not yet."

"But you're mad! Prasville's on his way!"

"He can wait. I'm not done."

"Why, what more do you want? Clarisse shall have her brat. Isn't that enough for you?"

"No."

"Why not?"

"There is another son."

"Gilbert."

"Yes."

"Well?"

"I want you to save Gilbert."

"What are you saying? I save Gilbert!"

"You can, if you like; it only means taking a little trouble." Until that moment Daubrecq had remained quite calm. He now suddenly blazed out and, striking the table with his fist:

"No," he cried, "not that! Never! Don't reckon on me! No, that would be too idiotic!"

He walked up and down, in a state of intense excitement, with that queer step of his, which swayed him from right to left on each of his legs, like a wild beast, a heavy, clumsy bear. And, with a hoarse voice and distorted features, he shouted:

"Let her come here! Let her come and beg for her son's pardon! But let her come unarmed, not with criminal intentions, like last time! Let her come as a supplicant, as a tamed woman, as a submissive woman, who understands and accepts the situation... Gilbert? Gilbert's sentence? The scaffold? Why, that is where my strength lies! What! For more than twenty years have I awaited my hour; and, when that hour strikes, when fortune brings me this unhoped-for chance, when I am at last about to know the joy of a full revenge – and such a revenge! – you think that I will give it up, give up the thing which I have been pursuing for twenty years?

I save Gilbert? I? For nothing? For love? I, Daubrecq? No, no, you can't have studied my features!"

He laughed, with a fierce and hateful laugh. Visibly, he saw before him, within reach of his hand, the prey which he had been hunting down so long. And Lupin also summoned up the vision of Clarisse, as he had seen her several days before, fainting, already beaten, fatally conquered, because all the hostile powers were in league against her.

He contained himself and said:

"Listen to me."

And, when Daubrecq moved away impatiently, he took him by the two shoulders, with that superhuman strength which Daubrecq knew, from having felt it in the box at the Vaudeville, and, holding him motionless in his grip, he said:

"One last word."

"You're wasting your breath," growled the deputy.

"One last word. Listen, Daubrecq: forget Madame Mergy, give up all the nonsensical and imprudent acts which your pride and your passions are making you commit; put all that on one side and think only of your interest ..."

"My interest," said Daubrecq, jestingly, "always coincides with my pride and with what you call my passions."

"Up to the present, perhaps. But not now, not now that I have taken a hand in the business. That constitutes a new factor, which you choose to ignore. You are wrong. Gilbert is my pal. Gilbert is my chum. Gilbert has to be saved from the scaffold. Use your influence to that end, and I swear to you, do you hear, I swear that we will leave you in peace. Gilbert's safety, that's all I ask. You will have no more battles to wage with Madame Mergy, with me; there will be no more traps laid for you. You will be the master, free to act as you please. Gilbert's safety, Daubrecq! If you refuse ..."

"What then?"

"If you refuse, it will be war, relentless war; in other words, a certain defeat for you."

"Meaning thereby ..."

"Meaning thereby that I shall take the list of the twenty-seven from you."

"Rot! You think so, do you?"

"I swear it."

"What Prasville and all his men, what Clarisse Mergy, what nobody has been able to do, you think that you will do!"

"I shall!"

"And why? By favour of what saint will you succeed where everybody else has failed? There must be a reason?"

"There is."

"What is it?"

"My name is Arsène Lupin."

He had let go of Daubrecq, but held him for a time under the dominion of his authoritative glance and will. At last, Daubrecq drew himself up, gave him a couple of sharp taps on the shoulder and, with the same calm, the same intense obstinacy, said:

"And my name's Daubrecq. My whole life has been one desperate battle, one long series of catastrophes and routs in which I spent all my energies until victory came: complete, decisive, crushing, irrevocable victory. I have against me the police, the government, France, the world. What difference do you expect it to make to me if I have Monsieur Arsène Lupin against me into the bargain? I will go further: the more numerous and skilful my enemies, the more cautiously I am obliged to play. And that is why, my dear sir, instead of having you arrested, as I might have done – yes, as I might have done and very easily – I let you remain at large and beg charitably to remind you that you must quit in less than three minutes."

"Then the answer is no?"

"The answer is no."

"You won't do anything for Gilbert?"

"Yes, I shall continue to do what I have been doing since his arrest – that is to say, to exercise indirect influence with the minister of justice, so that the trial may be hurried on and end in the way in which I want to see it end."

"What!" cried Lupin, beside himself with indignation. "It's because of you, it's for you ..."

"Yes, it's for me, Daubrecq; yes, by Jove! I have a trump card, the son's head, and I am playing it. When I have procured a nice little death sentence for Gilbert, when the days go by and Gilbert's petition for a reprieve is rejected by my good offices, you shall see, Monsieur Lupin, that his mummy will drop all her objections to calling herself Madame Alexis Daubrecq and giving me an unexceptionable pledge of her good will. That fortunate issue is inevitable, whether you like it or not.

It is foredoomed. All I can do for you is to invite you to the wedding and the breakfast. Does that suit you? No? You persist in your sinister designs? Well, good luck, lay your traps, spread your nets, rub up your weapons and grind away at the Complete Foreign-Post Paper Burglar's Handbook. You'll need it. And now, good night. The rules of open-handed and disinterested hospitality demand that I should turn you out of doors. Hop it!"

Lupin remained silent for some time. With his eyes fixed on Daubrecq, he seemed to be taking his adversary's size, gauging his weight, estimating his physical strength, discussing, in fine, in which exact part to attack him. Daubrecq clenched his fists and worked out his plan of defence to meet the attack when it came.

Half a minute passed. Lupin put his hand to his hip-pocket. Daubrecq did the same and grasped the handle of his revolver.

A few seconds more. Coolly, Lupin produced a little gold box of the kind that ladies use for holding sweets, opened it and handed it to Daubrecq:

"A lozenge?"

"What's that?" asked the other, in surprise.

"Cough drops."

"What for?"

"For the draught you're going to feel!"

And, taking advantage of the momentary fluster into which Daubrecq was thrown by his sally, he quickly took his hat and slipped away.

"Of course," he said, as he crossed the hall, "I am knocked into fits. But all the same, that bit of commercial-traveller's waggery was rather novel, in the circumstances. To expect a pill and receive a cough drop is by way of being a sort of disappointment. It left the old chimpanzee quite flummoxed."

As he closed the gate, a motor car drove up and a man sprang out briskly, followed by several others.

Lupin recognised Prasville:

"Monsieur le Secretaire General," he muttered, "your humble servant. I have an idea that, someday, fate will bring us face to face: and I am sorry, for your sake; for you do not inspire me with any particular esteem and you have a bad time before you, on that day. Meanwhile, if I were not in such a hurry, I should wait till you leave and I should follow Daubrecq to find out in whose charge he has placed the child whom he is going to hand back to me. But I am in a hurry. Besides, I can't tell that Daubrecq won't act by telephone. So let us not waste ourselves in vain efforts, but rather join Victoire, Achille and our precious bag."

Two hours later, Lupin, after taking all his measures, was on the lookout in his shed at Neuilly and saw Daubrecq turn out of an adjoining street and walk along with a distrustful air.

Lupin himself opened the double doors:

"Your things are in here, Monsieur le député," he said. "You can go round and look. There is a job-master's yard next door: you have only to ask for a van and a few men. Where is the child?"

Daubrecq first inspected the articles and then took Lupin to the avenue de Neuilly, where two closely veiled old ladies stood waiting with little Jacques.

Lupin carried the child to his car, where Victoire was waiting for him.

All this was done swiftly, without useless words and as though the parts had been got by heart and the various movements settled in advance, like so many stage entrances and exits.

At ten o'clock in the evening Lupin kept his promise and handed little Jacques to his mother. But the doctor had to be hurriedly called in, for the child, upset by all those happenings, showed great signs of excitement and terror. It was more than a fortnight before he was sufficiently recovered to bear the strain of the removal which Lupin considered necessary. Madame Mergy herself was only just fit to travel when the time came. The journey took place at night, with every possible precaution and under Lupin's escort.

He took the mother and son to a little seaside place in Brittany and entrusted them to Victoire's care and vigilance.

"At last," he reflected, when he had seen them settled, "there is no one between the Daubrecq bird and me. He can do nothing more to Madame Mergy and the kid; and she no longer runs the risk of diverting the struggle through her intervention. By Jingo, we have made blunders enough! First, I have had to disclose myself to Daubrecq. Secondly, I have had to surrender my share of the Enghien movables. True, I shall get those back, sooner or later; of that there is not the least doubt. But, all the same, we are not getting on; and, in a week from now, Gilbert and Vaucheray will be up for trial."

What Lupin felt most in the whole business was

Daubrecq's revelation of the whereabouts of the flat. The police had entered his place in the rue Chateaubriand. The identity of Lupin and Michel Beaumont had been recognised and certain papers discovered; and Lupin, while pursuing his aim, while, at the same time, managing various enterprises on which he had embarked, while avoiding the searches of the police, which were becoming more zealous and persistent than ever, had to set to work and reorganise his affairs throughout on a fresh basis.

His rage with Daubrecq, therefore, increased in proportion to the worry which the deputy caused him. He had but one longing, to pocket him, as he put it, to have him at his bidding by fair means or foul, to extract his secret from him. He dreamt of tortures fit to unloose the tongue of the most silent of men. The boot, the rack, red-hot pincers, nailed planks: no form of suffering, he thought, was more than the enemy deserved; and the end to be attained justified every means.

"Oh," he said to himself, "oh, for a decent bench of inquisitors and a couple of bold executioners! What a time we should have!"

Every afternoon the Growler and the Masher watched the road which Daubrecq took between the Square Lamartine, the Chamber of Deputies and his club. Their instructions were to choose the most deserted street and the most favourable moment and, one evening, to hustle him into a motor car.

Lupin, on his side, got ready an old building, standing in the middle of a large garden, not far from Paris, which presented all the necessary conditions of safety and isolation and which he called the Monkey's Cage.

Unfortunately, Daubrecq must have suspected something, for every time, so to speak, he changed his route, or took the underground or a tram; and the cage remained unoccupied.

Lupin devised another plan. He sent to Marseilles for one of his associates, an elderly retired grocer called Brindebois, who happened to live in Daubrecq's electoral district and interested himself in politics. Old Brindebois wrote to Daubrecq from Marseilles, announcing his visit. Daubrecq gave this important constituent a hearty welcome, and a dinner was arranged for the following week.

The elector suggested a little restaurant on the left bank of the Seine, where the food, he said, was something wonderful. Daubrecq accepted.

This was what Lupin wanted. The proprietor of the restaurant was one of his friends. The attempt, which was to take place on the following Thursday, was this time bound to succeed.

Meanwhile, on the Monday of the same week, the trial of Gilbert and Vaucheray opened.

The reader will remember – and the case took place too recently for me to recapitulate its details – the really incomprehensible partiality which the presiding judge showed in his cross-examination of Gilbert. The thing was noticed and severely criticised at the time. Lupin recognised Daubrecq's hateful influence.

The attitude observed by the two prisoners differed greatly. Vaucheray was gloomy, silent, hard-faced. He cynically, in curt, sneering, almost defiant phrases, admitted the crimes of which he had formerly been guilty.

But, with an inconsistency which puzzled everybody except Lupin, he denied any participation in the murder of Leonard the valet and violently accused Gilbert. His object, in thus linking his fate with Gilbert's, was to force Lupin to take identical measures for the rescue of both his accomplices.

Gilbert, on the other hand, whose frank countenance and dreamy, melancholy eyes won every sympathy, was unable to protect himself against the traps laid for him by the judge or to counteract Vaucheray's lies. He burst into tears, talked too much, or else did not talk when he should have talked. Moreover, his counsel, one of the Leaders of the bar, was taken ill at the last moment – and here again Lupin saw the hand of Daubrecq – and he was replaced by a junior who spoke badly, muddied the whole case, set the jury against him and failed to wipe out the impression produced by the speeches of the advocate-general and of Vaucheray's counsel.

Lupin, who had the inconceivable audacity to be present on the last day of the trial, the Thursday, had no doubt as to the result. A verdict of guilty was certain in both cases.

It was certain because all the efforts of the prosecution, thus supporting Vaucheray's tactics, had tended to link the two prisoners closely together. It was certain, also and above all, because it concerned two of Lupin's accomplices. From the opening of the inquiry before the magistrate until the delivery of the verdict, all the proceedings had been directed against Lupin; and this in spite of the fact that the prosecution, for want of sufficient evidence and also in order not to scatter its efforts over too wide an area, had decided not to include Lupin in the indictment. He was the adversary aimed at, the leader who must be punished in the person of his friends, the famous and popular scoundrel whose fascination in the eyes of the crowd must be destroyed for good and all. With Gilbert and Vaucheray executed, Lupin's halo would fade away and the legend would be exploded.

Lupin ... Lupin ... Arsène Lupin: it was the one name heard throughout the four days. The advocate general, the presiding judge, the jury, the counsel, the witnesses had no other words on their lips. Every moment, Lupin was mentioned and cursed at, scoffed at, insulted and held responsible for all the crimes committed. It was as though Gilbert and Vaucheray figured only as supernumeraries, while the real criminal undergoing trial was he, Lupin, Master Lupin, Lupin the burglar, the leader of a gang of thieves, the forger, the incendiary, the hardened offender, the ex-convict, Lupin the murderer, Lupin stained with the blood of his victim, Lupin lurking in the shade, like a coward, after sending his friends to the foot of the scaffold.

"Oh, the rascals know what they're about!" he muttered. "It's my debt which they are making my poor old Gilbert pay."

And the terrible tragedy went on.

At seven o'clock in the evening, after a long deliberation, the jury returned to court and the foreman read out the answers to the questions put from the bench. The answer was 'Yes' to every count of the indictment, a verdict of guilty without extenuating circumstances.

The prisoners were brought in. Standing up, but staggering and white-faced, they received their sentence of death.

And, amid the great, solemn silence, in which the anxiety of the onlookers was mingled with pity, the assize-president asked:

"Have you anything more to say, Vaucheray?"

"Nothing, Monsieur le President. Now that my mate is sentenced as well as myself, I am easy ... We are both on the same footing ... The governor must find a way to save the two of us."

"The governor?"

"Yes, Arsène Lupin."

There was a laugh among the crowd.

The President asked:

"And you, Gilbert?"

Tears streamed down the poor lad's cheeks and he stammered a few inarticulate sentences. But, when the judge repeated his question, he succeeded in mastering himself and replied, in a trembling voice:

"I wish to say, Monsieur le President, that I am guilty of many things, that's true ... I have done a lot of harm ... But, all the same, not this. No, I have not committed murder ... I have never committed murder ... And I don't want to die ... it would be too horrible ..."

He swayed from side to side, supported by the warders, and he was heard to cry, like a child calling for help:

"Governor ... save me! Save me! I don't want to die!"

Then, in the crowd, amid the general excitement, a voice rose above the surrounding clamour:

"Don't be afraid, little 'un! The governor's here!"

A tumult and hustling followed. The municipal guards and the policemen rushed into court and laid hold of a big, red-faced man, who was stated by his neighbours to be the author of that outburst and who struggled hand and foot.

Questioned without delay, he gave his name, Philippe Bonel, an undertaker's man, and declared that someone sitting beside him had offered him a hundred-franc note if he would consent, at the proper moment, to shout a few words which his neighbour scribbled on a bit of paper. How could he refuse?

In proof of his statements, he produced the hundred-franc note and the scrap of paper.

Philippe Bonel was let go.

Meanwhile, Lupin, who of course had assisted energetically in the individual's arrest and handed him over to the guards, left the law-courts, his heart heavy with anguish. His car was waiting for him on the quay. He flung himself into it, in despair, seized with so great a sorrow that he had to make an effort to restrain his tears. Gilbert's cry, his voice wrung with affliction, his distorted features, his tottering frame: all this haunted his brain; and he felt as if he would never, for a single second, forget those impressions.

He drove home to the new place which he had selected among his different residences and which occupied a corner of the place de Clichy. He expected to find the Growler and the Masher, with whom he was to kidnap Daubrecq that evening. But he had hardly opened the door of his flat, when a cry escaped him: Clarisse stood before him; Clarisse, who had returned from Brittany at the moment of the verdict.

He at once gathered from her attitude and her pallor that she knew. And, at once, recovering his courage in her presence, without giving her time to speak, he exclaimed:

"Yes, yes, yes ... but it doesn't matter. We foresaw that. We couldn't prevent it. What we have to do is to stop the mischief. And tonight, you understand, tonight, the thing will be done."

Motionless and tragic in her sorrow, she stammered:

"Tonight?"

"Yes. I have prepared everything. In two hours, Daubrecq will be in my hands. Tonight, whatever means I have to employ, he shall speak."

"Do you mean that?" she asked, faintly, while a ray of hope began to light up her face.

"He shall speak. I shall have his secret. I shall tear the list of the twenty-seven from him. And that list will set your son free."

"Too late," Clarisse murmured.

"Too late? Why? Do you think that, in exchange for such a document, I shall not obtain Gilbert's pretended escape? Why, Gilbert will be at liberty in three days! In three days ..."

He was interrupted by a ring at the bell:

"Listen, here are our friends. Trust me. Remember that I keep my promises. I gave you back your little Jacques. I shall give you back Gilbert."

He went to let the Growler and the Masher in and said:

"Is everything ready? Is old Brindebois at the restaurant? Quick, let us be off!"

"It's no use, governor," replied the Masher.

"No use? What do you mean?"

"There's news."

"What news? Speak, man!"

"Daubrecq has disappeared."

"Eh? What's that? Daubrecq disappeared?"

"Yes, carried off from his house, in broad daylight."

"The devil! By whom?"

"Nobody knows ... four men ... there were pistols fired ... The police are on the spot. Prasville is directing the investigations."

Lupin did not move a limb. He looked at Clarisse Mergy, who lay huddled in a chair.

He himself had to bow his head. Daubrecq being carried off meant one more chance of success lost ...

THE PROFILE
OF NAPOLEON

As soon as the prefect of police, the chief of the criminal investigation department and the examining-magistrates had left Daubrecq's house, after a preliminary and entirely fruitless inquiry, Prasville resumed his personal search.

He was examining the study and the traces of the struggle which had taken place there, when the portress brought him a visiting-card, with a few words in pencil scribbled upon it.

"Show the lady in," he said.

"The lady has someone with her," said the portress.

"Oh? Well, show the other person in as well."

Clarisse Mergy entered at once and introduced the gentleman with her, a gentleman in a black frock coat, which was too tight for him and which looked as though it had not been brushed for ages. He was shy in his manner and seemed greatly embarrassed about how to dispose of his old, rusty top hat, his gingham umbrella, his one and only glove and his body generally.

"Monsieur Nicole," said Clarisse, "a private teacher,

who is acting as tutor to my little Jacques. Monsieur Nicole has been of the greatest help to me with his advice during the past year. He worked out the whole story of the crystal stopper. I should like him, as well as myself – if you see no objection to telling me – to know the details of this kidnapping business, which alarms me and upsets my plans; yours too, I expect?"

Prasville had every confidence in Clarisse Mergy. He knew her relentless hatred of Daubrecq and appreciated the assistance which she had rendered in the case. He therefore made no difficulties about telling her what he knew, thanks to certain clues and especially to the evidence of the portress.

For that matter, the thing was exceedingly simple. Daubrecq, who had attended the trial of Gilbert and Vaucheray as a witness and who was seen in court during the speeches, had returned home at six o'clock. The portress affirmed that he came in alone and that there was nobody in the house at the time. Nevertheless, a few minutes later, she heard shouts, followed by the sound of a struggle and two pistol shots; and from her lodge she saw four masked men scuttle down the front steps, carrying Daubrecq the deputy, and hurry towards the gate. They opened the gate. At the same moment, a motor car arrived outside the house. The four men bundled themselves into it; and the motor car, which had hardly had time to stop, set off at full speed.

"Were there not always two policemen on duty?" asked Clarisse.

"They were there," said Prasville, "but at a hundred and fifty yards' distance; and Daubrecq was carried off so quickly that they were unable to interfere, although they hastened up as fast as they could."

"And did they discover nothing, find nothing?"

"Nothing, or hardly anything … Merely this."

"What is that?"

"A little piece of ivory, which they picked up on the ground. There was a fifth party in the car; and the portress saw him get down while the others were hoisting Daubrecq in. As he was stepping back into the car, he dropped something and picked it up again at once. But the thing, whatever it was, must have been broken on the pavement; for this is the bit of ivory which my men found."

"But how did the four men manage to enter the house?" asked Clarisse.

"By means of false keys, evidently, while the portress was doing her shopping, in the course of the afternoon; and they had no difficulty in secreting themselves, as Daubrecq keeps no other servants. I have every reason to believe that they hid in the room next door, which is the dining room, and afterward attacked Daubrecq here, in the study. The disturbance of the furniture and other articles proves how violent the struggle was. We found a large-bore revolver, belonging to Daubrecq, on the carpet. One of the bullets had smashed the glass over the mantelpiece, as you see."

Clarisse turned to her companion for him to express an opinion. But Monsieur Nicole, with his eyes obstinately lowered, had not budged from his chair and sat fumbling at the rim of his hat, as though he had not yet found a proper place for it.

Prasville gave a smile. It was evident that he did not look upon Clarisse's adviser as a man of first-rate intelligence:

"The case is somewhat puzzling, monsieur," he said, "is it not?"

"Yes ... yes," Monsieur Nicole confessed, "most puzzling."

"Then you have no little theory of your own upon the matter?"

"Well, Monsieur le Secretaire General, I'm thinking that Daubrecq has many enemies."

"Ah, capital!"

"And that several of those enemies, who are interested in his disappearance, must have banded themselves against him."

"Capital, capital!" said Prasville, with satirical approval. "Capital! Everything is becoming clear as daylight. It only remains for you to furnish us with a little suggestion that will enable us to turn our search in the right direction."

"Don't you think, Monsieur le Secretaire General, that this broken bit of ivory which was picked up on the ground ..."

"No, Monsieur Nicole, no. That bit of ivory belongs to something which we do not know and which its owner will at once make it his business to conceal. In order to trace the owner, we should at least be able to define the nature of the thing itself."

Monsieur Nicole reflected and then began:

"Monsieur le Secretaire General, when Napoleon I fell from power ..."

"Oh, Monsieur Nicole, oh, a lesson in French history!"

"Only a sentence, Monsieur le Secretaire General, just one sentence which I will ask your leave to complete. When Napoleon I fell from power, the Restoration placed a certain number of officers on half-pay. These officers were suspected by the authorities and kept under observation by the police. They remained faithful to the emperor's memory; and they contrived to reproduce the features of their idol on all sorts of objects of everyday use; snuff-boxes, rings, breastpins, penknives and so on."

"Well?"

"Well, this bit comes from a walking stick, or rather a sort of loaded cane, or life preserver, the knob of which is formed of a piece of carved ivory. When you look at the knob in a certain way, you end by seeing that the outline represents the profile of the Little Corporal. What you have in your hand, Monsieur le Secretaire General, is a bit of the ivory knob at the top of a half-pay officer's life preserver."

"Yes," said Prasville, examining the exhibit, "yes, I can make out a profile ... but I don't see the inference ..."

"The inference is very simple. Among Daubrecq's victims, among those whose names are inscribed on the famous list, is the descendant of a Corsican family in Napoleon's service, which derived its wealth and title from the emperor and was afterward ruined under the Restoration. It is ten to one that this descendant, who was the leader of the Bonapartist party a few years ago, was the fifth person hiding in the motor car. Need I state his name?"

"The Marquis d'Albufex?" said Prasville.

"The Marquis d'Albufex," said Monsieur Nicole.

Monsieur Nicole, who no longer seemed in the least worried with his hat, his glove and his umbrella, rose and said to Prasville:

"Monsieur le Secretaire General, I might have kept my discovery to myself, and not told you of it until after the final victory, that is, after bringing you the list of the twenty-seven. But matters are urgent. Daubrecq's disappearance, contrary to what his kidnappers expect, may hasten on the catastrophe which you wish to avert. We must therefore act with all speed. Monsieur le Secretaire General, I ask for your immediate and practical assistance."

"In what way can I help you?" asked Prasville, who was beginning to be impressed by his quaint visitor.

"By giving me, tomorrow, those particulars about the Marquis d'Albufex which it would take me personally several days to collect."

Prasville seemed to hesitate and turned his head towards Madame Mergy. Clarisse said:

"I beg of you to accept Monsieur Nicole's services. He is an invaluable and devoted ally. I will answer for him as I would for myself."

"What particulars do you require, Monsieur?" asked Prasville.

"Everything that concerns the Marquis d'Albufex: the position of his family, the way in which he spends his time, his family connections, the properties which he owns in Paris and in the country."

Prasville objected:

"After all, whether it's the Marquis or another,

Daubrecq's kidnapper is working on our behalf, seeing that, by capturing the list, he disarms Daubrecq."

"And who says, Monsieur le Secretaire General, that he is not working on his own behalf?"

"That is not possible, as his name is on the list."

"And suppose he erases it? Suppose you then find yourself dealing with a second blackmailer, even more grasping and more powerful than the first and one who, as a political adversary, is in a better position than Daubrecq to maintain the contest?"

The secretary general was struck by the argument. After a moment's thought, he said:

"Come and see me in my office at four o'clock tomorrow. I will give you the particulars. What is your address, in case I should want you?"

"Monsieur Nicole, 25, place de Clichy. I am staying at a friend's flat, which he has lent me during his absence."

The interview was at an end. Monsieur Nicole thanked the secretary general, with a very low bow, and walked out, accompanied by Madame Mergy:

"That's an excellent piece of work," he said, outside, rubbing his hands. "I can march into the police office whenever I like, and set the whole lot to work."

Madame Mergy, who was less hopefully inclined, said:

"Alas, will you be in time? What terrifies me is the thought that the list may be destroyed."

"Goodness gracious me, by whom? By Daubrecq?"

"No, but by the Marquis, when he gets hold of it."

"He hasn't got it yet! Daubrecq will resist long enough, at any rate, for us to reach him. Just think! Prasville is at my orders!"

"Suppose he discovers who you are? The least inquiry will prove that there is no such person as Monsieur Nicole."

"But it will not prove that Monsieur Nicole is the same person as Arsène Lupin. Besides, make yourself easy. Prasville is not only beneath contempt as a detective: he has but one aim in life, which is to destroy his old enemy, Daubrecq. To achieve that aim, all means are equally good; and he will not waste time in verifying the identity of a Monsieur Nicole who promises him Daubrecq. Not to mention that I was brought by you and that, when all is said, my little gifts did dazzle him to some extent. So let us go ahead boldly."

Clarisse always recovered confidence in Lupin's presence. The future seemed less appalling to her; and she admitted, she forced herself to admit, that the chances of saving Gilbert were not lessened by that hideous death sentence. But he could not prevail upon her to return to Brittany. She wanted to fight by his side. She wanted to be there and share all his hopes and all his disappointments.

The next day the inquiries of the police confirmed what Prasville and Lupin already knew. The Marquis d'Albufex had been very deeply involved in the business of the canal, so deeply that Prince Napoleon was obliged to remove him from the management of his political campaign in France; and he kept up his very extravagant style of living only by dint of constant loans and makeshifts. On the other hand, in so far as concerned the kidnapping of Daubrecq, it was ascertained that, contrary to his usual custom, the Marquis had not appeared in his club between six and seven that evening and had not dined at home. He did not come back until midnight; and then he came on foot.

Monsieur Nicole's accusation, therefore, was receiving an early proof. Unfortunately – and Lupin was no more successful in his own attempts – it was impossible to obtain the least clue as to the motor car, the chauffeur and the four people who had entered Daubrecq's house. Were they associates of the Marquis, compromised in the canal affair like himself? Were they men in his pay? Nobody knew.

The whole search, consequently, had to be concentrated upon the Marquis and the country-seats and houses which he might possess at a certain distance from Paris, a distance which, allowing for the average speed of a motor car and the inevitable stoppages, could be put at sixty to ninety miles.

Now d'Albufex, having sold everything that he ever had, possessed neither country houses nor landed estates.

They turned their attention to the Marquis' relations and intimate friends. Was he able on this side to dispose of some safe retreat in which to imprison Daubrecq?

The result was equally fruitless.

And the days passed. And what days for Clarisse Mergy! Each of them brought Gilbert nearer to the terrible day of reckoning. Each of them meant twenty-four hours less from the date which Clarisse had instinctively fixed in her mind. And she said to Lupin, who was racked with the same anxiety:

"Fifty-five days more ... Fifty days more ... What can one do in so few days? Oh, I beg of you ... I beg of you ..."

What could they do indeed? Lupin, who would not

leave the task of watching the Marquis to any one but himself, practically lived without sleeping. But the Marquis had resumed his regular life; and, doubtless suspecting something, did not risk going away.

Once alone, he went down to the Duc de Montmaur's, in the daytime. The Duke kept a pack of boar-hounds, with which he hunted the Forest of Durlaine. D'Albufex maintained no relations with him outside the hunt.

"It is hardly likely," said Prasville, "that the Duc de Montmaur, an exceedingly wealthy man, who is interested only in his estates and his hunting and takes no part in politics, should lend himself to the illegal detention of Daubrecq the deputy in his chateau."

Lupin agreed; but, as he did not wish to leave anything to chance, the next week, seeing d'Albufex go out one morning in riding dress, he followed him to the Gare du Nord and took the same train.

He got out at Aumale, where d'Albufex found a carriage at the station which took him to the Chateau de Montmaur.

Lupin lunched quietly, hired a bicycle and came in view of the house at the moment when the guests were going into the park, in motor cars or mounted. The Marquis d'Albufex was one of the horsemen.

Thrice, in the course of the day, Lupin saw him cantering along. And he found him, in the evening, at the station, where d'Albufex rode up, followed by a huntsman.

The proof, therefore, was conclusive; and there was nothing suspicious on that side. Why did Lupin, nevertheless, resolve not to be satisfied with appearances?

And why, next day, did he send the Masher to find out things in the neighbourhood of Montmaur? It was an additional precaution, based upon no logical reason, but agreeing with his methodical and careful manner of acting.

Two days later he received from the Masher, among other information of less importance, a list of the house-party at Montmaur and of all the servants and keepers.

One name struck him, among those of the huntsmen. He at once wired:

Enquire about huntsman Sebastiani.

The Masher's answer was received the next day:

Sebastiani, a Corsican, was recommended to the Duc de Montmaur by the Marquis d'Albufex. He lives at two or three miles from the house, in a hunting-lodge built among the ruins of the feudal stronghold which was the cradle of the Montmaur family.

"That's it," said Lupin to Clarisse Mergy, showing her the Masher's letter. "That name, Sebastiani, at once reminded me that d'Albufex is of Corsican descent. There was a connection ..."

"Then what do you intend to do?"

"If Daubrecq is imprisoned in those ruins, I intend to enter into communication with him."

"He will distrust you."

"No. Lately, acting on the information of the police, I ended by discovering the two old ladies who carried off your little Jacques at Saint-Germain and who brought him, the same evening, to Neuilly. They are two old maids, cousins of Daubrecq, who makes them a small monthly allowance. I have been to call on those Demoiselles Rousselot; remember the name and the address: 134 bis, rue du Bac. I inspired them with confidence, promised them to find their cousin and benefactor; and the elder sister, Euphrasie Rousselot, gave me a letter in which she begs Daubrecq to trust Monsieur Nicole entirely. So you see, I have taken every precaution. I shall leave tonight."

"We, you mean," said Clarisse.

"You!"

"Can I go on living like this, in feverish inaction?" And she whispered, "I am no longer counting the days, the thirty-eight or forty days that remain to us: I am counting the hours."

Lupin felt that her resolution was too strong for him to try to combat it. They both started at five o'clock in the morning, by motor car. The Growler went with them.

So as not to arouse suspicion, Lupin chose a large town as his headquarters. At Amiens, where he installed Clarisse, he was only eighteen miles from Montmaur.

At eight o'clock he met the Masher not far from the old fortress, which was known in the neighbourhood by the name of Mortepierre, and he examined the locality under his guidance.

On the confines of the forest, the little river Ligier, which has dug itself a deep valley at this spot, forms a loop which is overhung by the enormous cliff of Mortepierre.

"Nothing to be done on this side," said Lupin. "The cliff is steep, over two hundred feet high, and the river hugs it all round."

Not far away they found a bridge that led to the foot of a path which wound, through the oaks and pines, up to a little esplanade, where stood a massive, iron-bound gate, studded with nails and flanked on either side by a large tower.

"Is this where Sebastiani the huntsman lives?" asked Lupin.

"Yes," said the Masher, "with his wife, in a lodge standing in the midst of the ruins. I also learnt that he has three tall sons and that all the four were supposed to be away for a holiday on the day when Daubrecq was carried off."

"Oho!" said Lupin. "The coincidence is worth remembering. It seems likely enough that the business was done by those chaps and their father."

Towards the end of the afternoon Lupin availed himself of a breach to the right of the towers to scale the curtain. From there he was able to see the huntsman's lodge and the few remains of the old fortress: here, a bit of wall, suggesting the mantel of a chimney; further away, a water tank; on this side, the arches of a chapel; on the other, a heap of fallen stones.

A patrol path edged the cliff in front; and, at one of the ends of this patrol path, there were the remains of a formidable donjon keep razed almost level with the ground.

Lupin returned to Clarisse Mergy in the evening. And from that time he went backwards and forwards between Amiens and Mortepierre, leaving the Growler and the Masher permanently on the watch.

And six days passed. Sebastiani's habits seemed to be subject solely to the duties of his post. He would go up to the Chateau de Montmaur, walk about in the forest, note the tracks of the game and go about his rounds at night.

But, on the seventh day, learning that there was to be a meet and that a carriage had been sent to Aumale Station in the morning, Lupin took up his post in a cluster of box and laurels which surrounded the little esplanade in front of the gate.

At two o'clock he heard the pack give tongue. They approached, accompanied by hunting cries, and then drew farther away. He heard them again, about the middle of the afternoon, not quite so distinctly; and that was all. But suddenly, amid the silence, the sound of galloping horses reached his ears; and, a few minutes later, he saw two riders climbing the river path.

He recognised the Marquis d'Albufex and Sebastiani. On reaching the esplanade, they both alighted; and a woman – the huntsman's wife, no doubt – opened the gate. Sebastiani fastened the horses' bridles to rings fixed on a post at a few yards from Lupin and ran to join the Marquis. The gate closed behind them.

Lupin did not hesitate; and, though it was still broad daylight, relying upon the solitude of the place, he hoisted himself to the hollow of the breach. Passing his head through cautiously, he saw the two men and Sebastiani's wife hurrying towards the ruins of the keep.

The huntsman drew aside a hanging screen of ivy and revealed the entrance to a stairway, which he went down, as did d'Albufex, leaving his wife on guard on the terrace.

There was no question of going in after them; and Lupin returned to his hiding place. He did not wait long before the gate opened again.

The Marquis d'Albufex seemed in a great rage. He was striking the leg of his boot with his whip and mumbling angry words which Lupin was able to distinguish when the distance became less great:

"Ah, the hound! I'll make him speak ... I'll come back tonight ... tonight, at ten o'clock, do you hear, Sebastiani? And we shall do what's necessary ... Oh, the brute!"

Sebastiani unfastened the horses. D'Albufex turned to the woman:

"See that your sons keep a good watch ... If anyone attempts to deliver him, so much the worse for him. The trapdoor is there. Can I rely upon them?"

"As thoroughly as on myself, Monsieur le Marquis," declared the huntsman. "They know what Monsieur le Marquis has done for me and what he means to do for them. They will shrink at nothing."

"Let us mount and get back to the hounds," said d'Albufex.

So things were going as Lupin had supposed. During these runs, d'Albufex, taking a line of his own, would push off to Mortepierre, without anybody's suspecting his trick. Sebastiani, who was devoted to him body and soul, for reasons connected with the past into which it was not worthwhile to enquire, accompanied him; and together they went to see the captive, who was closely watched by the huntsman's wife and his three sons.

"That's where we stand," said Lupin to Clarisse Mergy, when he joined her at a neighbouring inn. "This evening the Marquis will put Daubrecq to the question – a little brutally, but indispensably – as I intended to do myself."

"And Daubrecq will give up his secret," said Clarisse, already quite upset.

"I'm afraid so."

"Then ..."

"I am hesitating between two plans," said Lupin, who seemed very calm. "Either to prevent the interview ..."

"How?"

"By forestalling d'Albufex. At nine o'clock, the Growler, the Masher and I climb the ramparts, burst into the fortress, attack the keep, disarm the garrison ... and the thing's done: Daubrecq is ours."

"Unless Sebastiani's sons fling him through the trapdoor to which the Marquis alluded ..."

"For that reason," said Lupin, "I intend to risk that violent measure only as a last resort and in case my other plan should not be practicable."

"What is the other plan?"

"To witness the interview. If Daubrecq does not speak, it will give us the time to prepare to carry him off under more favourable conditions. If he speaks, if they compel him to reveal the place where the list of the twenty-seven is hidden, I shall know the truth at the same time as d'Albufex, and I swear to God that I shall turn it to account before he does."

"Yes, yes," said Clarisse. "But how do you propose to be present?"

"I don't know yet," Lupin confessed. "It depends on certain particulars which the Masher is to bring me and on some which I shall find out for myself."

He left the inn and did not return until an hour later as night was falling. The Masher joined him.

"Have you the little book?" asked Lupin.

"Yes, governor. It was what I saw at the Aumale newspaper shop. I got it for ten sous."

"Give it me."

The Masher handed him an old, soiled, torn pamphlet, entitled, on the cover, *A Visit to Mortepierre, 1824, with Plans and Illustrations.*

Lupin at once looked for the plan of the donjon keep.

"That's it," he said. "Above the ground were three stories, which have been razed, and below the ground, dug out of the rock, two stories, one of which was blocked up by the rubbish, while the other ... There, that's where our friend Daubrecq lies. The name is significant: the torture chamber ... Poor, dear friend! Between the staircase and the torture chamber, two doors. Between those two doors, a recess in which the three brothers obviously sit, gun in hand."

"So it is impossible for you to get in that way without being seen."

"Impossible ... unless I come from above, by the story that has fallen in, and look for a means of entrance through the ceiling ... But that is very risky ..."

He continued to turn the pages of the book. Clarisse asked:

"Is there no window to the room?"

"Yes," he said. "From below, from the river – I have just been there – you can see a little opening, which is also marked on the plan. But it is fifty yards up, sheer; and even then the rock overhangs the water. So that again is out of the question."

He glanced through a few pages of the book. The title

of one chapter struck him: 'The Lovers' Towers'. He read the opening lines:

In the old days, the donjon was known to the people of the neighbourhood as the Lovers' Tower, in memory of a fatal tragedy that marked it in the Middle Ages. The Comte de Mortepierre, having received proofs of his wife's faithlessness, imprisoned her in the torture chamber, where she spent twenty years. One night, her lover, the Sire de Tancarville, with reckless courage, set up a ladder in the river and then clambered up the face of the cliff till he came to the window of the room. After filing the bars, he succeeded in releasing the woman he loved and bringing her down with him by means of a rope. They both reached the top of the ladder, which was watched by his friends, when a shot was fired from the patrol path and hit the man in the shoulder. The two lovers were hurled into the air ...

There was a pause, after he had read this, a long pause during which each of them drew a mental picture of the tragic escape. So, three or four centuries earlier, a man, risking his life, had attempted that surprising feat and would have succeeded but for the vigilance of some sentry who heard the noise. A man had ventured! A man had dared! A man done it!

Lupin raised his eyes to Clarisse. She was looking at him ... with such a desperate, such a beseeching look! The look of a mother who demanded the impossible and who would have sacrificed anything to save her son.

"Masher," he said, "get a strong rope, but very

slender, so that I can roll it round my waist, and very long: fifty or sixty yards. You, Growler, go and look for three or four ladders and fasten them end to end."

"Why, what are you thinking of, governor?" cried the two accomplices. "What, you mean to ... But it's madness!"

"Madness? Why? What another has done I can do."

"But it's a hundred chances to one that you break your neck."

"Well, you see, Masher, there's one chance that I don't."

"But, governor ..."

"That's enough, my friends. Meet me in an hour on the riverbank."

The preparations took long in the making. It was difficult to find the material for a fifty-foot ladder that would reach the first ledge of the cliff; and it required an endless effort and care to join the different sections.

At last, a little after nine o'clock, it was set up in the middle of the river and held in position by a boat, the bows of which were wedged between two of the rungs, while the stern was rammed into the bank.

The road through the river valley was little used, and nobody came to interrupt the work. The night was dark, the sky heavy with moveless clouds.

Lupin gave the Masher and the Growler their final instructions and said, with a laugh:

"I can't tell you how amused I am at the thought of seeing Daubrecq's face when they proceed to take his scalp or slice his skin into ribbons. Upon my word, it's worth the journey."

Clarisse also had taken a seat in the boat. He said to her:

"Until we meet again. And, above all, don't stir. Whatever happens, not a movement, not a cry."

"Can anything happen?" she asked.

"Why, remember the Sire de Tancarville! It was at the very moment when he was achieving his object, with his true love in his arms, that an accident betrayed him. But be easy: I shall be all right."

She made no reply. She seized his hand and grasped it warmly between her own.

He put his foot on the ladder and made sure that it did not sway too much. Then he went up.

He soon reached the top rung.

This was where the dangerous ascent began, a difficult ascent at the start, because of the excessive steepness, and developing, midway, into an absolute escalade.

Fortunately, here and there were little hollows, in which his feet found a resting place, and projecting stones, to which his hands clung. But twice those stones gave way and he slipped; and twice he firmly believed that all was lost. Finding a deeper hollow, he took a rest. He was worn out, felt quite ready to throw up the enterprise, asked himself if it was really worthwhile for him to expose himself to such danger:

"I say!" he thought. "Seems to me you're showing the white feather, Lupin, old boy. Throw up the enterprise? Then Daubrecq will babble his secret, the Marquis will possess himself of the list, Lupin will return empty-handed, and Gilbert ..."

The long rope which he had fastened round his waist caused him needless inconvenience and fatigue. He fixed one of the ends to the strap of his trousers and let the rope uncoil all the way down the ascent, so that he could use it, on returning, as a hand-rail.

Then he once more clutched at the rough surface of the cliff and continued the climb, with bruised nails and bleeding fingers. At every moment he expected the inevitable fall. And what discouraged him most was to hear the murmur of voices rising from the boat, murmurs so distinct that it seemed as though he were not increasing the distance between his companions and himself.

And he remembered the Sire de Tancarville, alone, he too, amid the darkness, who must have shivered at the noise of the stones which he loosened and sent bounding down the cliff. How the least sound reverberated through the silence! If one of Daubrecq's guards was peering into the gloom from the Lovers' Tower, it meant a shot ... and death.

And he climbed ... he climbed ... He had climbed so long that he ended by imagining that the goal was passed. Beyond a doubt, he had slanted unawares to the right or left and he would finish at the patrol path. What a stupid upshot! And what other upshot could there be to an attempt which the swift force of events had not allowed him to study and prepare?

Madly, he redoubled his efforts, raised himself by a number of yards, slipped, recovered the lost ground, clutched a bunch of roots that came loose in his hand, slipped once more and was abandoning the game in despair when, suddenly, stiffening himself and contracting his whole frame, his muscles and his will, he stopped still: the sound of voices seemed to issue from the very rock which he was grasping.

He listened. It came from the right. Turning his head, he thought that he saw a ray of light penetrating the darkness of space. By what effort of energy, by what imperceptible movements he succeeded in dragging himself to the spot he was never able exactly to realise. But suddenly he found himself on the ledge of a fairly wide opening, at least three yards deep, which dug into the wall of the cliff like a passage, while its other end, much narrower, was closed by three bars.

Lupin crawled along. His head reached the bars. And he saw ...

The Lovers' Tower

The torture chamber lay beneath him. It was a large, irregular room, divided into unequal portions by the four wide, massive pillars that supported its arched roof. A smell of damp and mildew came from its walls and from its flags moistened by the water that trickled from without. Its appearance at any time must have been gruesome. But, at that moment, with the tall figures of Sebastiani and his sons, with the slanting gleams of light that fell between the pillars, with the vision of the captive chained down upon the truckle bed, it assumed a sinister and barbarous aspect.

Daubrecq was in the front part of the room, four or five yards down from the window at which Lupin lurked. In addition to the ancient chains that had been used to fasten him to his bed and to fasten the bed to an iron hook in the wall, his wrists and ankles were restrained with leather straps; and an ingenious arrangement caused his least movement to set in motion a bell hung to the nearest pillar.

A lamp placed on a stool lit him full in the face.

The Marquis d'Albufex was standing beside him. Lupin could see his pale features, his grizzled moustache, his long, lean form as he looked at his prisoner with an expression of content and of gratified hatred.

A few minutes passed in profound silence. Then the Marquis gave an order:

"Light those three candles, Sebastiani, so that I can see him better."

And, when the three candles were lit and he had taken a long look at Daubrecq, he stooped over him and said, almost gently:

"I can't say what will be the end of you and me. But at any rate I shall have had some deuced happy moments in this room. You have done me so much harm, Daubrecq! The tears you have made me shed! Yes, real tears, real sobs of despair ... The money you have robbed me of! A fortune! And my terror at the thought that you might give me away! You had but to utter my name to complete my ruin and bring about my disgrace! Oh, you villain!"

Daubrecq did not budge. He had been deprived of his black glasses, but still kept his spectacles, which reflected the light from the candles. He had lost a good deal of flesh; and the bones stood out above his sunken cheeks.

"Come along," said d'Albufex. "The time has come to act. It seems that there are rogues prowling about the neighbourhood. Heaven forbid that they are here on your account and try to release you; for that would mean your immediate death, as you know ... Is the trapdoor still in working order, Sebastiani?"

Sebastiani came nearer, knelt on one knee and lifted

and turned a ring, at the foot of the bed, which Lupin had not noticed. One of the flagstones moved on a pivot, disclosing a black hole.

"You see," the Marquis continued, "everything is provided for; and I have all that I want at hand, including dungeons: bottomless dungeons, says the legend of the castle. So there is nothing to hope for, no help of any kind. Will you speak?"

Daubrecq did not reply; and he went on:

"This is the fourth time that I am questioning you, Daubrecq. It is the fourth time that I have troubled to ask you for the document which you possess, in order that I may escape your blackmailing proceedings. It is the fourth time and the last. Will you speak?"

The same silence as before. D'Albufex made a sign to Sebastiani. The huntsman stepped forwards, followed by two of his sons. One of them held a stick in his hand.

"Go ahead," said d'Albufex, after waiting a few seconds.

Sebastiani slackened the straps that bound Daubrecq's wrists and inserted and fixed the stick between the straps.

"Shall I turn, Monsieur le Marquis?"

A further silence. The Marquis waited. Seeing that Daubrecq did not flinch, he whispered:

"Can't you speak? Why expose yourself to physical suffering?"

No reply.

"Turn away, Sebastiani."

Sebastiani made the stick turn a complete circle. The straps stretched and tightened. Daubrecq gave a groan.

"You won't speak? Still, you know that I won't give way, that I can't give way, that I hold you and that, if necessary, I shall torture you till you die of it. You won't speak? You won't? Sebastiani, once more."

The huntsman obeyed. Daubrecq gave a violent start of pain and fell back on his bed with a rattle in his throat.

"You fool!" cried the Marquis, shaking with rage. "Why don't you speak? What, haven't you had enough of that list? Surely it's somebody else's turn! Come, speak ... Where is it? One word. One word only ... and we will leave you in peace. And, tomorrow, when I have the list, you shall be free. Free, do you understand? But, in Heaven's name, speak! Oh, the brute! Sebastiani, one more turn."

Sebastiani made a fresh effort. The bones cracked.

"Help! Help!" cried Daubrecq, in a hoarse voice, vainly struggling to release himself. And, in a spluttering whisper, "Mercy ... mercy."

It was a dreadful sight ... The faces of the three sons were horror-struck. Lupin shuddered, sick at heart, and realised that he himself could never have accomplished that abominable thing. He listened for the words that were bound to come. He must learn the truth. Daubrecq's secret was about to be expressed in syllables, in words wrung from him by pain. And Lupin began to think of his retreat, of the car which was waiting for him, of the wild rush to Paris, of the victory at hand.

"Speak," whispered d'Albufex. "Speak and it will be over."

"Yes ... yes ..." gasped Daubrecq.

"Well ...?"

"Later ... tomorrow ..."

"Oh, you're mad! What are you talking about: tomorrow? Sebastiani, another turn!"

"No, no!" yelled Daubrecq. "Stop!"

"Speak!"

"Well, then ... the paper ... I have hidden the paper ..."

But his pain was too great. He raised his head with a last effort, uttered incoherent words, succeeded in twice saying, "Marie ... Marie ..." and fell back, exhausted and lifeless.

"Let go at once!" said d'Albufex to Sebastiani. "Hang it all, can we have overdone it?"

But a rapid examination showed him that Daubrecq had only fainted. Thereupon, he himself, worn out with the excitement, dropped on the foot of the bed and, wiping the beads of perspiration from his forehead, stammered:

"Oh, what a dirty business!"

"Perhaps that's enough for today," said the huntsman, whose rough face betrayed a certain emotion. "We might try again tomorrow or the next day ..."

The Marquis was silent. One of the sons handed him a flask of brandy. He poured out half a glass and drank it down at a draught:

"Tomorrow?" he said. "No. Here and now. One little effort more. At the stage which he has reached, it won't be difficult." And, taking the huntsman aside, "Did you hear what he said? What did he mean by that word, 'Marie'? He repeated it twice."

"Yes, twice," said the huntsman. "Perhaps he entrusted the document to a person called Marie."

"Not he!" protested d'Albufex. "He never entrusts anything to anybody. It means something different."

"But what, Monsieur le Marquis?"

"We'll soon find out, I'll answer for it."

At that moment, Daubrecq drew a long breath and stirred on his couch.

D'Albufex, who had now recovered all his composure and who did not take his eyes off the enemy, went up to him and said:

"You see, Daubrecq, it's madness to resist ... Once you're beaten, there's nothing for it but to submit to your conqueror, instead of allowing yourself to be tortured like an idiot ... Come, be sensible."

He turned to Sebastiani:

"Tighten the rope ... let him feel it a little that will wake him up ... He's shamming death ..." Sebastiani took hold of the stick again and turned until the cord touched the swollen flesh. Daubrecq gave a start.

"That'll do, Sebastiani," said the Marquis. "Our friend seems favourably disposed and understands the need for coming to terms. That's so, Daubrecq, is it not? You prefer to have done with it? And you're quite right!"

The two men were leaning over the sufferer, Sebastiani with his hand on the stick, d'Albufex holding the lamp so as to throw the light on Daubrecq's face: "His lips are moving ... he's going to speak. Loosen the rope a little, Sebastiani: I don't want our friend to be hurt ... No, tighten it: I believe our friend is hesitating ... One turn more ... stop! That's done it! Oh, my dear Daubrecq, if you can't speak plainer than that, it's no use! What? What did you say?"

Arsène Lupin muttered an oath. Daubrecq was speaking and he, Lupin, could not hear a word of what he said! In vain, he pricked up his ears, suppressed the beating of his heart and the throbbing of his temples: not a sound reached him.

"Confound it!" he thought. "I never expected this. What am I to do?"

He was within an ace of covering Daubrecq with his revolver and putting a bullet into him which would cut short any explanation. But he reflected that he himself would then be none the wiser and that it was better to trust to events in the hope of making the most of them.

Meanwhile the confession continued beneath him, indistinctly, interrupted by silences and mingled with moans. D'Albufex clung to his prey:

"Go on! Finish, can't you?"

And he punctuated the sentences with exclamations of approval:

"Good ...! Capital! Oh, how funny ...! And no one suspected ...? Not even Prasville ...? What an ass! Loosen a bit, Sebastiani: don't you see that our friend is out of breath? Keep calm, Daubrecq ... don't tire yourself ... And so, my dear fellow, you were saying ..."

That was the last. There was a long whispering to which d'Albufex listened without further interruption and of which Arsène Lupin could not catch the least syllable. Then the Marquis drew himself up and exclaimed, joyfully:

"That's it! Thank you, Daubrecq. And, believe me, I shall never forget what you have just done. If ever you're in need, you have only to knock at my door and there will always be a crust of bread for you in the kitchen and a glass of water from the filter. Sebastiani, look after Monsieur le député as if he were one of your sons. And, first of all, release him from his bonds. It's a heartless thing to truss one's fellow man like that, like a chicken on the spit!"

"Shall we give him something to drink?" suggested the huntsman.

"Yes, that's it, give him a drink."

Sebastiani and his sons undid the leather straps, rubbed the bruised wrists, dressed them with an ointment and bandaged them. Then Daubrecq swallowed a few drops of brandy.

"Feeling better?" said the Marquis. "Pooh, it's nothing much! In a few hours, it won't show; and you'll be able to boast of having been tortured, as in the good old days of the Inquisition. You lucky dog!"

He took out his watch. "Enough said! Sebastiani, let your sons watch him in turns. You, take me to the station for the last train."

"Then are we to leave him like that, Monsieur le Marquis, free to move as he pleases?"

"Why not? You don't imagine that we are going to keep him here to the day of his death? No, Daubrecq, sleep quietly. I shall go to your place tomorrow afternoon; and, if the document is where you told me, a telegram shall be sent off at once and you shall be set free. You haven't told me a lie, I suppose?"

He went back to Daubrecq and, stooping over him again:

"No humbug, eh? That would be very silly of you. I should lose a day, that's all. Whereas you would lose all the days that remain to you to live. But no, the hiding place is too good. A fellow doesn't invent a thing like that for fun. Come on, Sebastiani. You shall have the telegram tomorrow."

"And suppose they don't let you into the house, Monsieur le Marquis?"

"Why shouldn't they?"

"The house in the Square Lamartine is occupied by Prasville's men."

"Don't worry, Sebastiani. I shall get in. If they don't open the door, there's always the window. And, if the window won't open, I shall arrange with one of Prasville's men. It's a question of money, that's all. And, thank goodness, I shan't be short of that, henceforth! Goodnight, Daubrecq."

He went out, accompanied by Sebastiani, and the heavy door closed after them.

Lupin at once effected his retreat, in accordance with a plan which he had worked out during this scene.

The plan was simple enough: to scramble, by means of his rope, to the bottom of the cliff, take his friends with him, jump into the motor car and attack d'Albufex and Sebastiani on the deserted road that leads to Aumale Station. There could be no doubt about the issue of the contest. With d'Albufex and Sebastiani prisoners; it would be an easy matter to make one of them speak. D'Albufex had shown him how to set about it; and Clarisse Mergy would be inflexible where it was a question of saving her son.

He took the rope with which he had provided himself and groped about to find a jagged piece of rock round which to pass it, so as to leave two equal lengths hanging, by which he could let himself down. But, when he found what he wanted, instead of acting swiftly – for the business was urgent – he stood motionless, thinking. His scheme failed to satisfy him at the last moment.

"It's absurd, what I'm proposing," he said to himself. "Absurd and illogical. How can I tell that d'Albufex and Sebastiani will not escape me? How can I even tell that, once they are in my power, they will speak? No, I shall stay. There are better things to try ... much better things. It's not those two I must be at, but Daubrecq. He's done for; he has not a kick left in him. If he has told the Marquis his secret, there is no reason why he shouldn't tell it to Clarisse and me, when we employ the same methods. That's settled! We'll kidnap the Daubrecq bird." And he continued, "Besides, what do I risk? If the scheme miscarries, Clarisse and I will rush off to Paris and, together with Prasville, organise a careful watch in the Square Lamartine to prevent d'Albufex from benefiting by Daubrecq's revelations. The great thing is for Prasville to be warned of the danger. He shall be."

The church clock in a neighbouring village struck twelve. That gave Lupin six or seven hours to put his new plan into execution. He set to work forthwith.

When moving away from the embrasure which had the window at the bottom of it, he had come upon a clump of small shrubs in one of the hollows of the cliff. He cut away a dozen of these, with his knife, and whittled them all down to the same size. Then he cut off two equal lengths from his rope. These were the uprights of the ladder. He fastened the twelve little sticks between the uprights and thus contrived a rope ladder about six yards long.

When he returned to this post, there was only one of the three sons beside Daubrecq's bed in the torture chamber. He was smoking his pipe by the lamp. Daubrecq was asleep.

"Hang it!" thought Lupin. "Is the fellow going to sit there all night? In that case, there's nothing for me to do but to slip off ..."

The idea that d'Albufex was in possession of the secret vexed him mightily. The interview at which he had assisted had left the clear impression in his mind that the Marquis was working "on his own" and that, in securing the list, he intended not only to escape Daubrecq's activity, but also to gain Daubrecq's power and build up his fortune anew by the identical means which Daubrecq had employed.

That would have meant, for Lupin, a fresh battle to wage against a fresh enemy. The rapid march of events did not allow of the contemplation of such a possibility. He must at all costs spike the Marquis d'Albufex' guns by warning Prasville.

However, Lupin remained held back by the stubborn hope of some incident that would give him the opportunity of acting.

The clock struck half-past twelve.

It struck one.

The waiting became terrible, all the more so as an icy mist rose from the valley and Lupin felt the cold penetrate to his very marrow.

He heard the trot of a horse in the distance:

"Sebastiani returning from the station," he thought.

But the son who was watching in the torture chamber, having finished his packet of tobacco, opened the door and asked his brothers if they had a pipeful for him. They made some reply; and he went out to go to the lodge.

And Lupin was astounded. No sooner was the door closed than Daubrecq, who had been so sound asleep, sat up on his couch, listened, put one foot to the ground, followed by the other, and, standing up, tottering a little, but firmer on his legs than one would have expected, tried his strength.

"Well," said Lupin, "the beggar doesn't take long recovering. He can very well help in his own escape. There's just one point that ruffles me: will he allow himself to be convinced? Will he consent to go with me? Will he not think that this miraculous assistance which comes to him straight from heaven is a trap laid by the Marquis?"

But suddenly Lupin remembered the letter which he had made Daubrecq's old cousins write, the letter of recommendation, so to speak, which the elder of the two sisters Rousselot had signed with her Christian name, Euphrasie.

It was in his pocket. He took it and listened. Not a sound, except the faint noise of Daubrecq's footsteps on the flagstones. Lupin considered that the moment had come. He thrust his arm through the bars and threw the letter in.

Daubrecq seemed thunderstruck.

The letter had fluttered through the room and lay on the floor, at three steps from him. Where did it come from? He raised his head towards the window and tried to pierce the darkness that hid all the upper part of the room from his eyes. Then he looked at the envelope, without yet daring to touch it, as though he dreaded a snare. Then, suddenly, after a glance at the door, he stooped briskly, seized the envelope and opened it.

"Ah," he said, with a sigh of delight, when he saw the signature.

He read the letter half-aloud:

Rely implicitly on the bearer of this note. He has succeeded in discovering the Marquis' secret, with the money which we gave him, and has contrived a plan of escape. Everything is prepared for your flight.
Euphrasie Rousselot

He read the letter again, repeated, "Euphrasie ... Euphrasie ..." and raised his head once more.

Lupin whispered:

"It will take me two or three hours to file through one of the bars. Are Sebastiani and his sons coming back?"

"Yes, they are sure to," replied Daubrecq, in the same low voice, "but I expect they will leave me to myself."

"But they sleep next door?"

"Yes."

"Won't they hear?"

"No, the door is too thick."

"Very well. In that case, it will soon be done. I have a rope ladder. Will you be able to climb up alone, without my assistance?"

"I think so ... I'll try ... It's my wrists that they've

broken ... Oh, the brutes! I can hardly move my hands ... and I have very little strength left. But I'll try all the same ... needs must ..."

He stopped, listened and, with his finger to his mouth, whispered:

"Hush!"

When Sebastiani and his sons entered the room, Daubrecq, who had hidden the letter and lain down on his bed, pretended to wake with a start.

The huntsman brought him a bottle of wine, a glass and some food:

"How goes it, Monsieur le député?" he cried. "Well, perhaps we did squeeze a little hard ... It's very painful, that thumb screwing. Seems they often did it at the time of the Great Revolution and Bonaparte ... in the days of the chauffeurs. A pretty invention! Nice and clean ... no bloodshed ... And it didn't last long either! In twenty minutes, you came out with the missing word!" Sebastiani burst out laughing. "By the way, Monsieur le député, my congratulations! A capital hiding place. Who would ever suspect it? You see, what put us off, Monsieur le Marquis and me, was that name of Marie which you let out at first. You weren't telling a lie; but there you are, you know: the word was only half finished. We had to know the rest. Say what you like, it's amusing! Just think, on your study table! Upon my word, what a joke!"

The huntsman rose and walked up and down the room, rubbing his hands:

"Monsieur le Marquis is jolly well pleased, so pleased, in fact, that he himself is coming tomorrow evening to let you out. Yes, he has thought it over; there will be a few formalities: you may have to sign a cheque or two, stump up, what, and make good Monsieur le Marquis' expense and trouble. But what's that to you? A trifle! Not to mention that, from now on, there will be no more chains, no more straps round your wrists; in short, you will be treated like a king! And I've even been told – look here! – to allow you a good bottle of old wine and a flask of brandy."

Sebastiani let fly a few more jests, then took the lamp, made a last examination of the room and said to his sons:

"Let's leave him to sleep. You also, take a rest, all three of you. But sleep with one eye open. One never can tell ..." They withdrew.

Lupin waited a little longer and asked, in a low voice:

"Can I begin?"

"Yes, but be careful. It's not impossible that they may go on a round in an hour or two."

Lupin set to work. He had a very powerful file; and the iron of the bars, rusted and gnawed away by time, was, in places, almost reduced to dust. Twice Lupin stopped to listen, with ears pricked up. But it was only the patter of a rat over the rubbish in the upper story, or the flight of some night-bird; and he continued his task, encouraged by Daubrecq, who stood by the door, ready to warn him at the least alarm.

"Oof!" he said, giving a last stroke of the file. "I'm glad that's over, for, on my word, I've been a bit cramped in this cursed tunnel ... to say nothing of the cold ..."

He bore with all his strength upon the bar, which he had sawn from below, and succeeded in forcing it down sufficiently for a man's body to slip between the two remaining bars. Next, he had to go back to the end of the embrasure, the wider part, where he had left the rope ladder. After fixing it to the bars, he called Daubrecq:

"Psst! It's all right ... Are you ready?"

"Yes ... coming ... One more second, while I listen ... All right ... They're asleep ... give me the ladder."

Lupin lowered it and asked:

"Must I come down?"

"No ... I feel a little weak ... but I shall manage."

Indeed, he reached the window of the embrasure pretty quickly and crept along the passage in the wake of his rescuer. The open air, however, seemed to make him giddy. Also, to give himself strength, he had drunk half the bottle of wine; and he had a fainting fit that kept him lying on the stones of the embrasure for half an hour. Lupin, losing patience, was fastening him to one end of the rope, of which the other end was knotted round the bars and was preparing to let him down like a bale of goods, when Daubrecq woke up, in better condition:

"That's over," he said. "I feel fit now. Will it take long?"

"Pretty long. We are a hundred and fifty yards up."

"How was it that d'Albufex did not foresee that it was possible to escape this way?"

"The cliff is perpendicular."

"And you were able to ..."

"Well, your cousins insisted ... And then one has to live, you know, and they were free with their money."

"The dear, good souls!" said Daubrecq. "Where are they?"

"Down below, in a boat."

"Is there a river, then?"

"Yes, but we won't talk, if you don't mind. It's dangerous."

"One word more. Had you been there long when you threw me the letter?"

"No, no. A quarter of an hour or so. I'll tell you all about it ... Meanwhile, we must hurry."

Lupin went first, after recommending Daubrecq to hold tight to the rope and to come down backwards. He would give him a hand at the difficult places.

It took them over forty minutes to reach the platform of the ledge formed by the cliff; and Lupin had several times to help his companion, whose wrists, still bruised from the torture, had lost all their strength and suppleness.

Over and over again, he groaned:

"Oh, the swine, they've done for me! The swine! Ah, d'Albufex, I'll make you pay dear for this ...!"

"Ssh!" said Lupin.

"What's the matter?"

"A noise ... up above ..."

Standing motionless on the platform, they listened. Lupin thought of the Sire de Tancarville and the sentry who had killed him with a shot from his harquebus. He shivered, feeling all the anguish of the silence and the darkness.

"No," he said, "I was mistaken ... Besides, it's absurd ... They can't hit us here."

"Who would hit us?"

"No one ... no one ... it was a silly notion ..."

He groped about till he found the uprights of the ladder; then he said:

"There, here's the ladder. It is fixed in the bed of the river. A friend of mine is looking after it, as well as your cousins."

He whistled:

"Here I am," he said, in a low voice. "Hold the ladder fast." And, to Daubrecq, "I'll go first."

Daubrecq objected:

"Perhaps it would be better for me to go down first."

"Why?"

"I am very tired. You can tie your rope round my waist and hold me ... Otherwise, there is a danger that I might ..."

"Yes, you are right," said Lupin. "Come nearer."

Daubrecq came nearer and knelt down on the rock. Lupin fastened the rope to him and then, stooping over, grasped one of the uprights in both hands to keep the ladder from shaking:

"Off you go," he said.

At the same moment, he felt a violent pain in the shoulder:

"Blast it!" he said, sinking to the ground.

Daubrecq had stabbed him with a knife below the nape of the neck, a little to the right.

"You blackguard! You blackguard!"

He half-saw Daubrecq, in the dark, ridding himself of his rope, and heard him whisper:

"You're a bit of a fool, you know! You bring me a letter from my Rousselot cousins, in which I recognise the writing of the elder, Adelaide, but which that sly puss of an Adelaide, suspecting something and meaning to put me on my guard, if necessary, took care to sign with the name of the younger sister, Euphrasie Rousselot. You see, I tumbled to it! So, with a little reflection ... you are Master Arsène Lupin, are you not? Clarisse's protector, Gilbert's saviour ... Poor Lupin, I fear you're in a bad way ... I don't use the knife often; but, when I do, I use it with a vengeance."

He bent over the wounded man and felt in his pockets:

"Give me your revolver, can't you? You see, your friends will know at once that it is not their governor; and they will try to secure me ... And, as I have not much strength left, a bullet or two ... Goodbye, Lupin. We shall meet in the next world, eh? Book me a nice flat, with all the latest conveniences.

"Goodbye, Lupin. And my best thanks. For really I don't know what I should have done without you. By Jove, d'Albufex was hitting me hard! It'll be a joke to meet the beggar again!"

Daubrecq had completed his preparations. He whistled once more. A reply came from the boat.

"Here I am," he said.

With a last effort, Lupin put out his arm to stop him. But his hand touched nothing but space. He tried to call out, to warn his accomplices: his voice choked in his throat.

He felt a terrible numbness creep over his whole being. His temples buzzed.

Suddenly, shouts below. Then a shot. Then another, followed by a triumphant chuckle. And a woman's wail and moans. And, soon after, two more shots.

Lupin thought of Clarisse, wounded, dead perhaps; of Daubrecq, fleeing victoriously; of d'Albufex; of the crystal stopper, which one or other of the two adversaries would recover unresisted. Then a sudden vision showed him the Sire de Tancarville falling with the woman he loved. Then he murmured, time after time:

"Clarisse ... Clarisse ... Gilbert ..." A great silence overcame him; an infinite peace entered into him; and, without the least revolt, he received the impression that his exhausted body, with nothing now to hold it back, was rolling to the very edge of the rock, towards the abyss.

A Hotel
Bedroom
at Amiens

Lupin was recovering a little consciousness for the first time. Clarisse and the Masher were seated by his bedside.

Both were talking; and Lupin listened to them, without opening his eyes. He learned that they had feared for his life, but that all danger was now removed. Next, in the course of the conversation, he caught certain words that revealed to him what had happened in the tragic night at Mortepierre: Daubrecq's descent; the dismay of the accomplices, when they saw that it was not the governor; then the short struggle: Clarisse flinging herself on Daubrecq and receiving a wound in the shoulder; Daubrecq leaping to the bank; the Growler firing two revolver shots and darting off in pursuit of him; the Masher clambering up the ladder and finding the governor in a swoon:

"True as I live," said the Masher, "I can't make out even now how he did not roll over. There was a sort of hollow at that place, but it was a sloping hollow; and, half dead as he was, he must have hung on with his ten fingers. Crikey, it was time I came!"

Lupin listened, listened in despair. He collected his strength to grasp and understand the words. But suddenly a terrible sentence was uttered: Clarisse, weeping, spoke of the eighteen days that had elapsed, eighteen more days lost to Gilbert's safety.

Eighteen days! The figure terrified Lupin. He felt that all was over, that he would never be able to recover his strength and resume the struggle and that Gilbert and Vaucheray were doomed ... His brain slipped away from him. The fever returned and the delirium.

And more days came and went. It was perhaps the time of his life of which Lupin speaks with the greatest horror. He retained just enough consciousness and had sufficiently lucid moments to realise the position exactly. But he was not able to coordinate his ideas, to follow a line of argument nor to instruct or forbid his friends to adopt this or that line of conduct.

Often, when he emerged from his torpor, he found his hand in Clarisse's and, in that half-slumbering condition in which a fever keeps you, he would address strange words to her, words of love and passion, imploring her and thanking her and blessing her for all the light and joy which she had brought into his darkness.

Then, growing calmer and not fully understanding what he had said, he tried to jest:

"I have been delirious, have I not? What a heap of nonsense I must have talked!"

But Lupin felt by Clarisse's silence that he could safely talk as much nonsense as ever his fever suggested to him. She did not hear. The care and attention which she lavished on the patient, her devotion, her vigilance, her alarm at the least relapse: all this was meant not for him, but for the possible saviour of Gilbert. She anxiously watched the progress of his convalescence. How soon would he be fit to resume the campaign? Was it not madness to linger by his side, when every day carried away a little hope?

Lupin never ceased repeating to himself, with the inward belief that, by so doing, he could influence the course of his illness:

"I will get well ... I will get well ..."

And he lay for days on end without moving, so as not to disturb the dressing of his wound nor increase the excitement of his nerves in the smallest degree.

He also strove not to think of Daubrecq. But the image of his dire adversary haunted him; and he reconstituted the various phases of the escape, the descent of the cliff ... One day, struck by a terrible memory, he exclaimed:

"The list! The list of the twenty-seven! Daubrecq must have it by now ... or else d'Albufex. It was on the table!"

Clarisse reassured him:

"No one can have taken it," she declared. "The Growler was in Paris that same day, with a note from me for Prasville, entreating him to redouble his watch in the Square Lamartine, so that no one should enter, especially d'Albufex ..."

"But Daubrecq?"

"He is wounded. He cannot have gone home."

"Ah, well," he said, "that's all right! But you too were wounded ..."

"A mere scratch on the shoulder."

Lupin was easier in his mind after these revelations. Nevertheless, he was pursued by stubborn notions which he was unable either to drive from his brain or to put into words. Above all, he thought incessantly of that name of 'Marie' which Daubrecq's sufferings had drawn from him. What did the name refer to? Was it the title of one of the books on the shelves, or a part of the title? Would the book in question supply the key to the mystery? Or was it the combination word of a safe? Was it a series of letters written somewhere: on a wall, on a paper, on a wooden panel, on the mount of a drawing, on an invoice?

These questions, to which he was unable to find a reply, obsessed and exhausted him.

One morning Arsène Lupin woke feeling a great deal better. The wound was closed, the temperature almost normal. The doctor, a personal friend, who came every day from Paris, promised that he might get up two days later. And, on that day, in the absence of his accomplices and of Madame Mergy, all three of whom had left two days before, in quest of information, he had himself moved to the open window.

He felt life return to him with the sunlight, with the balmy air that announced the approach of spring. He recovered the concatenation of his ideas; and facts once more took their place in his brain in their logical sequence and in accordance with their relations one to the other.

In the evening he received a telegram from Clarisse to say that things were going badly and that she, the Growler and the Masher were all staying in Paris. He was much disturbed by this wire and had a less quiet night. What could the news be that had given rise to Clarisse's telegram?

But, the next day, she arrived in his room looking very pale, her eyes red with weeping, and, utterly worn out, dropped into a chair:

"The appeal has been rejected," she stammered.

He mastered his emotion and asked, in a voice of surprise:

"Were you relying on that?"

"No, no," she said, "but, all the same ... one hopes in spite of one's self."

"Was it rejected yesterday?"

"A week ago. The Masher kept it from me; and I have not dared to read the papers lately."

"There is always the commutation of sentence," he suggested.

"The commutation? Do you imagine that they will commute the sentence of Arsène Lupin's accomplices?"

She ejaculated the words with a violence and a bitterness which he pretended not to notice; and he said:

"Vaucheray perhaps not ... But they will take pity on Gilbert, on his youth ..."

"They will do nothing of the sort."

"How do you know?"

"I have seen his counsel."

"You have seen his counsel! And you told him ..."

"I told him that I was Gilbert's mother and I asked him whether, by proclaiming my son's identity, we could not influence the result ... or at least delay it."

"You would do that?" he whispered. "You would admit ..."

"Gilbert's life comes before everything. What do I care about my name! What do I care about my husband's name!"

"And your little Jacques?" he objected. "Have you the right to ruin Jacques, to make him the brother of a man condemned to death?"

She hung her head. And he resumed:

"What did the counsel say?"

"He said that an act of that sort would not help Gilbert in the remotest degree. And, in spite of all his protests, I could see that, as far as he was concerned, he had no illusions left and that the pardoning commission are bound to find in favour of the execution."

"The commission, I grant you; but what of the President of the Republic?"

"The President always goes by the advice of the commission."

"He will not do so this time."

"And why not?"

"Because we shall bring influence to bear upon him."

"How?"

"By the conditional surrender of the list of the twenty-seven!"

"Have you it?"

"No, but I shall have it."

His certainty had not wavered. He made the statement with equal calmness and faith in the infinite power of his will.

She had lost some part of her confidence in him and she shrugged her shoulders lightly:

"If d'Albufex has not purloined the list, one man alone can exercise any influence; one man alone: Daubrecq."

She spoke these words in a low and absent voice that made him shudder. Was she still thinking, as he had often seemed to feel, of going back to Daubrecq and paying him for Gilbert's life?

"You have sworn an oath to me," he said. "I'm reminding you of it. It was agreed that the struggle with Daubrecq should be directed by me and that there would never be a possibility of any arrangement between you and him."

She retorted:

"I don't even know where he is. If I knew, wouldn't you know?"

It was an evasive answer. But he did not insist, resolving to watch her at the opportune time; and he asked her, for he had not yet been told all the details:

"Then it's not known what became of Daubrecq?"

"No. Of course, one of the Growler's bullets struck him. For, next day, we picked up, in a coppice, a handkerchief covered with blood. Also, it seems that a man was seen at Aumale Station, looking very tired and walking with great difficulty. He took a ticket for Paris, stepped into the first train and that is all ..."

"He must be seriously wounded," said Lupin, "and he is nursing himself in some safe retreat. Perhaps, also, he considers it wise to lie low for a few weeks and avoid any traps on the part of the police, d'Albufex, you, myself and all his other enemies."

He stopped to think and continued:

"What has happened at Mortepierre since Daubrecq's escape? Has there been no talk in the neighbourhood?"

"No, the rope was removed before daybreak, which proves that Sebastiani or his sons discovered Daubrecq's flight on the same night. Sebastiani was away the whole of the next day."

"Yes, he will have informed the Marquis. And where is the Marquis himself?"

"At home. And, from what the Growler has heard, there is nothing suspicious there either."

"Are they certain that he has not been inside Daubrecq's house?"

"As certain as they can be."

"Nor Daubrecq?"

"Nor Daubrecq."

"Have you seen Prasville?"

"Prasville is away on leave. But Chief Inspector Blanchon, who has charge of the case, and the detectives who are guarding the house declare that, in accordance with Prasville's instructions, their watch is not relaxed for a moment, even at night; that one of them, turn and turn about, is always on duty in the study; and that no one, therefore, can have gone in."

"So, on principle," Arsène Lupin concluded, "the crystal stopper must still be in Daubrecq's study?"

"If it was there before Daubrecq's disappearance, it should be there now."

"And on the study table."

"On the study table? Why do you say that?"

"Because I know," said Lupin, who had not forgotten Sebastiani's words.

"But you don't know the article in which the stopper is hidden?"

"No. But a study table, a writing desk, is a limited space. One can explore it in twenty minutes. One can demolish it, if necessary, in ten."

The conversation had tired Arsène Lupin a little. As he did not wish to commit the least imprudence, he said to Clarisse:

"Listen. I will ask you to give me two or three days more. This is Monday, the fourth of March. On Wednesday or Thursday, at latest, I shall be up and about. And you can be sure that we shall succeed."

"And, in the meantime ..."

"In the meantime, go back to Paris. Take rooms, with the Growler and the Masher, in the Hotel Franklin, near the Trocadero, and keep a watch on Daubrecq's house. You are free to go in and out as you please. Stimulate the zeal of the detectives on duty."

"Suppose Daubrecq returns?"

"If he returns, that will be so much the better: we shall have him."

"And, if he only passes?"

"In that case, the Growler and the Masher must follow him."

"And if they lose sight of him?"

Lupin did not reply. No one felt more than he how fatal it was to remain inactive in a hotel bedroom and how useful his presence would have been on the battlefield! Perhaps even this vague idea had already prolonged his illness beyond the ordinary limits.

He murmured:

"Go now, please."

There was a constraint between them which increased as the awful day drew nigh. In her injustice, forgetting or wishing to forget that it was she who had forced her son into the Enghien enterprise, Madame Mergy did not forget that the law was pursuing Gilbert with such rigour not so much because he was a criminal as because he was an accomplice of Arsène Lupin's. And then, notwithstanding all his efforts, notwithstanding his prodigious expenditure of energy, what result had Lupin achieved, when all was said? How far had his intervention benefited Gilbert?

After a pause, she rose and left him alone.

The next day he was feeling rather low. But on the day after, the Wednesday, when his doctor wanted him to keep quiet until the end of the week, he said:

"If not, what have I to fear?"

"A return of the fever."

"Nothing worse?"

"No. The wound is pretty well healed."

"Then I don't care. I'll go back with you in your car. We shall be in Paris by midday."

What decided Lupin to start at once was, first, a letter in which Clarisse told him that she had found Daubrecq's traces, and, also, a telegram, published in the Amiens papers, which stated that the Marquis d'Albufex had been arrested for his complicity in the affair of the canal.

Daubrecq was taking his revenge.

Now the fact that Daubrecq was taking his revenge proved that the Marquis had not been able to prevent that revenge by seizing the document which was on the writing desk in the study. It proved that Chief Inspector Blanchon and the detectives had kept a good watch. It proved that the crystal stopper was still in the Square Lamartine.

It was still there; and this showed either that Daubrecq had not ventured to go home, or else that his state of health hindered him from doing so, or else again that he had sufficient confidence in the hiding place not to trouble to put himself out.

In any case, there was no doubt as to the course to be pursued: Lupin must act and he must act smartly. He must forestall Daubrecq and get hold of the crystal stopper.

When they had crossed the Bois de Boulogne and were nearing the Square Lamartine, Lupin took leave of the doctor and stopped the car. The Growler and the Masher, to whom he had wired, met him.

"Where's Madame Mergy?" he asked.

"She has not been back since yesterday; she sent us an express message to say that she saw Daubrecq leaving his cousins' place and getting into a cab. She knows the number of the cab and will keep us informed."

"Nothing further?"

"Nothing further."

"No other news?"

"Yes, the *Paris-Midi* says that d'Albufex opened his veins last night, with a piece of broken glass, in his cell at the Sante. He seems to have left a long letter behind him, confessing his fault, but accusing Daubrecq of his death and exposing the part played by Daubrecq in the canal affair."

"Is that all?"

"No. The same paper stated that it has reason to believe that the pardoning commission, after examining the record, has rejected Vaucheray and Gilbert's petition and that their counsel will probably be received in audience by the President on Friday."

Lupin gave a shudder.

"They're losing no time," he said. "I can see that Daubrecq, on the very first day, put the screw on the old judicial machine. One short week more ... and the knife falls. My poor Gilbert! If, on Friday next, the papers which your counsel submits to the President of the Republic do not contain the conditional offer of the list of the twenty-seven, then, my poor Gilbert, you are done for!"

"Come, come, governor, are you losing courage?"

"I? Rot! I shall have the crystal stopper in an hour. In two hours, I shall see Gilbert's counsel. And the nightmare will be over."

"Well done, governor! That's like your old self. Shall we wait for you here?"

"No, go back to your hotel. I'll join you later."

They parted. Lupin walked straight to the house and rang the bell.

A detective opened the door and recognised him:

"Monsieur Nicole, I believe?"

"Yes," he said. "Is Chief Inspector Blanchon here?"

"He is."

"Can I speak to him?"

The man took him to the study, where Chief Inspector Blanchon welcomed him with obvious pleasure.

"Well, Chief Inspector, one would say there was something new?"

"Monsieur Nicole, my orders are to place myself entirely at your disposal; and I may say that I am very glad to see you today."

"Why so?"

"Because there is something new."

"Something serious?"

"Something very serious."

"Quick, speak."

"Daubrecq has returned."

"Eh, what!" exclaimed Lupin, with a start. "Daubrecq returned? Is he here?"

"No, he has gone."

"And did he come in here, in the study?"

"Yes."

"This morning."

"And you did not prevent him?"

"What right had I?"

"And you left him alone?"

"By his positive orders, yes, we left him alone."

Lupin felt himself turn pale. Daubrecq had come back to fetch the crystal stopper!

He was silent for some time and repeated to himself:

"He came back to fetch it … He was afraid that it would be found and he has taken it … Of course, it was inevitable … with d'Albufex arrested, with d'Albufex accused and accusing him, Daubrecq was bound to defend himself. It's a difficult game for him. After months and months of mystery, the public is at last learning that the infernal being who contrived the whole tragedy of the Twenty-Seven and who ruins and kills his adversaries is he, Daubrecq. What would become of him if, by a miracle, his talisman did not protect him? He has taken it back."

And, trying to make his voice sound firm, he asked:

"Did he stay long?"

"Twenty seconds, perhaps."

"What! Twenty seconds? No longer?"

"No longer."

"What time was it?"

"Ten o'clock."

"Could he have known of the Marquis d'Albufex' suicide by then?"

"Yes. I saw the special edition of the *Paris-Midi* in his pocket."

"That's it, that's it," said Lupin. And he asked, "Did Monsieur Prasville give you no special instructions in case Daubrecq should return?"

"No. So, in Monsieur Prasville's absence, I telephoned the police office and I am waiting. The disappearance of Daubrecq the deputy caused a great stir, as you know, and our presence here has a reason, in the eyes of the public, as long as that disappearance continues. But, now that Daubrecq has returned, now that we have proofs that he is neither under restraint nor dead, how can we stay in the house?"

"It doesn't matter," said Lupin, absently. "It doesn't matter whether the house is guarded or not. Daubrecq has been; therefore the crystal stopper is no longer here."

He had not finished the sentence, when a question quite naturally forced itself upon his mind. If the crystal stopper was no longer there, would this not be obvious from some material sign? Had the removal of that object, doubtless contained within another object, left no trace, no void?

It was easy to ascertain. Lupin had simply to examine the writing desk, for he knew, from Sebastiani's chaff, that this was the spot of the hiding place. And the hiding place could not be a complicated one, seeing that Daubrecq had not remained in the study for more than twenty seconds, just long enough, so to speak, to walk in and walk out again.

Lupin looked. And the result was immediate. His memory had so faithfully recorded the picture of the desk, with all the articles lying on it, that the absence of one of them struck him instantaneously, as though that article and that alone were the characteristic sign which distinguished this particular writing table from every other table in the world.

"Oh," he thought, quivering with delight, "everything fits in! Everything! Down to that half-word which the torture drew from Daubrecq in the tower at Mortepierre! The riddle is solved. There need be no more hesitation, no more groping in the dark. The end is in sight."

And, without answering the inspector's questions, he thought of the simplicity of the hiding place and remembered Edgar Allan Poe's wonderful story in which the stolen letter, so eagerly sought for, is, in a manner of speaking, displayed to all eyes. People do not suspect what does not appear to be hidden.

"Well, well," said Lupin, as he went out, greatly excited by his discovery, "I seem doomed, in this confounded adventure, to knock up against disappointments to the finish. Everything that I build crumbles to pieces at once.

Every victory ends in disaster."

Nevertheless, he did not allow himself to be cast down. On the one hand, he now knew where Daubrecq the deputy hid the crystal stopper. On the other hand, he would soon learn from Clarisse Mergy where Daubrecq himself was lurking. The rest, to him, would be child's play.

The Growler and the Masher were waiting for him in the drawing room of the Hotel Franklin, a small family hotel near the Trocadero. Madame Mergy had not yet written to him.

"Oh," he said, "I can trust her! She will hang on to Daubrecq until she is certain."

However, towards the end of the afternoon, he began to grow impatient and anxious. He was fighting one of those battles – the last, he hoped – in which the least delay might jeopardise everything. If Daubrecq threw Madame Mergy off the scent, how was he to be caught again? They no longer had weeks or days, but only a few hours, a terribly limited number of hours, in which to repair any mistakes that they might commit.

He saw the proprietor of the hotel and asked him:

"Are you sure that there is no express letter for my two friends?"

"Quite sure, sir."

"Nor for me, Monsieur Nicole?"

"No, sir."

"That's curious," said Lupin. "We were certain that we should hear from Madame Audran."

Audran was the name under which Clarisse was staying at the hotel.

"But the lady has been," said the proprietor.

"What's that?"

"She came some time ago and, as the gentlemen were not there, left a letter in her room. Didn't the porter tell you?"

Lupin and his friends hurried upstairs. There was a letter on the table.

"Hullo!" said Lupin. "It's been opened! How is that? And why has it been cut about with scissors?"

The letter contained the following lines:

Daubrecq has spent the week at the Hotel Central. This morning he had his luggage taken to the Gare de — and telephoned to reserve a berth in the sleeping car — for — I do not know when the train starts. But I shall be at the station all the afternoon. Come as soon as you can, all three of you. We will arrange to kidnap him.

"What next?" said the Masher. "At which station? And where's the sleeping car for? She has cut out just the words we wanted!"

"Yes," said the Growler. "Two snips with the scissors in each place; and the words which we most want are gone. Who ever saw such a thing? Has Madame Mergy lost her head?"

Lupin did not move. A rush of blood was beating at his temples with such violence that he glued his fists to them and pressed with all his might. His fever returned, burning and riotous, and his will, incensed to the verge of physical suffering, concentrated itself upon that stealthy enemy, which must be controlled then and there, if he himself did not wish to be irretrievably beaten.

He muttered, very calmly:

"Daubrecq has been here."

"Daubrecq!"

"We can't suppose that Madame Mergy has been amusing herself by cutting out those words. Daubrecq has been here. Madame Mergy thought that she was watching him. He was watching her instead."

"How?"

"Doubtless through that hall-porter who did not tell us that Madame Mergy had been to the hotel, but who must have told Daubrecq. He came. He read the letter. And, by way of getting at us, he contented himself with cutting out the essential words."

"We can find out ... we can ask ..."

"What's the good? What's the use of finding out how he came, when we know that he did come?"

He examined the letter for some time, turned it over and over, then stood up and said:

"Come along."

"Where to?"

"Gare de Lyon."

"Are you sure?"

"I am sure of nothing with Daubrecq. But, as we have to choose, according to the contents of the letter, between the Gare de l'Est and the Gare de Lyon, I am presuming that his business, his pleasure and his health are more likely to take Daubrecq in the direction of Marseilles and the Riviera than to the Gare de l'Est."

It was past seven when Lupin and his companions left the Hotel Franklin. A motor car took them across Paris at full speed, but they soon saw that Clarisse Mergy was not outside the station, nor in the waiting-rooms, nor on any of the platforms.

"Still," muttered Lupin, whose agitation grew as the obstacles increased, "still, if Daubrecq booked a berth in a sleeping car, it can only have been in an evening train. And it is barely half-past seven!"

A train was starting, the night express. They had time to rush along the corridor. Nobody ... neither Madame Mergy nor Daubrecq ...

But, as they were all three going, a porter accosted them near the refreshment room:

"Is one of you gentlemen looking for a lady?"

"Yes, yes ... I am," said Lupin. "Quick, what is it?"

"Oh, it's you, sir! The lady told me there might be three of you or two of you ... And I didn't know ..."

"But, in heaven's name, speak, man! What lady?"

"The lady who spent the whole day on the pavement, with the luggage, waiting."

"Well, out with it! Has she taken a train?"

"Yes, the train-de-luxe, at six-thirty: she made up her mind at the last moment, she told me to say. And I was also to say that the gentleman was in the same train and that they were going to Monte Carlo."

"Damn it!" muttered Lupin. "We ought to have taken the express just now! There's nothing left but the evening trains, and they crawl! We've lost over three hours."

The wait seemed interminable. They booked their seats. They telephoned to the proprietor of the Hotel Franklin to send on their letters to Monte Carlo. They dined. They read the papers. At last, at half-past nine, the train started.

And so, by a really tragic series of circumstances, at the most critical moment of the contest, Lupin was turning his back on the battlefield and going away, at haphazard, to seek, he knew not where, and beat, he knew not how, the most formidable and elusive enemy that he had ever fought.

And this was happening four days, five days at most, before the inevitable execution of Gilbert and Vaucheray.

It was a bad and painful night for Lupin. The more he studied the situation the more terrible it appeared to him. On every side he was faced with uncertainty, darkness, confusion, helplessness.

True, he knew the secret of the crystal stopper. But how was he to know that Daubrecq would not change or had not already changed his tactics? How was he to know that the list of the twenty-seven was still inside that crystal stopper or that the crystal stopper was still inside the object where Daubrecq had first hidden it?

And there was a further serious reason for alarm in the fact that Clarisse Mergy thought that she was shadowing and watching Daubrecq at a time when, on the contrary, Daubrecq was watching her, having her shadowed and dragging her, with diabolical cleverness, towards the places selected by himself, far from all help or hope of help.

Oh, Daubrecq's game was clear as daylight! Did not Lupin know the unhappy woman's hesitations? Did he not know – and the Growler and the Masher confirmed it most positively – that Clarisse looked upon the infamous bargain planned by Daubrecq in the light of a possible, an acceptable thing? In that case, how could he, Lupin, succeed? The logic of events, so powerfully moulded by Daubrecq, led to a fatal result: the mother must sacrifice herself and, to save her son, throw her scruples, her repugnance, her very honour, to the winds!

"Oh, you scoundrel!" snarled Lupin, in a fit of rage. "If I get hold of you, I'll make you dance to a pretty tune! I wouldn't be in your shoes for a great deal, when that happens."

They reached Monte Carlo at three o'clock in the afternoon. Lupin was at once disappointed not to see Clarisse on the platform at the station.

He waited. No messenger came up to him.

He asked the porters and ticket collectors if they had noticed, among the crowd, two travellers answering to the description of Daubrecq and Clarisse. They had not.

He had, therefore, to set to work and hunt through all the hotels and lodging-houses in the principality. Oh, the time wasted!

By the following evening, Lupin knew, beyond a doubt, that Daubrecq and Clarisse were not at Monte Carlo, nor at Monaco, nor at the Cap d'Ail, nor at La Turbie, nor at Cap Martin.

"Where can they be then?" he wondered, trembling with rage.

At last, on the Saturday, he received, at the poste restante, a telegram which had been readdressed from the Hotel Franklin and which said:

He got out at Cannes and is going on to San Remo, Hotel Palace des Ambassadeurs. Clarisse.

The telegram was dated the day before.

"Hang it!" exclaimed Lupin. "They passed through Monte Carlo. One of us ought to have remained at the station. I did think of it; but, in the midst of all that bustle..."

Lupin and his friends took the first train for Italy.

They crossed the frontier at twelve o'clock. The train entered the station at San Remo at twelve-forty.

They at once saw an hotel-porter, with "Ambassadeurs-Palace" on his braided cap, who seemed to be looking for someone among the arrivals.

Lupin went up to him:

"Are you looking for Monsieur Nicole?"

"Yes, Monsieur Nicole and two gentlemen."

"From a lady?"

"Yes, Madame Mergy."

"Is she staying at your hotel?"

"No. She did not get out. She beckoned to me, described you three gentlemen and told me to say that she was going on to Genoa, to the Hotel Continental."

"Was she by herself?"

"Yes."

Lupin tipped the man, dismissed him and turned to his friends:

"This is Saturday. If the execution takes place on Monday, there's nothing to be done. But Monday is not a likely day ... What I have to do is to lay hands on Daubrecq tonight and to be in Paris on Monday, with the document. It's our last chance. Let's take it."

The Growler went to the booking-office and returned with three tickets for Genoa.

The engine whistled.

Lupin had a last hesitation:

"No, really, it's too childish! What are we doing? We ought to be in Paris, not here! Just think!"

He was in a point of opening the door and jumping out on the permanent way. But his companions held him back. The train started. He sat down again.

And they continued their mad pursuit, travelling at random, towards the unknown ...

And this happened two days before the inevitable execution of Gilbert and Vaucheray.

Extra-Dry?

On one of the hills that girdle Nice with the finest scenery in the world, between the Vallon de Saint-Silvestre and the Vallon de La Mantega, stands a huge hotel which overlooks the town and the wonderful Baie des Anges. A crowd flocks to it from all parts, forming a medley of every class and nation.

On the evening of the same Saturday when Lupin, the Growler and the Masher were plunging into Italy, Clarisse Mergy entered this hotel, asked for a bedroom facing south and selected No. 130, on the second floor, a room which had been vacant since that morning.

The room was separated from No. 129 by two partition doors. As soon as she was alone, Clarisse pulled back the curtain that concealed the first door, noiselessly drew the bolt and put her ear to the second door:

"He is here," she thought. "He is dressing to go to the club ... as he did yesterday."

When her neighbour had gone, she went into the passage and, availing herself of a moment when there was no one in sight, walked up to the door of No. 129. The door was locked.

She waited all the evening for her neighbour's return and did not go to bed until two o'clock. On Sunday morning, she resumed her watch.

The neighbour went out at eleven. This time he left the key in the door.

Hurriedly turning the key, Clarisse entered boldly, went to the partition door, raised the curtain, drew the bolt and found herself in her own room.

In a few minutes, she heard two chambermaids doing the room in No. 129.

She waited until they were gone. Then, feeling sure that she would not be disturbed, she once more slipped into the other room.

Her excitement made her lean against a chair. After days and nights of stubborn pursuit, after alternate hopes and disappointments, she had at last succeeded in entering a room occupied by Daubrecq. She could look about at her ease; and, if she did not discover the crystal stopper, she could at least hide in the space between the partition doors, behind the hanging, see Daubrecq, spy upon his movements and surprise his secret.

She looked around her. A travelling bag at once caught her attention. She managed to open it; but her search was useless.

She ransacked the trays of a trunk and the compartments of a portmanteau. She searched the wardrobe, the writing table, the chest of drawers, the bathroom, all the tables, all the furniture. She found nothing.

She gave a start when she saw a scrap of paper on the balcony, lying as though flung there by accident:

"Can it be a trick of Daubrecq's?" she thought, out loud. "Can that scrap of paper contain ..."

"No," said a voice behind her, as she put her hand on the latch.

She turned and saw Daubrecq.

She felt neither astonishment nor alarm, nor even any embarrassment at finding herself face to face with him. She had suffered too deeply for months to trouble about what Daubrecq could think of her or say, at catching her in the act of spying.

She sat down wearily.

He grinned:

"No, you're out of it, dear friend. As the children say, you're not 'burning' at all. Oh, not a bit of it! And it's so easy! Shall I help you? It's next to you, dear friend, on that little table ... And yet, by Jove, there's not much on that little table! Something to read, something to write with, something to smoke, something to eat ... and that's all ... Will you have one of these candied fruits? Or perhaps you would rather wait for the more substantial meal which I have ordered?"

Clarisse made no reply. She did not even seem to listen to what he was saying, as though she expected other words, more serious words, which he could not fail to utter.

He cleared the table of all the things that lay upon it and put them on the mantelpiece. Then he rang the bell.

A head waiter appeared. Daubrecq asked:

"Is the lunch which I ordered ready?"

"Yes, sir."

"It's for two, isn't it?"

"Yes, sir."

"And the champagne?"

"Yes, sir."

"Extra-dry?"

"Yes, sir."

Another waiter brought a tray and laid two covers on the table: a cold lunch, some fruit and a bottle of champagne in an ice pail.

Then the two waiters withdrew.

"Sit down, dear lady. As you see, I was thinking of you and your cover is laid."

And, without seeming to observe that Clarisse was not at all prepared to do honour to his invitation, he sat down, began to eat and continued:

"Yes, upon my word, I hoped that you would end by consenting to this little private meeting. During the past week, while you were keeping so assiduous a watch upon me, I did nothing but say to myself, 'I wonder which she prefers: sweet champagne, dry champagne, or extra-dry?' I was really puzzled. Especially after our departure from Paris. I had lost your tracks, that is to say, I feared that you had lost mine and abandoned the pursuit which was so gratifying to me. When I went for a walk, I missed your beautiful dark eyes, gleaming with hatred under your hair just touched with grey. But, this morning, I understood: the room next to mine was empty at last; and my friend Clarisse was able to take up her quarters, so to speak, by my bedside. From that moment I was reassured. I felt certain that, on coming back – instead of lunching in the restaurant as usual – I should find you arranging my things to your convenience and suiting your own taste. That was why I ordered two covers: one for your humble servant, the other for his fair friend."

She was listening to him now and in the greatest terror. So Daubrecq knew that he was spied upon! For a whole week he had seen through her and all her schemes!

In a low voice, anxious-eyed, she asked:

"You did it on purpose, did you not? You only went away to drag me with you?"

"Yes," he said.

"But why? Why?"

"Do you mean to say that you don't know?" retorted Daubrecq, laughing with a little cluck of delight.

She half-rose from her chair and, bending towards him, thought, as she thought each time, of the murder which she could commit, of the murder which she would commit. One revolver shot and the odious brute was done for.

Slowly her hand glided to the weapon concealed in her bodice.

Daubrecq said:

"One second, dear friend ... You can shoot presently; but I beg you first to read this wire which I have just received."

She hesitated, not knowing what trap he was laying for her; but he went on, as he produced a telegram:

"It's about your son."

"Gilbert?" she asked, greatly concerned.

"Yes, Gilbert ... Here, read it."

She gave a yell of dismay. She had read:

Execution on Tuesday morning.

And she at once flung herself on Daubrecq, crying:

"It's not true! It's a lie ... to madden me ... Oh, I know you: you are capable of anything! Confess! It won't be on Tuesday, will it? In two days! No, no ... I tell you, we have four days yet, five days, in which to save him ... Confess it, confess it!"

She had no strength left, exhausted by this fit of rebellion; and her voice uttered none but inarticulate sounds.

He looked at her for a moment, then poured himself out a glass of champagne and drank it down at a gulp. He took a few steps up and down the room, came back to her and said:

"Listen to me, darling ..."

The insult made her quiver with an unexpected energy. She drew herself up and, panting with indignation, said:

"I forbid you ... I forbid you to speak to me like that. I will not accept such an outrage. You wretch!"

He shrugged his shoulders and resumed:

"Pah, I see you're not quite alive to the position. That comes, of course, because you still hope for assistance in some quarter. Prasville, perhaps? The excellent Prasville, whose right hand you are ... My dear friend, a forlorn hope ... You must know that Prasville is mixed up in the Canal affair! Not directly: that is to say, his name is not on the list of the twenty-seven; but it is there under the name of one of his friends, an ex-deputy called Vorenglade, Stanislas Vorenglade, his man of straw, apparently: a penniless individual whom I left alone and rightly.

I knew nothing of all that until this morning, when, lo and behold, I received a letter informing me of the existence of a bundle of documents which prove the complicity of our one and only Prasville! And who is my informant? Vorenglade himself! Vorenglade, who, tired of living in poverty, wants to extort money from Prasville, at the risk of being arrested, and who will be delighted to come to terms with me. And Prasville will get the sack. Oh, what a lark! I swear to you that he will get the sack, the villain! By Jove, but he's annoyed me long enough! Prasville, old boy, you've deserved it ..."

He rubbed his hands together, revelling in his coming revenge. And he continued:

"You see, my dear Clarisse ... there's nothing to be done in that direction. What then? What straw will you cling to? Why, I was forgetting: Monsieur Arsène Lupin! Mr. Growler! Mr. Masher! Pah, you'll admit that those gentlemen have not shone and that all their feats of prowess have not prevented me from going my own little way. It was bound to be. Those fellows imagine that there's no one to equal them. When they meet an adversary like myself, one who is not to be bounced, it upsets them and they make blunder after blunder, while still believing that they are hoodwinking him like mad. Schoolboys, that's what they are! However, as you seem to have some illusions left about the aforesaid Lupin, as you are counting on that poor devil to crush me and to work a miracle in favour of your innocent Gilbert, come, let's dispel that illusion. Oh! Lupin! Lord above, she believes in Lupin! She places her last hopes in Lupin! Lupin! Just wait till I prick you, my illustrious windbag!"

He took up the receiver of the telephone which communicated with the hall of the hotel and said:

"I'm No. 129, mademoiselle. Would you kindly ask the person sitting opposite your office to come up to me? Huh! Yes, mademoiselle, the gentleman in a grey felt hat. He knows. Thank you, mademoiselle."

Hanging up the receiver, he turned to Clarisse:

"Don't be afraid. The man is discretion itself. Besides, it's the motto of his trade: 'Discretion and dispatch'. As a retired detective, he has done me a number of services, including that of following you while you were following me. Since our arrival in the south, he has been less busy with you; but that was because he was more busy elsewhere. Come in, Jacob."

He himself opened the door, and a short, thin man, with a red moustache, entered the room.

"Please tell this lady, Jacob, in a few brief words, what you have done since Wednesday evening, when, after letting her get into the train-de-luxe which was taking me from the Gare de Lyon to the south, you yourself remained on the platform at the station. Of course, I am not asking how you spent your time, except in so far as concerns the lady and the business with which I entrusted you."

Jacob dived into the inside pocket of his jacket and produced a little notebook of which he turned over the pages and read them aloud in the voice of a man reading a report:

"Wednesday evening, 8.15. Gare de Lyon. Wait for two gents, Growler and Masher. They come with another whom I don't know yet, but who can only be Monsieur Nicole.

Give a porter ten francs for the loan of his cap and blouse. Accost the gents and tell them, from a lady, 'that they were gone to Monte Carlo'. Next, telephone to the porter at the Hotel Franklin. All telegrams sent to his boss and dispatched by said boss will be read by said hotel porter and, if necessary, intercepted.

"Thursday. Monte Carlo. The three gents search the hotels.

"Friday. Flying visits to La Turbie, the Cap d'Ail, Cap Martin. Monsieur Daubrecq rings me up. Thinks it wiser to send the gents to Italy. Make the porter of the Hotel Franklin send them a telegram appointing a meeting at San Remo.

"Saturday. San Remo. Station platform. Give the porter of the Ambassadeurs-Palace ten francs for the loan of his cap. The three gents arrive. They speak to me. Explain to them that a lady traveller, Madame Mergy, is going on to Genoa, to the Hotel Continental. The gents hesitate. Monsieur Nicole wants to get out. The others hold him back. The train starts. Good luck, gents! An hour later, I take the train for France and get out at Nice, to await fresh orders."

Jacob closed his notebook and concluded:

"That's all. Today's doings will be entered this evening."

"You can enter them now, Monsieur Jacob. '12 noon. Monsieur Daubrecq sends me to the Wagon-Lits Co. I book two berths in the Paris sleeping car, by the 2.48 train, and send them to Monsieur Daubrecq by express messenger. Then I take the 12.58 train for Vintimille, the frontier station, where I spend the day on the platform watching all the travellers who come to France.

Should Messrs. Nicole, Growler and Masher take it into their heads to leave Italy and return to Paris by way of Nice, my instructions are to telegraph to the headquarters of police that Master Arsène Lupin and two of his accomplices are in train number so-and-so."

While speaking, Daubrecq led Jacob to the door. He closed it after him, turned the key, pushed the bolt and, going up to Clarisse, said:

"And now, darling, listen to me."

This time, she uttered no protest. What could she do against such an enemy, so powerful, so resourceful, who provided for everything, down to the minutest details, and who toyed with his adversaries in such an airy fashion? Even if she had hoped till then for Lupin's interference, how could she do so now, when he was wandering through Italy in pursuit of a shadow?

She understood at last why three telegrams which she had sent to the Hotel Franklin had remained unanswered. Daubrecq was there, lurking in the dark, watching, establishing a void around her, separating her from her comrades in the fight, bringing her gradually, a beaten prisoner, within the four walls of that room.

She felt her weakness. She was at the monster's mercy. She must be silent and resigned.

He repeated, with an evil delight:

"Listen to me, darling. Listen to the irrevocable words which I am about to speak. Listen to them well. It is now twelve o'clock. The last train starts at 2.48: you understand, the last train that can bring me to Paris tomorrow, Monday, in time to save your son. The evening-trains would arrive too late. The trains-de-luxe are full up. Therefore I shall have to start at 2.48. Am I to start?"

"Yes."

"Our berths are booked. Will you come with me?"

"Yes."

"You know my conditions for interfering?"

"Yes."

"Do you accept them?"

"Yes."

"You will marry me?"

"Yes."

Oh, those horrible answers! The unhappy woman gave them in a sort of awful torpor, refusing even to understand what she was promising. Let him start first, let him snatch Gilbert from the engine of death whose vision haunted her day and night ... And then ... and then ... let what must come, come ...

He burst out laughing:

"Oh, you rogue, it's easily said! You're ready to pledge yourself to anything, eh? The great thing is to save Gilbert, isn't it? Afterward, when that noodle of a Daubrecq comes with his engagement ring, not a bit of it! Nothing doing! We'll laugh in his face! No, no, enough of empty words. I don't want promises that won't be kept: I want facts, immediate facts."

He came and sat close beside her and stated, plainly:

"This is what I propose ... what must be ... what shall be ... I will ask, or rather I will demand, not Gilbert's pardon, to begin with, but a reprieve, a postponement of the execution, a postponement of three or four weeks. They will invent a pretext of some sort: that's not my affair.

And, when Madame Mergy has become Madame Daubrecq, then and not till then will I ask for his pardon, that is to say, the commutation of his sentence. And make yourself quite easy: they'll grant it."

"I accept ... I accept," she stammered.

He laughed once more:

"Yes, you accept, because that will happen in a month's time ... and meanwhile you reckon on finding some trick, an assistance of some kind or another ... Monsieur Arsène Lupin ..."

"I swear it on the head of my son."

"The head of your son! Why, my poor pet, you would sell yourself to the devil to save it from falling!"

"Oh, yes," she whispered, shuddering. "I would gladly sell my soul!"

He sidled up against her and, in a low voice:

"Clarisse, it's not your soul I ask for ... It's something else ... For more than twenty years my life has spun around that longing. You are the only woman I have ever loved ... Loathe me, hate me – I don't care – but do not spurn me ... Am I to wait? To wait another month? No, Clarisse, I have waited too many years already ..."

He ventured to touch her hand. Clarisse shrank back with such disgust that he was seized with fury and cried:

"Oh, I swear to heaven, my beauty, the executioner won't stand on such ceremony when he catches hold of your son! And you give yourself airs! Why, think, it'll happen in forty hours! Forty hours, no more, and you hesitate ... and you have scruples, when your son's life is at stake! Come, come, no whimpering, no silly sentimentality. Look things in the face. By your own oath, you are my wife, you are my bride from this moment ... Clarisse, Clarisse, give me your lips ..."

Half-fainting, she had hardly the strength to put out her arm and push him away; and, with a cynicism in which all his abominable nature stood revealed, Daubrecq, mingling words of cruelty and words of passion, continued:

"Save your son! Think of the last morning: the preparations for the scaffold, when they snip away his shirt and cut his hair ... Clarisse, Clarisse, I will save him ... Be sure of it ... All my life shall be yours ... Clarisse ..."

She no longer resisted. It was over. The loathsome brute's lips were about to touch hers; and it had to be, and nothing could prevent it. It was her duty to obey the decree of fate. She had long known it. She understood it; and, closing her eyes, so as not to see the foul face that was slowly raised to hers, she repeated to herself:

"My son ... my poor son."

A few seconds passed: ten, twenty perhaps. Daubrecq did not move. Daubrecq did not speak. And she was astounded at that great silence and that sudden quiet. Did the monster, at the last moment, feel a scruple of remorse?

She raised her eyelids.

The sight which she beheld struck her with stupefaction. Instead of the grinning features which she expected to see, she saw a motionless, unrecognisable face, contorted by an expression of unspeakable terror: and the eyes, invisible under the double impediment of the spectacles, seemed to be staring above her head, above the chair in which she lay prostrate.

Clarisse turned her face. Two revolver barrels, pointed at Daubrecq, showed on the right, a little above the chair. She saw only that: those two huge, formidable revolvers, gripped in two clenched hands. She saw only that and also Daubrecq's face, which fear was discolouring little by little, until it turned livid. And, almost at the same time, someone slipped behind Daubrecq, sprang up fiercely, flung one of his arms round Daubrecq's neck, threw him to the ground with incredible violence and applied a pad of cotton wool to his face. A sudden smell of chloroform filled the room.

Clarisse had recognised Monsieur Nicole.

"Come along, Growler!" he cried. "Come along, Masher! Drop your shooters: I've got him! He's a limp rag ... Tie him up."

Daubrecq, in fact, was bending in two and falling on his knees like a disjointed doll. Under the action of the chloroform, the fearsome brute sank into impotence, became harmless and grotesque.

The Growler and the Masher rolled him in one of the blankets of the bed and tied him up securely.

"That's it! That's it!" shouted Lupin, leaping to his feet.

And, in a sudden reaction of mad delight, he began to dance a wild jig in the middle of the room, a jig mingled with bits of can-can and the contortions of the cakewalk and the whirls of a dancing dervish and the acrobatic movements of a clown and the lurching steps of a drunken man. And he announced, as though they were the numbers in a music hall performance:

"The prisoner's dance! The captive's hornpipe! A fantasia on the corpse of a representative of the people!

The chloroform polka! The two-step of the conquered goggles! Olle! Olle! The blackmailer's fandango! Hoot! Hoot! The McDaubrecq's fling! The turkey trot! And the bunny hug! And the grizzly bear! The Tyrolean dance: tra-la-liety! Allons, enfants de la partie! Zing, boum, boum! Zing, boum, boum!"

All his rascally nature, all his instincts of gaiety, so long suppressed by his constant anxiety and disappointment, came out and betrayed themselves in roars of laughter, bursts of animal spirits and a picturesque need for childlike exuberance and riot.

He gave a last high kick, turned a series of cartwheels round the room and ended by standing with his hands on his hips and one foot on Daubrecq's lifeless body.

"An allegorical tableau!" he announced. "The angel of virtue destroying the hydra of vice!"

And the humour of the scene was twice as great because Lupin was appearing under the aspect of Monsieur Nicole, in the clothes and figure of that wizened, awkward, nervous private tutor.

A sad smile flickered across Madame Mergy's face, her first smile for many a long month. But, at once returning to the reality of things, she besought him:

"Please, please ... think of Gilbert!"

He ran up to her, caught her in his arms and, obeying a spontaneous impulse, so frank that she could but laugh at it, gave her a resounding kiss on either cheek:

"There, lady, that's the kiss of a decent man! Instead of Daubrecq, it's I kissing you ... Another word and I'll do it again ... and I'll call you darling next ... Be angry with me, if you dare. Oh, how happy I am!"

He knelt before her on one knee. And, respectfully:

"I beg your pardon, Madame. The fit is over."

And, getting up again, resuming his whimsical manner, he continued, while Clarisse wondered what he was driving at:

"What's the next article, Madame? Your son's pardon, perhaps? Certainly! Madame, I have the honour to grant you the pardon of your son, the commutation of his sentence to penal servitude for life and, to wind up with, his early escape. It's settled, eh, Growler? Settled, Masher, what? You'll both go with the boy to New Caledonia and arrange for everything. Oh, my dear Daubrecq, we owe you a great debt! But I'm not forgetting you, believe me! What would you like? A last pipe? Coming, coming!"

He took one of the pipes from the mantelpiece, stooped over the prisoner, shifted his pad and thrust the amber mouthpiece between his teeth:

"Draw, old chap, draw. Lord, how funny you look, with your plug over your nose and your cutty in your mouth. Come, puff away. By Jove, I forgot to fill your pipe! Where's your tobacco, your favourite Maryland? Oh, here we are ...!"

He took from the chimney an unopened yellow packet and tore off the government band:

"His lordship's tobacco! Ladies and gentlemen, keep your eyes on me! This is a great moment. I am about to fill his lordship's pipe: by Jupiter, what an honour! Observe my movements! You see, I have nothing in my hands, nothing up my sleeves!"

He turned back his cuffs and stuck out his elbows.

Then he opened the packet and inserted his thumb and forefinger, slowly, gingerly, like a conjurer performing a sleight-of-hand trick before a puzzled audience, and, beaming all over his face, extracted from the tobacco a glittering object which he held out before the spectators.

Clarisse uttered a cry.

It was the crystal stopper.

She rushed at Lupin and snatched it from him:

"That's it; that's the one!" she exclaimed, feverishly. "There's no scratch on the stem! And look at this line running down the middle, where the gilt finishes ... That's it; it unscrews! Oh, dear, my strength's going ..." She trembled so violently that Lupin took back the stopper and unscrewed it himself.

The inside of the knob was hollow; and in the hollow space was a piece of paper rolled into a tiny pellet.

"The foreign-post paper," he whispered, himself greatly excited, with quivering hands.

There was a long silence. All four felt as if their hearts were ready to burst from their bodies; and they were afraid of what was coming.

"Please, please ..." stammered Clarisse.

Lupin unfolded the paper.

There was a set of names written one below the other, twenty-seven of them, the twenty-seven names of the famous list: Langeroux, Dechaumont, Vorenglade, d'Albufex, Victorien Mergy and the rest.

And, at the foot, the signature of the chairman of the Two-Seas Canal Company, the signature written in letters of blood.

Lupin looked at his watch:

"A quarter to one," he said. "We have twenty minutes to spare. Let's have some lunch."

"But," said Clarisse, who was already beginning to lose her head, "don't forget ..."

He simply said:

"All I know is that I'm dying of hunger."

He sat down at the table, cut himself a large slice of cold pie and said to his accomplices:

"Growler? A bite? You, Masher?"

"I could do with a mouthful, governor."

"Then hurry up, lads. And a glass of champage to wash it down with: it's the chloroform patient's treat. Your health, Daubrecq! Sweet champagne? Dry champagne? Extra-dry?"

THE CROSS
OF LORRAINE

The moment Lupin had finished lunch, he at once and, so to speak, without transition, recovered all his mastery and authority. The time for joking was past; and he must no longer yield to his love of astonishing people with claptrap and conjuring tricks. Now that he had discovered the crystal stopper in the hiding place which he had guessed with absolute certainty, now that he possessed the list of the twenty-seven, it became a question of playing off the last game of the rubber without delay.

It was child's play, no doubt, and what remained to be done presented no difficulty. Nevertheless, it was essential that he should perform these final actions with promptness, decision and infallible perspicacity. The smallest blunder was irretrievable. Lupin knew this; but his strangely lucid brain had allowed for every contingency. And the movements and words which he was now about to make and utter were all fully prepared and matured:

"Growler, the commissionaire is waiting on the boulevard Gambetta with his barrow and the trunk which we bought. Bring him here and have the trunk carried up. If the people of the hotel ask any questions, say it's for the lady in No. 130."

Then, addressing his other companion:

"Masher, go back to the station and take over the limousine. The price is arranged: ten thousand francs. Buy a chauffeur's cap and overcoat and bring the car to the hotel."

"The money, governor."

Lupin opened a pocketbook which had been removed from Daubrecq's jacket and produced a huge bundle of banknotes. He separated ten of them:

"Here you are. Our friend appears to have been doing well at the club. Off with you, Masher!"

The two men went out through Clarisse's room Lupin availed himself of a moment when Clarisse Mergy was not looking to stow away the pocketbook with the greatest satisfaction:

"I shall have done a fair stroke of business," he said to himself. "When all the expenses are paid, I shall still be well to the good; and it's not over yet."

Then turning to Clarisse Mergy, he asked:

"Have you a bag?"

"Yes, I bought one when I reached Nice, with some linen and a few necessaries; for I left Paris unprepared."

"Get all that ready. Then go down to the office. Say that you are expecting a trunk which a commissionaire is bringing from the station cloakroom and that you will want to unpack and pack it again in your room; and tell them that you are leaving."

When alone, Lupin examined Daubrecq carefully, felt in all his pockets and appropriated everything that seemed to present any sort of interest.

The Growler was the first to return. The trunk, a large wicker hamper covered with black moleskin, was taken into Clarisse's room. Assisted by Clarisse and the Growler, Lupin moved Daubrecq and put him in the trunk, in a sitting posture, but with his head bent so as to allow of the lid being fastened:

"I don't say that it's as comfortable as your berth in a sleeping car, my dear deputy," Lupin observed. "But, all the same, it's better than a coffin. At least, you can breathe. Three little holes in each side. You have nothing to complain of!"

Then, unstopping a flask:

"A drop more chloroform? You seem to love it!"

He soaked the pad once more, while, by his orders, Clarisse and the Growler propped up the deputy with linen, rugs and pillows, which they had taken the precaution to heap in the trunk.

"Capital!" said Lupin. "That trunk is fit to go round the world. Lock it and strap it."

The Masher arrived, in a chauffeur's livery:

"The car's below, governor."

"Good," he said. "Take the trunk down between you. It would be dangerous to give it to the hotel servants."

"But if any one meets us?"

"Well, what then, Masher? Aren't you a chauffeur? You're carrying the trunk of your employer here present, the lady in No. 130, who will also go down, step into her motor ... and wait for me two hundred yards farther on.

Growler, you help to hoist the trunk up. Oh, first lock the partition door!"

Lupin went to the next room, closed the other door, shot the bolt, walked out, locked the door behind him and went down in the lift.

In the office, he said:

"Monsieur Daubrecq has suddenly been called away to Monte Carlo. He asked me to say that he would not be back until Tuesday and that you were to keep his room for him. His things are all there. Here is the key."

He walked away quietly and went after the car, where he found Clarisse lamenting:

"We shall never be in Paris tomorrow! It's madness! The least breakdown ..."

"That's why you and I are going to take the train. It's safer ..."

He put her into a cab and gave his parting instructions to the two men:

"Thirty miles an hour, on the average, do you understand? You're to drive and rest, turn and turn about. At that rate, you ought to be in Paris between six and seven tomorrow evening. But don't force the pace. I'm keeping Daubrecq, not because I want him for my plans, but as a hostage ... and then by way of precaution – I like to feel that I can lay my hands on him during the next few days. So look after the dear fellow. Give him a few drops of chloroform every three or four hours: it's his one weakness ... Off with you, Masher! And you, Daubrecq, don't get excited up there. The roof'll bear you all right ... If you feel at all sick, don't mind ... Off you go, Masher!"

He watched the car move into the distance and then told the cabman to drive to a post office, where he dispatched a telegram in these words:

Monsieur Prasville, Prefecture de Police, Paris: Person found. Will bring you document eleven o'clock tomorrow morning. Urgent communication. Clarisse.

Clarisse and Lupin reached the station by half-past two.

"If only there's room!" said Clarisse, who was alarmed at the least thing.

"Room? Why, our berths are booked!"

"By whom?"

"By Jacob ... by Daubrecq."

"How?"

"Why, at the office of the hotel they gave me a letter which had come for Daubrecq by express. It was the two berths which Jacob had sent him. Also, I have his deputy's pass. So we shall travel under the name of Monsieur and Madame Daubrecq and we shall receive all the attention due to our rank and station. You see, my dear madam, that everything's arranged."

The journey, this time, seemed short to Lupin. Clarisse told him what she had done during the past few days. He himself explained the miracle of his sudden appearance in Daubrecq's bedroom at the moment when his adversary believed him in Italy:

"A miracle, no," he said. "But still a remarkable phenomenon took place in me when I left San Remo, a sort of mysterious intuition which prompted me first to try and jump out of the train – and the Masher prevented me

– and next to rush to the window, let down the glass and follow the porter of the Ambassadeurs-Palace, who had given me your message, with my eyes. Well, at that very minute, the porter aforesaid was rubbing his hands with an air of such satisfaction that, for no other reason, suddenly, I understood everything: I had been diddled, taken in by Daubrecq, as you yourself were. Heaps of little details flashed across my mind. My adversary's scheme became clear to me from start to finish. Another minute ... and the disaster would have been beyond remedy. I had, I confess, a few moments of real despair, at the thought that I should not be able to repair all the mistakes that had been made. It depended simply on the timetable of the trains, which would either allow me or would not allow me to find Daubrecq's emissary on the railway platform at San Remo. This time, at last, chance favoured me. We had hardly alighted at the first station when a train passed, for France. When we arrived at San Remo, the man was there. I had guessed right. He no longer wore his hotel porter's cap and frock coat, but a jacket and bowler. He stepped into a second-class compartment. From that moment, victory was assured."

"But ... how ...?" asked Clarisse, who, in spite of the thoughts that obsessed her, was interested in Lupin's story.

"How did I find you? Lord, simply by not losing sight of Master Jacob, while leaving him free to move about as he pleased, knowing that he was bound to account for his actions to Daubrecq. In point of fact, this morning, after spending the night in a small hotel at Nice, he met Daubrecq on the promenade des Anglais. They talked for some time. I followed them. Daubrecq went back to the hotel, planted Jacob in one of the passages on the ground floor, opposite the telephone office, and went up in the lift. Ten minutes later I knew the number of his room and knew that a lady had been occupying the next room, No. 130, since the day before. 'I believe we've done it,' I said to the Growler and the Masher. I tapped lightly at your door. No answer. And the door was locked."

"Well?" asked Clarisse.

"Well, we opened it. Do you think there's only one key in the world that will work a lock? So I walked in. Nobody in your room. But the partition door was ajar. I slipped through it. Thenceforth, a mere hanging separated me from you, from Daubrecq and from the packet of tobacco which I saw on the chimney slab."

"Then you knew the hiding place?"

"A look round Daubrecq's study in Paris showed me that that packet of tobacco had disappeared. Besides ..."

"What?"

"I knew, from certain confessions wrung from Daubrecq in the Lovers' Tower, that the word Marie held the key to the riddle. Since then I had certainly thought of this word, but with the preconceived notion that it was spelt M A R I E. Well, it was really the first two syllables of another word, which I guessed, so to speak, only at the moment when I was struck by the absence of the packet of tobacco."

"What word do you mean?"

"Maryland, Maryland tobacco, the only tobacco that Daubrecq smokes."

And Lupin began to laugh:

"Wasn't it silly? And, at the same time, wasn't it clever of Daubrecq? We looked everywhere, we ransacked everything. Didn't I unscrew the brass sockets of the electric lights to see if they contained a crystal stopper? But how could I have thought, how could anyone, however great his perspicacity, have thought of tearing off the paper band of a packet of Maryland, a band put on, gummed, sealed, stamped and dated by the State, under the control of the Inland Revenue Office? Only think! The State, the accomplice of such an act of infamy! The Inland R-r-r-revenue Awfice lending itself to such a trick! No, a thousand times no! The Regie is not perfect. It makes matches that won't light and cigarettes filled with hay. But there's all the difference in the world between recognising that fact and believing the Inland Revenue to be in league with Daubrecq with the object of hiding the list of the twenty-seven from the legitimate curiosity of the government and the enterprising efforts of Arsène Lupin! Observe that all Daubrecq had to do, in order to introduce the crystal stopper, was to bear upon the band a little, loosen it, draw it back, unfold the yellow paper, remove the tobacco and fasten it up again. Observe also that all we had to do, in Paris, was to take the packet in our hands and examine it, in order to discover the hiding place. No matter! The packet itself, the plug of Maryland made up and passed by the State and by the Inland Revenue Office, was a sacred, intangible thing, a thing above suspicion! And nobody opened it. That was how that demon of a Daubrecq allowed that untouched packet of tobacco to lie about for months on his table, among his pipes and among other unopened packets of tobacco. And no power on earth could have given any one even the vaguest notion of looking into that harmless little cube. I would have you observe, besides ..." Lupin went on pursuing his remarks relative to the packet of Maryland and the crystal stopper. His adversary's ingenuity and shrewdness interested him all the more inasmuch as Lupin had ended by getting the better of him. But to Clarisse these topics mattered much less than did her anxiety as to the acts which must be performed to save her son; and she sat wrapped in her own thoughts and hardly listened to him.

"Are you sure," she kept on repeating, "that you will succeed?"

"Absolutely sure."

"But Prasville is not in Paris."

"If he's not there, he's at the Havre. I saw it in the paper yesterday. In any case, a telegram will bring him to Paris at once."

"And do you think that he has enough influence?"

"To obtain the pardon of Vaucheray and Gilbert personally? No. If he had, we should have set him to work before now. But he is intelligent enough to understand the value of what we are bringing him and to act without a moment's delay."

"But, to be clear, are you not deceived as to that value?"

"Was Daubrecq deceived? Was Daubrecq not in a better position than any of us to know the full power of that paper? Did he not have twenty proofs of it, each more convincing than the last? Think of all that he was able to do, for the sole reason that people knew him to possess the list. They knew it; and that was all. He did not use the list, but he had it. And, having it, he killed your husband. He built up his fortune on the ruin and the disgrace of the twenty-seven. Only last week, one of the gamest of the lot, d'Albufex, cut his throat in a prison. No, take it from me, as the price of handing over that list, we could ask for anything we pleased. And we are asking for what? Almost nothing ... less than nothing ... the pardon of a child of twenty. In other words, they will take us for idiots. What! We have in our hands ..."

He stopped. Clarisse, exhausted by so much excitement, sat fast asleep in front of him.

They reached Paris at eight o'clock in the morning.

Lupin found two telegrams awaiting him at his flat in the Place de Clichy.

One was from the Masher, dispatched from Avignon on the previous day and stating that all was going well and that they hoped to keep their appointment punctually that evening. The other was from Prasville, dated from the Havre and addressed to Clarisse:

Impossible return tomorrow Monday morning. Come to my office five o'clock. Reckon on you absolutely.

"Five o'clock!" said Clarisse. "How late!"

"It's a first-rate hour," declared Lupin.

"Still, if ..."

"If the execution is to take place tomorrow morning: is that what you mean to say? Don't be afraid to speak out, for the execution will not take place."

"The newspapers ..."

"You haven't read the newspapers and you are not to

read them. Nothing that they can say matters in the least. One thing alone matters: our interview with Prasville. Besides ..."

He took a little bottle from a cupboard and, putting his hand on Clarisse's shoulder, said:

"Lie down here, on the sofa, and take a few drops of this mixture."

"What's it for?"

"It will make you sleep for a few hours ... and forget. That's always so much gained."

"No, no," protested Clarisse, "I don't want to. Gilbert is not asleep. He is not forgetting."

"Drink it," said Lupin, with gentle insistence. She yielded all of a sudden, from cowardice, from excessive suffering, and did as she was told and lay on the sofa and closed her eyes. In a few minutes she was asleep.

Lupin rang for his servant:

"The newspapers ... quick! Have you bought them?"

"Here they are, governor."

Lupin opened one of them and at once read the following lines:

ARSÈNE LUPIN'S ACCOMPLICES

We know from a positive source that Arsène Lupin's accomplices, Gilbert and Vaucheray, will be executed tomorrow, Tuesday, morning. Monsieur Deibler has inspected the scaffold. Everything is ready.

He raised his head with a defiant look.

"Arsène Lupin's accomplices! The execution of Arsène

Lupin's accomplices! What a fine spectacle! And what a crowd there will be to witness it! Sorry, gentlemen, but the curtain will not rise. Theatre closed by order of the authorities. And the authorities are myself!"

He struck his chest violently, with an arrogant gesture:

"The authorities are myself!"

At twelve o'clock Lupin received a telegram which the Masher had sent from Lyons:

"All well. Goods will arrive without damage."

At three o'clock Clarisse woke. Her first words were:

"Is it to be tomorrow?"

He did not answer. But she saw him look so calm and smiling that she felt herself permeated with an immense sense of peace and received the impression that everything was finished, disentangled, settled according to her companion's will.

They left the house at ten minutes past four. Prasville's secretary, who had received his chief's instructions by telephone, showed them into the office and asked them to wait. It was a quarter to five.

Prasville came running in at five o'clock exactly and, at once, cried:

"Have you the list?"

"Yes."

"Give it me."

He put out his hand. Clarisse, who had risen from her chair, did not stir.

Prasville looked at her for a moment, hesitated and sat down. He understood. In pursuing Daubrecq, Clarisse Mergy had not acted only from hatred and the desire for revenge. Another motive prompted her. The paper would not be handed over except upon conditions.

"Sit down, please," he said, thus showing that he accepted the discussion.

Clarisse resumed her seat and, when she remained silent, Prasville said:

"Speak, my friend, and speak quite frankly. I do not scruple to say that we wish to have that paper."

"If it is only a wish," remarked Clarisse, whom Lupin had coached in her part down to the least detail, "if it is only a wish, I fear that we shall not be able to come to an arrangement."

Prasville smiled:

"The wish, obviously, would lead us to make certain sacrifices."

"Every sacrifice," said Madame Mergy, correcting him.

"Every sacrifice, provided, of course, that we keep within the bounds of acceptable requirements."

"And even if we go beyond those bounds," said Clarisse, inflexibly.

Prasville began to lose patience:

"Come, what is it all about? Explain yourself."

"Forgive me, my friend, but I wanted above all to mark the great importance which you attach to that paper and, in view of the immediate transaction which we are about to conclude, to specify – what shall I say? – the value of my share in it. That value, which has no limits, must, I repeat, be exchanged for an unlimited value."

"Agreed," said Prasville, querulously.

"I presume, therefore, that it is unnecessary for me to trace the whole story of the business or to enumerate, on the one hand, the disasters which the possession of that paper would have allowed you to avert and, on the other hand, the incalculable advantages which you will be able to derive from its possession?"

Prasville had to make an effort to contain himself and to answer in a tone that was civil, or nearly so:

"I admit everything. Is that enough?"

"I beg your pardon, but we cannot explain ourselves too plainly. And there is one point that remains to be cleared up. Are you in a position to act, personally?"

"How do you mean?"

"I want to know not, of course, if you are empowered to settle this business here and now, but if, in dealing with me, you represent the views of those who know the business and who are qualified to settle it."

"Yes," declared Prasville, forcibly.

"So that I can have your answer within an hour after I have told you my conditions?"

"Yes."

"Will the answer be that of the government?"

"Yes."

Clarisse bent forwards and, sinking her voice:

"Will the answer be that of the Elysée?"

Prasville appeared surprised. He reflected for a moment and then said:

"Yes."

"It only remains for me to ask you to give me your word of honour that, however incomprehensible my conditions may appear to you, you will not insist on my revealing the reason. They are what they are. Your answer must be yes or no."

"I give you my word of honour," said Prasville, formally.

Clarisse underwent a momentary agitation that made her turn paler still. Then, mastering herself, with her eyes fixed on Prasville's eyes, she said:

"You shall have the list of the twenty-seven in exchange for the pardon of Gilbert and Vaucheray."

"Eh? What?"

Prasville leapt from his chair, looking absolutely dumbfounded:

"The pardon of Gilbert and Vaucheray? Of Arsène Lupin's accomplices?"

"Yes," she said.

"The murderers of the Villa Marie-Therese? The two who are due to die tomorrow?"

"Yes, those two," she said, in a loud voice. "I ask? I demand their pardon."

"But this is madness! Why? Why should you?"

"I must remind you, Prasville, that you gave me your word …"

"Yes … yes … I know … But the thing is so unexpected …"

"Why?"

"Why? For all sorts of reasons!"

"What reasons?"

"Well … well, but … think! Gilbert and Vaucheray have been sentenced to death!"

"Send them to penal servitude: that's all you have to do."

"Impossible! The case has created an enormous sensation. They are Arsène Lupin's accomplices. The whole world knows about the verdict."

"Well?"

"Well, we cannot, no, we cannot go against the decrees of justice."

"You are not asked to do that. You are asked for a commutation of punishment as an act of mercy. Mercy is a legal thing."

"The pardoning commission has given its finding ..."

"True, but there remains the President of the Republic."

"He has refused."

"He can reconsider his refusal."

"Impossible!"

"Why?"

"There's no excuse for it."

"He needs no excuse. The right of mercy is absolute. It is exercised without control, without reason, without excuse or explanation. It is a royal prerogative; the President of the Republic can wield it according to his good pleasure, or rather according to his conscience, in the best interests of the State."

"But it is too late! Everything is ready. The execution is to take place in a few hours."

"One hour is long enough to obtain your answer; you have just told us so."

"But this is confounded madness! There are insuperable obstacles to your conditions. I tell you again, it's impossible, physically impossible."

"Then the answer is no?"

"No! No! A thousand times no!"

"In that case, there is nothing left for us to do but to go."

She moved towards the door. Monsieur Nicole followed her. Prasville bounded across the room and barred their way:

"Where are you going?"

"Well, my friend, it seems to me that our conversation is at an end. As you appear to think, as, in fact, you are certain that the President of the Republic will not consider the famous list of the twenty-seven to be worth ..."

"Stay where you are," said Prasville.

He turned the key in the door and began to pace the room, with his hands behind his back and his eyes fixed on the floor.

And Lupin, who had not breathed a word during the whole of this scene and who had prudently contented himself with playing a colourless part, said to himself:

"What a fuss! What a lot of affectation to arrive at the inevitable result! As though Prasville, who is not a genius, but not an absolute blockhead either, would be likely to lose the chance of revenging himself on his mortal enemy! There, what did I say? The idea of hurling Daubrecq into the bottomless pit appeals to him. Come, we've won the rubber."

Prasville was opening a small inner door which led to the office of his private secretary.

He gave an order aloud:

"Monsieur Lartigue, telephone to the Elysée and say that I request the favour of an audience for a communication of the utmost importance."

He closed the door, came back to Clarisse and said:

"In any case, my intervention is limited to submitting your proposal."

"Once you submit it, it will be accepted."

A long silence followed. Clarisse's features expressed so profound a delight that Prasville was struck by it and looked at her with attentive curiosity. For what mysterious reason did Clarisse wish to save Gilbert and Vaucheray? What was the incomprehensible link that bound her to those two men? What tragedy connected those three lives and, no doubt, Daubrecq's in addition?

"Go ahead, old boy," thought Lupin, "cudgel your brains: you'll never spot it! Ah, if we had asked for Gilbert's pardon only, as Clarisse wished, you might have twigged the secret! But Vaucheray, that brute of a Vaucheray, there really could not be the least bond between Madame Mergy and him ... Aha, by Jingo, it's my turn now! He's watching me ... The inward soliloquy is turning upon myself ... I wonder who that Monsieur Nicole can be? Why has that little provincial usher devoted himself body and soul to Clarisse Mergy? Who is that old bore, if the truth were known? I made a mistake in not enquiring ... I must look into this .... I must rip off the beggar's mask. For, after all, it's not natural that a man should take so much trouble about a matter in which he is not directly interested. Why should he also wish to save Gilbert and Vaucheray? Why? Why should he?" Lupin turned his head away. "Look out! Look out! There's a notion passing through that red-tape merchant's skull: a confused notion which he can't put into words. Hang it all, he mustn't suspect Monsieur Lupin under Monsieur Nicole! The thing's complicated enough as it is, in all conscience!"

But there was a welcome interruption. Prasville's secretary came to say that the audience would take place in an hour's time.

"Very well. Thank you," said Prasville. "That will do."

And, resuming the interview, with no further

circumlocution, speaking like a man who means to put a thing through, he declared:

"I think that we shall be able to manage it. But, first of all, so that I may do what I have undertaken to do, I want more precise information, fuller details. Where was the paper?"

"In the crystal stopper, as we thought," said Madame Mergy.

"And where was the crystal stopper?"

"In an object which Daubrecq came and fetched, a few days ago, from the writing desk in his study in the Square Lamartine, an object which I took from him yesterday."

"What sort of object?"

"Simply a packet of tobacco, Maryland tobacco, which used to lie about on the desk."

Prasville was petrified. He muttered, guilelessly:

"Oh, if I had only known! I've had my hand on that packet of Maryland a dozen times! How stupid of me!"

"What does it matter?" said Clarisse. "The great thing is that the discovery is made."

Prasville pulled a face which implied that the discovery would have been much pleasanter if he himself had made it. Then he asked:

"So you have the list?"

"Yes."

"Show it to me."

And, when Clarisse hesitated, he added:

"Oh, please, don't be afraid! The list belongs to you, and I will give it back to you. But you must understand that I cannot take the step in question without making certain."

Clarisse consulted Monsieur Nicole with a glance which did not escape Prasville. Then she said:

"Here it is."

He seized the scrap of paper with a certain excitement, examined it and almost immediately said:

"Yes, yes ... the secretary's writing: I recognise it ... And the signature of the chairman of the company: the signature in red ... Besides, I have other proof ... For instance, the torn piece which completes the left-hand top corner of this sheet ..."

He opened his safe and, from a special cash-box, produced a tiny piece of paper which he put against the top left corner:

"That's right. The torn edges fit exactly. The proof is undeniable. All that remains is to verify the make of this foreign-post paper."

Clarisse was radiant with delight. No one would have believed that the most terrible torture had racked her for weeks and weeks and that she was still bleeding and quivering from its effects.

While Prasville was holding the paper against a window pane, she said to Lupin:

"I insist upon having Gilbert informed this evening. He must be so awfully unhappy!"

"Yes," said Lupin. "Besides, you can go to his lawyer and tell him."

She continued:

"And then I must see Gilbert tomorrow. Prasville can think what he likes."

"Of course. But he must first gain his cause at the Elysée."

"There can't be any difficulty, can there?"

"No. You saw that he gave way at once."

Prasville continued his examination with the aid of a magnifying-glass and compared the sheet with the scrap of torn paper. Next, he took from the cash box some other sheets of letter paper and examined one of these by holding it up to the light:

"That's done," he said. "My mind is made up. Forgive me, dear friend: it was a very difficult piece of work ... I passed through various stages. When all is said, I had my suspicions ... and not without cause ..."

"What do you mean?" asked Clarisse.

"One second ... I must give an order first."

He called his secretary:

"Please telephone at once to the Elysée, make my apologies and say that I shall not require the audience, for reasons which I will explain later."

He closed the door and returned to his desk. Clarisse and Lupin stood choking, looking at him in stupefaction, failing to understand this sudden change. Was he mad? Was it a trick on his part? A breach of faith? And was he refusing to keep his promise, now that he possessed the list?

He held it out to Clarisse:

"You can have it back."

"Have it back?"

"And return it to Daubrecq."

"To Daubrecq?"

"Unless you prefer to burn it."

"What do you say?"

"I say that, if I were in your place, I would burn it."

"Why do you say that? It's ridiculous!"

"On the contrary, it is very sensible."

"But why? Why?"

"Why? I will tell you. The list of the twenty-seven, as we know for absolutely certain, was written on a sheet of letter-paper belonging to the chairman of the Canal Company, of which there are a few samples in this cash-box. Now all these samples have as a watermark a little cross of Lorraine which is almost invisible, but which can just be seen in the thickness of the paper when you hold it up to the light. The sheet which you have brought me does not contain that little cross of Lorraine."

Lupin felt a nervous trembling shake him from head to foot and he dared not turn his eyes on Clarisse, realising what a terrible blow this was to her. He heard her stammer:

"Then are we to suppose ... that Daubrecq was taken in?"

"Not a bit of it!" exclaimed Prasville. "It is you who have been taken in, my poor friend. Daubrecq has the real list, the list which he stole from the dying man's safe."

"But this one ..."

"This one is a forgery."

"A forgery?"

"An undoubted forgery. It was an admirable piece of cunning on Daubrecq's part. Dazzled by the crystal stopper which he flashed before your eyes, you did nothing but look for that stopper in which he had stowed away no matter what, the first bit of paper that came to hand, while he quietly kept ..."

Prasville interrupted himself. Clarisse was walking up to him with short, stiff steps, like an automaton. She said:

"Then ..."

"Then what, dear friend?"

"You refuse?"

"Certainly, I am obliged to; I have no choice."

"You refuse to take that step?"

"Look here, how can I do what you ask? It's not possible, on the strength of a valueless document..."

"You won't do it? You won't do it? And, tomorrow morning ... in a few hours ... Gilbert ..."

She was frightfully pale, her face sunk, like the face of one dying. Her eyes opened wider and wider and her teeth chattered ...

Lupin, fearing the useless and dangerous words which she was about to utter, seized her by the shoulders and tried to drag her away. But she thrust him back with indomitable strength, took two or three more steps, staggered, as though on the point of falling, and, suddenly, in a burst of energy and despair, laid hold of Prasville and screamed:

"You shall go to the Elysée! You shall go at once ...! You must ...! You must save Gilbert!"

"Please, please, my dear friend, calm yourself ..."

She gave a strident laugh:

"Calm myself! When, tomorrow morning, Gilbert ... Ah, no, no, I am terrified ... it's appalling ... Oh, run, you wretch, run! Obtain his pardon! Don't you understand? Gilbert ... Gilbert is my son! My son! My son!"

Prasville gave a cry. The blade of a knife flashed in Clarisse's hand and she raised her arm to strike herself. But the movement was not completed. Monsieur Nicole caught her arm in its descent and, taking the knife from

Clarisse, reducing her to helplessness, he said, in a voice that rang through the room like steel:

"What you are doing is madness! When I gave you my oath that I would save him! You must ... live for him ... Gilbert shall not die ... How can he die, when ... I gave you my oath?"

"Gilbert ... my son ..." moaned Clarisse.

He clasped her fiercely, drew her against himself and put his hand over her mouth:

"Enough! Be quiet! I entreat you to be quiet ... Gilbert shall not die ..."

With irresistible authority, he dragged her away like a subdued child that suddenly becomes obedient; but, at the moment of opening the door, he turned to Prasville:

"Wait for me here, Monsieur," he commanded, in an imperative tone. "If you care about that list of the twenty-seven, the real list, wait for me. I shall be back in an hour, in two hours, at most; and then we will talk business."

And abruptly, to Clarisse:

"And you, Madame, a little courage yet. I command you to show courage, in Gilbert's name."

He went away, through the passages, down the stairs, with a jerky step, holding Clarisse under the arm, as he might have held a lay-figure, supporting her, carrying her almost. A courtyard, another courtyard, then the street.

Meanwhile, Prasville, surprised at first, bewildered by the course of events, was gradually recovering his composure and thinking. He thought of that Monsieur Nicole, a mere supernumerary at first, who played beside Clarisse the part of one of those advisers to whom we cling in the serious crises of our lives and who suddenly, shaking off his torpor, appeared in the full light of day, resolute, masterful, mettlesome, brimming over with daring, ready to overthrow all the obstacles that fate placed on his path.

Who was there that was capable of acting thus?

Prasville started. The question had no sooner occurred to his mind than the answer flashed on him, with absolute certainty. All the clues rose up, each more exact, each more convincing than the last.

Hurriedly he rang. Hurriedly he sent for the chief detective inspector on duty. And, feverishly:

"Were you in the waiting room, Chief Inspector?"

"Yes, Monsieur le Secretaire General."

"Did you see a gentleman and a lady go out?"

"Yes."

"Would you know the man again?"

"Yes."

"Then don't lose a moment, Chief Inspector. Take six inspectors with you. Go to the place de Clichy. Make inquiries about a man called Nicole and watch the house. The Nicole man is on his way back there."

"And if he comes out, Monsieur le Secretaire General?"

"Arrest him. Here's a warrant."

He sat down to his desk and wrote a name on a form:

"Here you are, Chief Inspector. I will let the chief detective know."

The Chief Inspector seemed staggered:

"But you spoke to me of a man called Nicole, Monsieur le Secretaire General."

"Well?"

"The warrant is in the name of Arsène Lupin."

"Arsène Lupin and the Nicole man are one and the same individual."

THE
SCAFFOLD

"I will save him, I will save him," Lupin repeated, without ceasing, in the taxicab in which he and Clarisse drove away. "I swear that I will save him."

Clarisse did not listen, sat as though numbed, as though possessed by some great nightmare of death, which left her ignorant of all that was happening outside her. And Lupin set forth his plans, perhaps more to reassure himself than to convince Clarisse. "No, no, the game is not lost yet. There is one trump left, a huge trump, in the shape of the letters and documents which Vorenglade, the ex-deputy, is offering to sell to Daubrecq and of which Daubrecq spoke to you yesterday at Nice. I shall buy those letters and documents of Stanislas Vorenglade at whatever price he chooses to name. Then we shall go back to the police office and I shall say to Prasville, 'Go to the Elysée at once ... Use the list as though it were genuine, save Gilbert from death and be content to acknowledge tomorrow, when Gilbert is saved, that the list is forged. Be off, quickly!

If you refuse, well, if you refuse, the Vorenglade letters and documents shall be reproduced tomorrow, Tuesday, morning in one of the leading newspapers.' Vorenglade will be arrested. And Monsieur Prasville will find himself in prison before night."

Lupin rubbed his hands:

"He'll do as he's told! He'll do as he's told! I felt that at once, when I was with him. The thing appeared to me as a dead certainty. And I found Vorenglade's address in Daubrecq's pocket books, so ... driver, boulevard Raspail!"

They went to the address given. Lupin sprang from the cab, ran up three flights of stairs.

The servant said that Monsieur Vorenglade was away and would not be back until dinner time next evening.

"And don't you know where he is?"

"Monsieur Vorenglade is in London, sir."

Lupin did not utter a word on returning to the cab. Clarisse, on her side, did not even ask him any questions, so indifferent had she become to everything, so absolutely did she look upon her son's death as an inevitable fact.

They drove to the place de Clichy. As Lupin entered the house he passed two men who were just leaving the porter's box. He was too much engrossed to notice them. They were Prasville's inspectors.

"No telegram?" he asked his servant.

"No, governor," replied Achille.

"No news of the Masher and the Growler?"

"No, governor, none."

"That's all right," he said to Clarisse, in a casual tone. "It's only seven o'clock and we mustn't reckon on seeing them before eight or nine. Prasville will have to wait, that's all. I will telephone to him to wait."

He did so and was hanging up the receiver, when he heard a moan behind him. Clarisse was standing by the table, reading an evening paper. She put her hand to her heart, staggered and fell.

"Achille, Achille!" cried Lupin, calling his man. "Help me put her on my bed ... And then go to the cupboard and get me the medicine-bottle marked number four, the bottle with the sleeping draught."

He forced open her teeth with the point of a knife and compelled her to swallow half the bottle:

"Good," he said. "Now the poor thing won't wake till tomorrow ... after."

He glanced through the paper, which was still clutched in Clarisse's hand, and read the following lines:

The strictest measures have been taken to keep order at the execution of Gilbert and Vaucheray, lest Arsène Lupin should make an attempt to rescue his accomplices from the last penalty. At twelve o'clock tonight a cordon of troops will be drawn across all the approaches to the Sante Prison. As already stated, the execution will take place outside the prison walls, in the square formed by the boulevard Arago and the rue de la Sante. We have succeeded in obtaining some details of the attitude of the two condemned men. Vaucheray observes a stolid sullenness and is awaiting the fatal event with no little courage:

'Crikey,' he says, 'I can't say I'm delighted; but I've got to go through it and I shall keep my end up.' And he adds, 'Death I don't care a hang about! What worries

me is the thought that they're going to cut my head off. Ah, if the governor could only hit on some trick to send me straight off to the next world before I had time to say knife! A drop of Prussic acid, governor, if you please!'

Gilbert's calmness is even more impressive, especially when we remember how he broke down at the trial. He retains an unshaken confidence in the omnipotence of Arsène Lupin:

'The governor shouted to me before everybody not to be afraid, that he was there, that he answered for everything. Well, I'm not afraid. I shall keep faith in him until the last day, until the last minute, at the very foot of the scaffold. I know the governor! There's no danger with him. He has promised and he will keep his word. If my head were off, he'd come and clap it on my shoulders and firmly! Arsène Lupin allow his chum Gilbert to die? Not he! Excuse my humour!'

There is a certain touching frankness in all this enthusiasm which is not without a dignity of its own. We shall see if Arsène Lupin deserves the confidence so blindly placed in him.

Lupin was hardly able to finish reading the article for the tears that dimmed his eyes: tears of affection, tears of pity, tears of distress.

No, he did not deserve the confidence of his chum Gilbert. Certainly, he had performed impossibilities; but there are circumstances in which we must perform more than impossibilities, in which we must show ourselves stronger than fate; and, this time, fate had been stronger than he. Ever since the first day and throughout this lamentable adventure, events had gone contrary to his anticipations, contrary to logic itself. Clarisse and he, though pursuing an identical aim, had wasted weeks in fighting each other. Then, at the moment when they were uniting their efforts, a series of ghastly disasters had come one after the other: the kidnapping of little Jacques, Daubrecq's disappearance, his imprisonment in the Lovers' Tower, Lupin's wound, his enforced inactivity, followed by the cunning manoeuvres that dragged Clarisse – and Lupin after her – to the south, to Italy. And then, as a crowning catastrophe, when, after prodigies of will-power, after miracles of perseverance, they were entitled to think that the Golden Fleece was won, it all came to nothing. The list of the twenty-seven had no more value than the most insignificant scrap of paper.

"The game's up!" said Lupin. "It's an absolute defeat. What if I do revenge myself on Daubrecq, ruin him and destroy him? He is the real victor, once Gilbert dies."

He wept anew, not with spite or rage, but with despair. Gilbert was going to die! The lad whom he called his chum, the best of his pals would be gone for ever, in a few hours. He could not save him. He was at the end of his tether. He did not even look round for a last expedient. What was the use?

And his persuasion of his own helplessness was so deep, so definite that he felt no shock of any kind on receiving a telegram from the Masher that said:

Motor accident. Essential part broken. Long repair. Arrive tomorrow morning.

It was a last proof to show that fate had uttered its decree. He no longer thought of rebelling against the decision.

He looked at Clarisse. She was peacefully sleeping; and this total oblivion, this absence of all consciousness, seemed to him so enviable that, suddenly yielding to a fit of cowardice, he seized the bottle, still half-filled with the sleeping-draught, and drank it down.

Then he stretched himself on a couch and rang for his man:

"Go to bed, Achille, and don't wake me on any pretext whatsoever."

"Then there's nothing to be done for Gilbert and Vaucheray, governor?" said Achille.

"Nothing."

"Are they going through it?"

"They are going through it."

Twenty minutes later Lupin fell into a heavy sleep. It was ten o'clock in the evening.

The night was full of incident and noise around the prison. At one o'clock in the morning the rue de la Sante, the boulevard Arago and all the streets abutting on the gaol were guarded by police, who allowed no one to pass without a regular cross-examination.

For that matter, it was raining in torrents; and it seemed as though the lovers of this sort of show would not be very numerous. The public houses were all closed by special order. At four o'clock three companies of infantry came and took up their positions along the pavements, while a battalion occupied the boulevard Arago in case of a surprise. Municipal guards cantered up and down between the lines; a whole staff of police-magistrates, officers and functionaries, brought together for the occasion, moved about among the troops.

The guillotine was set up in silence, in the middle of the square formed by the boulevard and the street; and the sinister sound of hammering was heard.

But, at five o'clock, the crowd gathered, notwithstanding the rain, and people began to sing. They shouted for the footlights, called for the curtain to rise, were exasperated to see that, at the distance at which the barriers had been fixed, they could hardly distinguish the uprights of the guillotine.

Several carriages drove up, bringing official persons dressed in black. There were cheers and hoots, whereupon a troop of mounted municipal guards scattered the groups and cleared the space to a distance of three hundred yards from the square. Two fresh companies of soldiers lined up.

And suddenly there was a great silence. A vague white light fell from the dark sky. The rain ceased abruptly.

Inside the prison, at the end of the passage containing the condemned cells, the men in black were conversing in low voices. Prasville was talking to the public prosecutor, who expressed his fears:

"No, no," declared Prasville, "I assure you, it will pass without an incident of any kind."

"Do your reports mention nothing at all suspicious, Monsieur le Secretaire General?"

"Nothing. And they can't mention anything, for the simple reason that we have Lupin."

"Do you mean that?"

"Yes, we know his hiding place. The house where he lives, on the place de Clichy, and where he went at seven o'clock last night, is surrounded. Moreover, I know the scheme by which he had contrived to save his two accomplices. The scheme miscarried at the last moment. We have nothing to fear, therefore. The law will take its course."

Meanwhile, the hour had struck.

They took Vaucheray first; and the governor of the prison ordered the door of his cell to be opened. Vaucheray leapt out of bed and cast eyes dilated with terror upon the men who entered.

"Vaucheray, we have come to tell you ..."

"Stow that, stow that," he muttered. "No words. I know all about it. Get on with the business."

One would have thought that he was in a hurry for it to be over as fast as possible, so readily did he submit to the usual preparations. But he would not allow any of them to speak to him:

"No words," he repeated. "What? Confess to the priest? Not worthwhile. I have shed blood. The law sheds my blood. It's the good old rule. We're quits."

Nevertheless, he stopped short for a moment:

"I say, is my mate going through it too?"

And, when he heard that Gilbert would go to the scaffold at the same time as himself, he had two or three seconds of hesitation, glanced at the bystanders, seemed about to speak, was silent and, at last, muttered:

"It's better so ... They'll pull us through together ... we'll clink glasses together."

Gilbert was not asleep either, when the men entered his cell.

Sitting on his bed, he listened to the terrible words,

tried to stand up, began to tremble frightfully, from head to foot, like a skeleton when shaken, and then fell back, sobbing:

"Oh, my poor mummy, poor mummy!" he stammered.

They tried to question him about that mother, of whom he had never spoken; but his tears were interrupted by a sudden fit of rebellion and he cried:

"I have done no murder ... I won't die. I have done no murder ..."

"Gilbert," they said, "show yourself a man."

"Yes, yes ... but I have done no murder ... Why should I die?"

His teeth chattered so loudly that words which he uttered became unintelligible. He let the men do their work, made his confession, heard mass and then, growing calmer and almost docile, with the voice of a little child resigning itself, murmured:

"Tell my mother that I beg her forgiveness."

"Your mother?"

"Yes ... Put what I say in the papers ... She will understand ... And then ..."

"What, Gilbert?"

"Well, I want the governor to know that I have not lost confidence."

He gazed at the bystanders, one after the other, as though he entertained the mad hope that 'the governor' was one of them, disguised beyond recognition and ready to carry him off in his arms:

"Yes," he said, gently and with a sort of religious piety, "yes, I still have confidence, even at this moment ... Be sure and let him know, won't you? I am positive that he will not let me die. I am certain of it ..."

They guessed, from the fixed look in his eyes, that he saw Lupin, that he felt Lupin's shadow prowling around and seeking an inlet through which to get to him. And never was anything more touching than the sight of that stripling – clad in a straitjacket, with his arms and legs bound, guarded by thousands of men – whom the executioner already held in his inexorable hand and who, nevertheless, hoped on.

Anguish wrung the hearts of all the beholders. Their eyes were dimmed with tears:

"Poor little chap!" stammered someone.

Prasville, touched like the rest and thinking of Clarisse, repeated, in a whisper:

"Poor little chap!"

But the hour struck, the preparations were finished. They set out.

The two processions met in the passage. Vaurheray, on seeing Gilbert, snapped out:

"I say, kiddie, the governor's chucked us!"

And he added a sentence which nobody, save Prasville, was able to understand:

"Expect he prefers to pocket the proceeds of the crystal stopper."

They went down the staircases. They crossed the prison yards. An endless, horrible distance.

And, suddenly, in the frame of the great doorway, the wan light of day, the rain, the street, the outlines of houses, while far-off sounds came through the awful silence.

They walked along the wall, to the corner of the boulevard.

A few steps farther Vaucheray started back: he had seen!

Gilbert crept along, with lowered head, supported by an executioner's assistant and by the chaplain, who made him kiss the crucifix as he went.

There stood the guillotine.

"No, no," shouted Gilbert, "I won't ... I won't ... Help! Help!"

A last appeal, hung in the air.

The executioner gave a signal. Vaucheray was laid hold of, lifted, dragged along, almost at a run.

And then came this staggering thing: a shot, a shot fired from the other side, from one of the houses opposite.

The assistants stopped short.

The burden which they were dragging had collapsed in their arms.

"What is it? What's happened?" asked everybody.

"He's wounded ..."

Blood spurted from Vaucheray's forehead and covered his face.

He spluttered:

"That's done it ... one in a thousand! Thank you, governor, thank you."

"Finish him off! Carry him there!" said a voice, amid the general confusion.

"But he's dead!"

"Get on with it ... finish him off!"

Tumult was at its height, in the little group of magistrates, officials and policemen. Everyone was giving orders:

"Execute him! The law must take its course! We have no right to delay! It would be cowardice! Execute him!"

"But the man's dead!"

"That makes no difference! The law must be obeyed! Execute him!"

The chaplain protested, while two warders and Prasville kept their eyes on Gilbert. In the meantime, the assistants had taken up the corpse again and were carrying it to the guillotine.

"Hurry up!" cried the executioner, scared and hoarse-voiced. "Hurry up! And the other one to follow ... Waste no time ..."

He had not finished speaking, when a second report rang out. He spun round on his heels and fell, groaning:

"It's nothing ... a wound in the shoulder ... Go on ... The next one's turn!"

But his assistants were running away, yelling with terror. The space around the guillotine was cleared. And the prefect of police, rallying his men, drove everybody back to the prison, helter-skelter, like a disordered rabble: the magistrates, the officials, the condemned man, the chaplain, all who had passed through the archway two or three minutes before.

In the meanwhile, a squad of policemen, detectives and soldiers were rushing upon the house, a little old-fashioned, three-storied house, with a ground floor occupied by two shops which happened to be empty. Immediately after the first shot, they had seen, vaguely, at one of the windows on the second floor, a man holding a rifle in his hand and surrounded with a cloud of smoke.

Revolver shots were fired at him, but missed him. He, standing calmly on a table, took aim a second time, fired from the shoulder; and the crack of the second report was heard. Then he withdrew into the room.

Down below, as nobody answered the peal at the bell, the assailants demolished the door, which gave way almost immediately. They made for the staircase, but their onrush was at once stopped, on the first floor, by an accumulation of beds, chairs and other furniture, forming a regular barricade and so close entangled that it took the aggressors four or five minutes to clear themselves a passage.

Those four or five minutes lost were enough to render all pursuit hopeless. When they reached the second floor they heard a voice shouting from above:

"This way, friends! Eighteen stairs more. A thousand apologies for giving you so much trouble!"

They ran up those eighteen stairs and nimbly at that! But, at the top, above the third story, was the garret, which was reached by a ladder and a trapdoor. And the fugitive had taken away the ladder and bolted the trapdoor.

The reader will not have forgotten the sensation created by this amazing action, the editions of the papers issued in quick succession, the newsboys tearing and shouting through the streets, the whole metropolis on edge with indignation and, we may say, with anxious curiosity.

But it was at the headquarters of police that the excitement developed into a paroxysm. Men flung themselves about on every side. Messages, telegrams, telephone calls followed one upon the other.

At last, at eleven o'clock in the morning, there was a meeting in the office of the prefect of police, and Prasville was there. The chief detective read a report of his inquiry, the results of which amounted to this: shortly before midnight yesterday someone had rung at the house on the boulevard Arago. The portress, who slept in a small room on the ground floor, behind one of the shops pulled the rope. A man came and tapped at her door. He said that he had come from the police on an urgent matter concerning tomorrow's execution. The portress opened the door and was at once attacked, gagged and bound.

Ten minutes later a lady and gentleman who lived on the first floor and who had just come home were also reduced to helplessness by the same individual and locked up, each in one of the two empty shops. The third floor tenant underwent a similar fate, but in his own flat and his own bedroom, which the man was able to enter without being heard. The second floor was unoccupied, and the man took up his quarters there. He was now master of the house.

"And there we are!" said the prefect of police, beginning to laugh, with a certain bitterness. "There we are! It's as simple as shelling peas. Only, what surprises me is that he was able to get away so easily."

"I will ask you to observe, Monsieur le Prefet, that, being absolute master of the house from one o'clock in the morning, he had until five o'clock to prepare his flight."

"And that flight took place ...?"

"Over the roofs. At that spot the houses in the next street, the rue de la Glaciere, are quite near and there is only one break in the roofs, about three yards wide, with a drop of one yard in height."

"Well?"

"Well, our man had taken away the ladder leading to the garret and used it as a footbridge. After crossing to the next block of buildings, all he had to do was to look through the windows until he found an empty attic, enter one of the houses in the rue de la Glaciere and walk out quietly with his hands in his pockets. In this way his flight, duly prepared beforehand, was effected very simply and without the least obstacle."

"But you had taken the necessary measures."

"Those which you ordered, Monsieur le Prefet. My men spent three hours last evening visiting all the houses, so as to make sure that there was no stranger hiding there. At the moment when they were leaving the last house I had the street barred. Our man must have slipped through during that few minutes' interval."

"Capital! Capital! And there is no doubt in your minds, of course: it's Arsène Lupin?"

"Not a doubt. In the first place, it was all a question of his accomplices. And then ... and then ... no one but Arsène Lupin was capable of contriving such a master stroke and carrying it out with that inconceivable boldness."

"But, in that case," muttered the prefect of police – and, turning to Prasville, he continued – "but, in that case, my dear Prasville, the fellow of whom you spoke to me, the fellow whom you and the chief detective have had watched since yesterday evening, in his flat in the place de Clichy, that fellow is not Arsène Lupin?"

"Yes, he is, monsieur le prefet. There is no doubt about that either."

"Then why wasn't he arrested when he went out last night?"

"He did not go out."

"I say, this is getting complicated!"

"It's quite simple, Monsieur le Prefet. Like all the

houses in which traces of Arsène Lupin are to be found, the house in the place de Clichy has two outlets."

"And you didn't know it?"

"I didn't know it. I only discovered it this morning, on inspecting the flat."

"Was there no one in the flat?"

"No. The servant, a man called Achille, went away this morning, taking with him a lady who was staying with Lupin."

"What was the lady's name?"

"I don't know," replied Prasville, after an imperceptible hesitation.

"But you know the name under which Arsène Lupin passed?"

"Yes. Monsieur Nicole, a private tutor, master of arts and so on. Here is his card."

As Prasville finished speaking, an office messenger came to tell the prefect of police that he was wanted immediately at the Elysee. The Prime Minister was there already.

"I'm coming," he said. And he added, between his teeth, "It's to decide upon Gilbert's fate."

Prasville ventured:

"Do you think they will pardon him, Monsieur le Prefet?"

"Never! After last night's affair, it would make a most deplorable impression. Gilbert must pay his debt tomorrow morning."

The messenger had, at the same time, handed Prasville a visiting card. Prasville now looked at it, gave a start and muttered:

"Well, I'm hanged! What a nerve!"

"What's the matter?" asked the prefect of police.

"Nothing, nothing, Monsieur le Prefet," declared Prasville, who did not wish to share with another the honour of seeing this business through. "Nothing ... an unexpected visit ... I hope soon to have the pleasure of telling you the result."

And he walked away, mumbling, with an air of amazement:

"Well, upon my word! What a nerve the beggar has! What a nerve!"

The visiting card which he held in his hand bore these words:

Monsieur Nicole, Master of Arts, Private Tutor.

THE LAST
BATTLE

When Prasville returned to his office he saw Monsieur Nicole sitting on a bench in the waiting-room, with his bent back, his ailing air, his gingham umbrella, his rusty hat and his single glove:

"It's he all right," said Prasville, who had feared for a moment that Lupin might have sent another Monsieur Nicole to see him. "And the fact that he has come in person proves that he does not suspect that I have seen through him." And, for the third time, he said, "All the same, what a nerve!"

He shut the door of his office and called his secretary:

"Monsieur Lartigue, I am having a rather dangerous person shown in here. The chances are that he will have to leave my office with the bracelets on. As soon as he is in my room, make all the necessary arrangements: send for a dozen inspectors and have them posted in the waiting-room and in your office. And take this as a definite instruction: the moment I ring, you are all to come in, revolvers in hand, and surround the fellow.

Do you quite understand?"

"Yes, Monsieur le Secretaire General."

"Above all, no hesitation. A sudden entrance, in a body, revolvers in hand. Send Monsieur Nicole in, please."

As soon as he was alone, Prasville covered the push of an electric bell on his desk with some papers and placed two revolvers of respectable dimensions behind a rampart of books.

"And now," he said to himself, "to sit tight. If he has the list, let's collar it. If he hasn't, let's collar him. And, if possible, let's collar both. Lupin and the list of the twenty-seven, on the same day, especially after the scandal of this morning, would be a scoop in a thousand."

There was a knock at the door.

"Come in!" said Prasville.

And, rising from his seat:

"Come in, Monsieur Nicole, come in."

Monsieur Nicole crept timidly into the room, sat down on the extreme edge of the chair to which Prasville pointed and said:

"I have come ... to resume ... our conversation of yesterday ... Please excuse the delay, Monsieur."

"One second," said Prasville. "Will you allow me?"

He stepped briskly to the outer room and, seeing his secretary:

"I was forgetting, Monsieur Lartigue. Have the staircases and passages searched ... in case of accomplices."

He returned, settled himself comfortably, as though for a long and interesting conversation, and began:

"You were saying, Monsieur Nicole?"

"I was saying, Monsieur le Secretaire General, that I must apologise for keeping you waiting yesterday evening. I was detained by different matters. First of all, Madame Mergy ..."

"Yes, you had to see Madame Mergy home."

"Just so, and to look after her. You can understand the poor thing's despair ... Her son Gilbert so near death ... And such a death! At that time we could only hope for a miracle ... an impossible miracle. I myself was resigned to the inevitable ... You know as well as I do, when fate shows itself implacable, one ends by despairing."

"But I thought," observed Prasville, "that your intention, on leaving me, was to drag Daubrecq's secret from him at all costs."

"Certainly. But Daubrecq was not in Paris."

"Oh?"

"No. He was on his way to Paris in a motor car."

"Have you a motor car, Monsieur Nicole?"

"Yes, when I need it: an out-of-date concern, an old tin kettle of sorts. Well, he was on his way to Paris in a motor car, or rather on the roof of a motor car, inside a trunk in which I packed him. But, unfortunately, the motor was unable to reach Paris until after the execution. Thereupon ..."

Prasville stared at Monsieur Nicole with an air of stupefaction. If he had retained the least doubt of the individual's real identity, this manner of dealing with Daubrecq would have removed it. By Jingo! To pack a man in a trunk and pitch him on the top of a motorcar! No one but Lupin would indulge in such a fancy, no one but Lupin would confess it with that ingenuous coolness!

"Thereupon," echoed Prasville, "you decided what?"

"I cast about for another method."

"What method?"

"Why, surely, Monsieur le Secretaire General, you know as well as I do!"

"How do you mean?"

"Why, weren't you at the execution?"

"I was."

"In that case, you saw both Vaucheray and the executioner hit, one mortally, the other with a slight wound. And you can't fail to see ..."

"Oh," exclaimed Prasville, dumbfounded, "you confess it? It was you who fired the shots, this morning?"

"Come, Monsieur le Secretaire General, think! What choice had I? The list of the twenty-seven which you examined was a forgery. Daubrecq, who possessed the genuine one, would not arrive until a few hours after the execution. There was therefore but one way for me to save Gilbert and obtain his pardon; and that was to delay the execution by a few hours."

"Obviously."

"Well, of course. By killing that infamous brute, that hardened criminal, Vaucheray, and wounding the executioner, I spread disorder and panic; I made Gilbert's execution physically and morally impossible; and I thus gained the few hours which were indispensable for my purpose."

"Obviously," repeated Prasville.

"Well, of course," repeated Lupin, "it gives us all – the government, the President and myself – time to reflect and to see the question in a clearer light. What do you think of it, Monsieur le Secretaire General?"

Prasville thought a number of things, especially that this Nicole was giving proof, to use a vulgar phrase, of the most infernal cheek, of a cheek so great that Prasville felt inclined to ask himself if he was really right in identifying Nicole with Lupin and Lupin with Nicole.

"I think, Monsieur Nicole, that a man has to be a jolly good shot to kill a person whom he wants to kill, at a distance of a hundred yards, and to wound another person whom he only wants to wound."

"I have had some little practice," said Monsieur Nicole, with modest air.

"And I also think that your plan can only be the fruit of a long preparation."

"Not at all! That's where you're wrong! It was absolutely spontaneous! If my servant, or rather the servant of the friend who lent me his flat in the place de Clichy, had not shaken me out of my sleep, to tell me that he had once served as a shopman in that little house on the boulevard Arago, that it did not hold many tenants and that there might be something to be done there, our poor Gilbert would have had his head cut off by now ... and Madame Mergy would most likely be dead."

"Oh, you think so?"

"I am sure of it. And that was why I jumped at that faithful retainer's suggestion. Only, you interfered with my plans, Monsieur le Secretaire General."

"I did?"

"Yes. You must needs go and take the three-cornered precaution of posting twelve men at the door of my house. I had to climb five flights of back stairs and go out through the servants' corridor and the next house. Such useless fatigue!"

"I am very sorry, Monsieur Nicole. Another time ..."

"It was the same thing at eight o'clock this morning, when I was waiting for the motor which was bringing Daubrecq to me in his trunk: I had to march up and down the place de Clichy, so as to prevent the car from stopping outside the door of my place and your men from interfering in my private affairs. Otherwise, once again, Gilbert and Clarisse Mergy would have been lost."

"But," said Prasville, "those painful events, it seems to me, are only delayed for a day, two days, three days at most. To avert them for good and all we should want ..."

"The real list, I suppose?"

"Exactly. And I daresay you haven't got it."

"Yes, I have."

"The genuine list?"

"The genuine, the undoubtedly genuine list."

"With the cross of Lorraine?"

"With the cross of Lorraine."

Prasville was silent. He was labouring under violent emotion, now that the duel was commencing with that adversary of whose terrifying superiority he was well aware; and he shuddered at the idea that Arsène Lupin, the formidable Arsène Lupin, was there, in front of him, calm and placid, pursuing his aims with as much coolness as though he had all the weapons in his hands and were face to face with a disarmed enemy.

Not yet daring to deliver a frontal attack, feeling almost intimidated, Prasville said:

"So Daubrecq gave it up to you?"

"Daubrecq gives nothing up. I took it."

"By main force, therefore?"

"Oh, dear, no!" said Monsieur Nicole, laughing. "Of course, I was ready to go to all lengths; and, when that worthy Daubrecq was dug out of the basket in which he had been travelling express, with an occasional dose of chloroform to keep his strength up, I had prepared things so that the fun might begin at once. Oh, no useless tortures ... no vain sufferings! No ... Death, simply. You press the point of a long needle on the chest, where the heart is, and insert it gradually, softly and gently. That's all but the point would have been driven by Madame Mergy. You understand: a mother is pitiless, a mother whose son is about to die! 'Speak, Daubrecq, or I'll go deeper ... You won't speak ...? Then I'll push another quarter of an inch ... and another still.' And the patient's heart stops beating, the heart that feels the needle coming ... And another quarter of an inch ... and one more ... I swear before Heaven that the villain would have spoken! We leant over him and waited for him to wake, trembling with impatience, so urgent was our hurry ... Can't you picture the scene, Monsieur le Secretaire General? The scoundrel lying on a sofa, well bound, bare-chested, making efforts to throw off the fumes of chloroform that dazed him. He breathes quicker ... He gasps ... He recovers consciousness ... his lips move ... Already, Clarisse Mergy whispers, 'It's I ... it's I, Clarisse ... Will you answer, you wretch?' She has put her finger on Daubrecq's chest, at the spot where the heart stirs like a little animal hidden under the skin. But she says to me, 'His eyes ... his eyes ... I can't see them under the spectacles ... I want to see them ... 'And I also want to see those eyes which I do not know, I want to see their anguish and I want to read in them, before I hear a word, the secret which is about to burst from the inmost recesses of the terrified body. I want to see. I long to see. The action which I am about to accomplish excites me beyond measure. It seems to me that, when I have seen the eyes, the veil will be rent asunder. I shall know things. It is a presentiment. It is the profound intuition of the truth that keeps me on tenterhooks. The eye glasses are gone. But the thick opaque spectacles are there still. And I snatch them off, suddenly. And, suddenly, startled by a disconcerting vision, dazzled by the quick light that breaks in upon me and laughing, oh, but laughing fit to break my jaws, with my thumb – do you understand? with my thumb – hop, I force out the left eye!"

Monsieur Nicole was really laughing, as he said, fit to break his jaws. And he was no longer the timid little unctuous and obsequious provincial usher, but a well-set-up fellow, who, after reciting and mimicking the whole scene with impressive ardour, was now laughing with a shrill laughter the sound of which made Prasville's flesh creep:

"Hop! Jump, Marquis! Out of your kennel, Towzer! What's the use of two eyes? It's one more than you want. Hop! I say, Clarisse, look at it rolling over the carpet! Mind Daubrecq's eye! Be careful with the grate!"

Monsieur Nicole, who had risen and pretended to be hunting after something across the room, now sat down again, took from his pocket a thing shaped like a marble, rolled it in the hollow of his hand, chucked it in the air, like a ball, put it back in his fob and said, coolly:

"Daubrecq's left eye."

Prasville was utterly bewildered. What was his strange visitor driving at? What did all this story mean? Pale with excitement, he said:

"Explain yourself."

"But it's all explained, it seems to me. And it fits in so well with things as they were, fits in with all the conjectures which I had been making in spite of myself and which would inevitably have led to my solving the mystery, if that damned Daubrecq had not so cleverly sent me astray! Yes, think, follow the trend of my suppositions: 'As the list is not to be discovered away from Daubrecq,' I said to myself, 'it cannot exist away from Daubrecq. And, as it is not to be discovered in the clothes he wears, it must be hidden deeper still, in himself, to speak plainly, in his flesh, under his skin ...'"

"In his eye, perhaps?" suggested Prasville, by way of a joke ...

"In his eye? Monsieur le Secretaire General, you have said the word."

"What?"

"I repeat, in his eye. And it is a truth that ought to have occurred to my mind logically, instead of being revealed to me by accident. And I will tell you why. Daubrecq knew that Clarisse had seen a letter from him instructing an English manufacturer to 'empty the crystal within, so as to leave a void which it was unpossible to suspect'. Daubrecq was bound, in prudence, to divert any attempt at search. And it was for this reason that he had a crystal stopper made, 'emptied within', after a model supplied by himself. And it is this crystal stopper which you and I have been after for months; and it is this crystal stopper which I dug out of a packet of tobacco. Whereas all I had to do ..."

"Was what?" asked Prasville, greatly puzzled.

Monsieur Nicole burst into a fresh fit of laughter:

"Was simply to go for Daubrecq's eye, that eye 'emptied within so as to leave a void which it is impossible to suspect,' the eye which you see before you."

And Monsieur Nicole once more took the thing from his pocket and rapped the table with it, producing the sound of a hard body with each rap.

Prasville whispered, in astonishment:

"A glass eye!"

"Why, of course!" cried Monsieur Nicole, laughing gaily. "A glass eye! A common or garden decanter stopper, which the rascal stuck into his eyesocket in the place of an eye which he had lost – a decanter stopper, or, if you prefer, a crystal stopper, but the real one, this time, which he faked, which he hid behind the double bulwark of his spectacles and eye glasses, which contained and still contains the talisman that enabled Daubrecq to work as he pleased in safety."

Prasville lowered his head and put his hand to his forehead to hide his flushed face: he was almost possessing the list of the twenty-seven. It lay before him, on the table.

Mastering his emotion, he said, in a casual tone:

"So it is there still?"

"At least, I suppose so," declared Monsieur Nicole.

"What! You suppose so?"

"I have not opened the hiding place. I thought, Monsieur le Secretaire General, I would reserve that honour for you."

Prasville put out his hand, took the thing up and inspected it. It was a block of crystal, imitating nature to perfection, with all the details of the eyeball, the iris, the pupil, the cornea.

He at once saw a movable part at the back, which slid in a groove. He pushed it. The eye was hollow.

There was a tiny ball of paper inside. He unfolded it, smoothed it out and, quickly, without delaying to make a preliminary examination of the names, the handwriting or the signatures, he raised his arms and turned the paper to the light from the windows.

"Is the cross of Lorraine there?" asked Monsieur Nicole.

"Yes, it is there," replied Prasville. "This is the genuine list."

He hesitated a few seconds and remained with his arms raised, while reflecting what he would do. Then he folded up the paper again, replaced it in its little crystal sheath and put the whole thing in his pocket. Monsieur Nicole, who was looking at him, asked:

"Are you convinced?"

"Absolutely."

"Then we are agreed?"

"We are agreed."

There was a pause, during which the two men watched each other without appearing to. Monsieur Nicole seemed to be waiting for the conversation to be resumed. Prasville, sheltered behind the piles of books on the table, sat with one hand grasping his revolver and the other touching the push of the electric bell. He felt the whole strength of his position with a keen zest. He held the list. He held Lupin:

"If he moves," he thought, "I cover him with my revolver and I ring. If he attacks me, I shoot."

And the situation appeared to him so pleasant that he prolonged it, with the exquisite relish of an epicure.

In the end, Monsieur Nicole took up the threads:

"As we are agreed, Monsieur le Secretaire General, I think there is nothing left for you to do but to hurry. Is the execution to take place tomorrow?"

"Yes, tomorrow."

"In that case, I shall wait here."

"Wait for what?"

"The answer from the Elysée."

"Oh, is someone to bring you an answer?"

"Yes."

"You, Monsieur le Secretaire General."

Prasville shook his head:

"You must not count on me, Monsieur Nicole."

"Really?" said Monsieur Nicole, with an air of surprise. "May I ask the reason?"

"I have changed my mind."

"Is that all?"

"That's all. I have come to the conclusion that, as things stand, after this last scandal, it is impossible to try to do anything in Gilbert's favour. Besides, an attempt in this direction at the Elysée, under present conditions, would constitute a regular case of blackmail, to which I absolutely decline to lend myself."

"You are free to do as you please, Monsieur. Your scruples do you honour, though they come rather late, for they did not trouble you yesterday. But, in that case, Monsieur le Secretaire General, as the compact between us is destroyed, give me back the list of the twenty-seven."

"What for?"

"So that I may apply to another spokesman."

"What's the good? Gilbert is lost."

"Not at all, not at all. On the contrary, I consider that, now that his accomplice is dead, it will be much easier to grant him a pardon which everybody will look upon as fair and humane. Give me back the list."

"Upon my word, Monsieur, you have a short memory and none too nice a conscience. Have you forgotten yesterday's promise?"

"Yesterday, I made a promise to a Monsieur Nicole."

"Well?"

"You are not Monsieur Nicole."

"Indeed! Then, pray, who am I?"

"Need I tell you?"

Monsieur Nicole made no reply, but began to laugh softly, as though pleased at the curious turn which the conversation was taking; and Prasville felt a vague misgiving at observing that fit of merriment. He grasped the butt end of his revolver and wondered whether he ought not to ring for help.

Monsieur Nicole drew his chair close to the desk, put his two elbows on the table, looked Prasville straight in the face and jeered:

"So, Monsieur Prasville, you know who I am and you have the assurance to play this game with me?"

"I have that assurance," said Prasville, accepting the sneer without flinching.

"Which proves that you consider me, Arsène Lupin – we may as well use the name: yes, Arsène Lupin – which proves that you consider me fool enough, dolt enough to deliver myself like this, bound hand and foot into your hands."

"Upon my word," said Prasville, airily, patting the waistcoat-pocket in which he had secreted the crystal ball, "I don't quite see what you can do, Monsieur Nicole, now that Daubrecq's eye is here, with the list of the twenty-seven inside it."

"What I can do?" echoed Monsieur Nicole, ironically.

"Yes! The talisman no longer protects you; and you are now no better off than any other man who might venture into the very heart of the police office, among some dozens of stalwart fellows posted behind each of those doors and some hundreds of others who will hasten up at the first signal."

Monsieur Nicole shrugged his shoulders and gave Prasville a look of great commiseration:

"Shall I tell you what is happening, Monsieur le Secretaire General? Well, you too are having your head turned by all this business. Now that you possess the list, your state of mind has suddenly sunk to that of a Daubrecq or a d'Albufex. There is no longer even a question, in your thoughts, of taking it to your superiors, so that this ferment of disgrace and discord may be ended. No, no; a sodden temptation has seized upon you and intoxicated you; and, losing your head, you say to yourself, 'It is here, in my pocket. With its aid,

I am omnipotent. It means wealth, absolute, unbounded power. Why not benefit by it? Why not let Gilbert and Clarisse Mergy die? Why not lock up that idiot of a Lupin? Why not seize this unparalleled piece of fortune by the forelock?'"

He bent towards Prasville and, very softly, in a friendly and confidential tone, said:

"Don't do that, my dear sir, don't do it."

"And why not?"

"It is not to your interest, believe me."

"Really!"

"No. Or, if you absolutely insist on doing it, have the kindness first to consult the twenty-seven names on the list of which you have just robbed me and reflect, for a moment, on the name of the third person on it."

"Oh? And what is the name of that third person?"

"It is the name of a friend of yours."

"What friend?"

"Stanislas Vorenglade, the ex-deputy."

"And then?" said Prasville, who seemed to be losing some of his self-confidence.

"Then? Ask yourself if an inquiry, however summary, would not end by discovering, behind that Stanislas Vorenglade, the name of one who shared certain little profits with him."

"And whose name is?"

"Louis Prasville."

Monsieur Nicole banged the table with his fist.

"Enough of this humbug, Monsieur! For twenty minutes, you and I have been beating about the bush. That will do. Let us understand each other. And, to begin with, drop your pistols. You can't imagine that I am frightened of those playthings! Stand up, sir, stand up, as I am doing, and finish the business: I am in a hurry."

He put his hand on Prasville's shoulder and, speaking with great deliberation, said:

"If, within an hour from now, you are not back from the Elysée, bringing with you a line to say that the decree of pardon has been signed; if, within one hour and ten minutes, I, Arsène Lupin, do not walk out of this building safe and sound and absolutely free, this evening four Paris newspapers will receive four letters selected from the correspondence exchanged between Stanislas Vorenglade and yourself, the correspondence which Stanislas Vorenglade sold me this morning. Here's your hat, here's your overcoat, here's your stick. Be off. I will wait for you."

Then happened this extraordinary and yet easily understood thing, that Prasville did not raise the slightest protest nor make the least show of fight. He received the sudden, far-reaching, utter conviction of what the personality known as Arsène Lupin meant, in all its breadth and fulness. He did not so much as think of carping, of pretending – as he had until then believed – that the letters had been destroyed by Vorenglade the deputy or, at any rate, that Vorenglade would not dare to hand them over, because, in so doing, Vorenglade was also working his own destruction. No, Prasville did not speak a word. He felt himself caught in a vice of which no human strength could force the jaws asunder. There was nothing to do but yield. He yielded.

"Here, in an hour," repeated Monsieur Nicole.

"In an hour," said Prasville, tamely. Nevertheless, in order to know exactly where he stood, he added, "The letters, of course, will be restored to me against Gilbert's pardon?"

"No."

"How do you mean, no? In that case, there is no object in ..."

"They will be restored to you, intact, two months after the day when my friends and I have brought about Gilbert's escape ... thanks to the very slack watch which will be kept upon him, in accordance with your orders."

"Is that all?"

"No, there are two further conditions: first, the immediate payment of a cheque for forty thousand francs."

"Forty thousand francs?"

"The sum for which Stanislas Vorenglade sold me the letters. It is only fair ..."

"And next?"

"Secondly, your resignation, within six months, of your present position."

"My resignation? But why?"

Monsieur Nicole made a very dignified gesture:

"Because it is against public morals that one of the highest positions in the police service should be occupied by a man whose hands are not absolutely clean. Make them send you to parliament or appoint you a minister, a councillor of State, an ambassador, in short, any post which your success in the Daubrecq case entitles you to demand. But not secretary general of police; anything but that! The very thought of it disgusts me."

Prasville reflected for a moment. He would have rejoiced in the sudden destruction of his adversary and he racked his brain for the means to effect it. But he was helpless.

He went to the door and called:

"Monsieur Lartigue." And, sinking his voice, but not very low, for he wished Monsieur Nicole to hear, "Monsieur Lartigue, dismiss your men. It's a mistake. And let no one come into my office while I am gone. This gentleman will wait for me here."

He came back, took the hat, stick and overcoat which Monsieur Nicole handed him and went out.

"Well done, sir," said Lupin, between his teeth, when the door was closed. "You have behaved like a sportsman and a gentleman ... So did I, for that matter ... perhaps with too obvious a touch of contempt ... and a little too bluntly. But, tush, this sort of business has to be carried through with a high hand! The enemy's got to be staggered! Besides, when one's own conscience is clear, one can't take up too bullying a tone with that sort of individual. Lift your head, Lupin. You have been the champion of outraged morality. Be proud of your work. And now take a chair, stretch out your legs and have a rest. You've deserved it."

When Prasville returned, he found Lupin sound asleep and had to tap him on the shoulder to wake him.

"Is it done?" asked Lupin.

"It's done. The pardon will be signed presently. Here is the written promise."

"The forty thousand francs?"

"Here's your cheque."

"Good. It but remains for me to thank you, Monsieur."

"So the correspondence ..."

"The Stanislas Vorenglade correspondence will be handed to you on the conditions stated. However, I am glad to be able to give you, here and now, as a sign of my gratitude, the four letters which I meant to send to the papers this evening."

"Oh, so you had them on you?" said Prasville.

"I felt so certain, Monsieur le Secretaire General, that we should end by coming to an understanding."

He took from his hat a fat envelope, sealed with five red seals, which was pinned inside the lining, and handed it to Prasville, who thrust it into his pocket. Then he said:

"Monsieur le Secretaire General, I don't know when I shall have the pleasure of seeing you again. If you have the least communication to make to me, one line in the agony column of the *Journal* will be sufficient. Just head it, 'Monsieur Nicole'. Good-day to you."

And he withdrew.

Prasville, when he was alone, felt as if he were waking from a nightmare during which he had performed incoherent actions over which his conscious mind had no control. He was almost thinking of ringing and causing a stir in the passages; but, just then, there was a tap at the door and one of the office messengers came hurrying in.

"What's the matter?" asked Prasville.

"Monsieur le Secretaire General, it's Monsieur le député Daubrecq asking to see you ... on a matter of the highest importance."

"Daubrecq!" exclaimed Prasville, in bewilderment. "Daubrecq here! Show him in."

Daubrecq had not waited for the order. He ran up to Prasville, out of breath, with his clothes in disorder, a bandage over his left eye, no tie, no collar, looking like an escaped lunatic; and the door was not closed before he caught hold of Prasville with his two enormous hands:

"Have you the list?"

"Yes."

"Have you bought it?"

"Yes."

"At the price of Gilbert's pardon?"

"Yes."

"Is it signed?"

"Yes."

Daubrecq made a furious gesture:

"You fool! You fool! You've been trapped! For hatred of me, I expect? And now you're going to take your revenge?"

"With a certain satisfaction, Daubrecq. Remember my little friend, the opera-dancer, at Nice ... It's your turn now to dance."

"So it means prison?"

"I should think so," said Prasville. "Besides, it doesn't matter. You're done for, anyhow. Deprived of the list, without defence of any kind, you're bound to fall to pieces under your own weight. And I shall be present at the break-up. That's my revenge."

"And you believe that!" yelled Daubrecq, furiously. "You believe that they will wring my neck like a chicken's and that I shall not know how to defend myself and that I have no claws left and no teeth to bite with! Well, my boy, if I do come to grief, there's always one who will fall with me and that is Master Prasville, the partner of Stanislas Vorenglade, who is going to hand me all the proof in existence against him, so that I may get him sent to gaol without delay. Aha, I've got you fixed, old chap! With those letters, you'll go as I please, hang it all, and there will be fine days yet for Daubrecq the deputy! What! You're laughing, are you? Perhaps those letters don't exist?"

Prasville shrugged his shoulders:

"Yes, they exist. But Vorenglade no longer has them in his possession."

"Since when?"

"Since this morning. Vorenglade sold them, two hours ago, for the sum of forty thousand francs; and I have bought them back at the same price."

Daubrecq burst into a great roar of laughter:

"Lord, how funny! Forty thousand francs! You've paid forty thousand francs! To Monsieur Nicole, I suppose, who sold you the list of the twenty-seven? Well, would you like me to tell you the real name of Monsieur Nicole? It's Arsène Lupin!"

"I know that."

"Very likely. But what you don't know, you silly ass, is that I have come straight from Stanislas Vorenglade's and that Stanislas Vorenglade left Paris four days ago! Oh, what a joke! They've sold you waste paper! And your forty thousand francs! What an ass! What an ass!"

He walked out of the room, screaming with laughter and leaving Prasville absolutely dumbfounded.

So Arsène Lupin possessed no proof at all; and, when he was threatening and commanding and treating

Prasville with that airy insolence, it was all a farce, all bluff!

"No, no, it's impossible," thought the secretary general. "I have the sealed envelope ... It's here ... I have only to open it."

He dared not open it. He handled it, weighed it, examined it ... And doubt made its way so swiftly into his mind that he was not in the least surprised, when he did open it, to find that it contained four blank sheets of notepaper.

"Well, well," he said, "I am no match for those rascals. But all is not over yet."

And, in point of fact, all was not over. If Lupin had acted so daringly, it showed that the letters existed and that he relied upon buying them from Stanislas Vorenglade. But, as, on the other hand, Vorenglade was not in Paris, Prasville's business was simply to forestall Lupin's steps with regard to Vorenglade and obtain the restitution of those dangerous letters from Vorenglade at all costs. The first to arrive would be the victor.

Prasville once more took his hat, coat and stick, went downstairs, stepped into a taxi and drove to Vorenglade's flat.

Here he was told that the ex-deputy was expected home from London at six o'clock that evening.

It was two o'clock in the afternoon. Prasville therefore had plenty of time to prepare his plan.

He arrived at the Gare du Nord at five o'clock and posted all around, in the waiting rooms and in the railway offices, the three or four dozen detectives whom he had brought with him.

This made him feel easy. If Monsieur Nicole tried to speak to Vorenglade, they would arrest Lupin. And, to make assurance doubly sure, they would arrest whosoever could be suspected of being either Lupin or one of Lupin's emissaries.

Moreover, Prasville made a close inspection of the whole station. He discovered nothing suspicious. But, at ten minutes to six, Chief Inspector Blanchon, who was with him, said:

"Look, there's Daubrecq."

Daubrecq it was; and the sight of his enemy exasperated the secretary general to such a pitch that he was on the verge of having him arrested. But he reflected that he had no excuse, no right, no warrant for the arrest.

Besides, Daubrecq's presence proved, with still greater force, that everything now depended on Stanislas Vorenglade. Vorenglade possessed the letters: who would end by having them? Daubrecq? Lupin? Or he, Prasville?

Lupin was not there and could not be there. Daubrecq was not in a position to fight. There could be no doubt, therefore, about the result: Prasville would reenter into possession of his letters and, through this very fact, would escape Daubrecq's threats and Lupin's threats and recover all his freedom of action against them.

The train arrived.

In accordance with orders, the stationmaster had issued instructions that no one was to be admitted to the platform. Prasville, therefore, walked on alone, in front of a number of his men, with Chief Inspector Blanchon at their head.

The train drew up.

Prasville almost at once saw Stanislas Vorenglade at the window of a first-class compartment, in the middle of the train.

The ex-deputy alighted and then held out his hand to assist an old gentleman who was travelling with him.

Prasville ran up to him and said, eagerly:

"Vorenglade ... I want to speak to you ..."

At the same moment, Daubrecq, who had managed to pass the barrier, appeared and exclaimed:

"Monsieur Vorenglade, I have had your letter. I am at your disposal."

Vorenglade looked at the two men, recognised Prasville, recognised Daubrecq, and smiled:

"Oho, it seems that my return was awaited with some impatience! What's it all about? Certain letters, I expect?"

"Yes ... yes ..." replied the two men, fussing around him.

"You're too late," he declared.

"Eh? What? What do you mean?"

"I mean that the letters are sold."

"Sold! To whom?"

"To this gentleman," said Vorenglade, pointing to his travelling companion, "to this gentleman, who thought that the business was worth going out of his way for and who came to Amiens to meet me."

The old gentleman, a very old man wrapped in furs and leaning on his stick, took off his hat and bowed.

"It's Lupin," thought Prasville, "it's Lupin, beyond a doubt."

And he glanced towards the detectives, was nearly calling them, but the old gentleman explained:

"Yes, I thought the letters were good enough to warrant a few hours' railway journey and the cost of two return tickets."

"Two tickets?"

"One for me and the other for one of my friends."

"One of your friends?"

"Yes, he left us a few minutes ago and reached the front part of the train through the corridor. He was in a great hurry."

Prasville understood: Lupin had taken the precaution to bring an accomplice, and the accomplice was carrying off the letters. The game was lost, to a certainty. Lupin had a firm grip on his victim. There was nothing to do but submit and accept the conqueror's conditions.

"Very well, sir," said Prasville. "We shall see each other when the time comes. Goodbye for the present, Daubrecq: you shall hear from me." And, drawing Vorenglade aside, "As for you, Vorenglade, you are playing a dangerous game."

"Dear me!" said the ex-deputy. "And why?"

The two men moved away.

Daubrecq had not uttered a word and stood motionless, as though rooted to the ground.

The old gentleman went up to him and whispered:

"I say, Daubrecq, wake up, old chap ... It's the chloroform, I expect ..."

Daubrecq clenched his fists and gave a muttered growl.

"Ah, I see you know me!" said the old gentleman. "Then you will remember our interview, some months ago, when I came to see you in the Square Lamartine and asked you to intercede in Gilbert's favour. I said to you that day, 'Lay down your arms, save Gilbert and I will leave you in peace. If not, I shall take the list of the twenty-seven from you; and then you're done for.' Well, I have a strong suspicion that done for is what you are. That comes of not making terms with kind Monsieur Lupin. Sooner or later, you're bound to lose your boots by it. However, let it be a lesson to you.

"By the way, here's your pocketbook which I forgot to give you. Excuse me if you find it lightened of its contents. There were not only a decent number of banknotes in it, but also the receipt from the warehouse where you stored the Enghien things which you took back from me. I thought I might as well save you the trouble of taking them out yourself. It ought to be done by now. No, don't thank me: it's not worth mentioning. Goodbye, Daubrecq. And, if you should want a louis or two, to buy yourself a new decanter-stopper, drop me a line. Goodbye, Daubrecq."

He walked away.

He had not gone fifty steps when he heard the sound of a shot.

He turned round.

Daubrecq had blown his brains out.

"De profundis," murmured Lupin, taking off his hat.

Two months later, Gilbert, whose sentence had been commuted to one of penal servitude for life, made his escape from the Ile de Re, on the day before that on which he was to have been transported to New Caledonia.

It was a strange escape. Its least details remained difficult to understand; and, like the two shots on the boulevard Arago, it greatly enhanced Arsène Lupin's prestige.

"Taken all round," said Lupin to me, one day, after telling me the different episodes of the story, "taken all around, no enterprise has ever given me more trouble or cost me greater exertions than that confounded adventure which, if you don't mind, we will call, 'The Crystal Stopper'; or, 'Never Say Die'. In twelve hours, between six o'clock in the morning and six o'clock in the evening, I made up for six months of bad luck, blunders, gropings in the dark and reverses. I certainly count those twelve hours among the finest and the most glorious of my life."

"And Gilbert?" I asked. "What became of him?"

"He is farming his own land, way down in Algeria, under his real name, his only name of Antoine Mergy. He is married to an Englishwoman, and they have a son whom he insisted on calling Arsène. I often receive a bright, chatty, warm-hearted letter from him."

"And Madame Mergy?"

"She and her little Jacques are living with them."

"Did you see her again?"

"I did not."

"Really!"

Lupin hesitated for a few moments and then said with a smile:

"My dear fellow, I will let you into a secret that will make me seem ridiculous in your eyes. But you know that I have always been as sentimental as a schoolboy and as silly as a goose. Well, on the evening when I went back to Clarisse Mergy and told her the news of the day – part of which, for that matter, she already knew – I felt two things very thoroughly. One was that I entertained for her a much deeper feeling than I thought; the other that she, on the contrary, entertained for me a feeling which was not without contempt, not without a rankling grudge nor even a certain aversion."

"Nonsense! Why?"

"Why? Because Clarisse Mergy is an exceedingly honest woman and because I am ... just Arsène Lupin."

"Oh!"

"Dear me, yes, an attractive bandit, a romantic and chivalrous cracksman, anything you please. For all that, in the eyes of a really honest woman, with an upright nature and a well-balanced mind, I am only the merest riffraff."

I saw that the wound was sharper than he was willing to admit, and I said:

"So you really loved her?"

"I even believe," he said, in a jesting tone, "that I asked her to marry me. After all, I had saved her son, had I not? So ... I thought. What a rebuff! It produced a coolness between us ... Since then ..."

"You have forgotten her?"

"Oh, certainly! But it required the consolations of one Italian, two Americans, three Russians, a German grand duchess and a Chinawoman to do it!"

"And, after that ...?"

"After that, so as to place an insuperable barrier between myself and her, I got married."

"Nonsense! You got married, you, Arsène Lupin?"

"Married, wedded, spliced, in the most lawful fashion. One of the greatest names in France. An only daughter. A colossal fortune ... What! You don't know the story?

Well, it's worth hearing."

And, straightway, Lupin, who was in a confidential vein, began to tell me the story of his marriage to Angelique de Sarzeau-Vendome, Princesse de Bourbon-Conde, today Sister Marie-Auguste, a humble nun in the Visitation Convent ...

But, after the first few words, he stopped, as though his narrative had suddenly ceased to interest him, and he remained pensive.

"What's the matter, Lupin?"

"The matter? Nothing."

"Yes, yes ... There ... now you're smiling ... Is it Daubrecq's secret receptacle, his glass eye, that's making you laugh?"

"Not at all."

"What then?"

"Nothing, I tell you ... only a memory."

"A pleasant memory?"

"Yes! Yes, a delightful memory even. It was at night, off the Ile de Re, on the fishing-smack in which Clarisse and I were taking Gilbert away ... We were alone, the two of us, in the stern of the boat ... And I remember ... I talked ... I spoke words and more words ... I said all that I had on my heart ... And then ... then came silence, a perturbing and disarming silence."

"Well?"

"Well, I swear to you that the woman whom I took in my arms that night and kissed on the lips – oh, not for long: a few seconds only, but no matter! – I swear before heaven that she was something more than a grateful mother, something more than a friend yielding to a moment of susceptibility, that she was a woman also, a woman quivering with emotion ..." And he continued, with a bitter laugh, "Who ran away next day, never to see me again."

He was silent once more. Then he whispered:

"Clarisse ... Clarisse ... On the day when I am tired and disappointed and weary of life, I will come to you down there, in your little house ... in that little white house, Clarisse, where you are waiting for me ..."